spirits that walk in shadow

VIKING

NINA KIRIKI HOFFMAN

spirits that walk in shadow

VIKING

VIKING
Published by Penguin Group
Penguin Group (USA) Inc., 345 Hudson Street, New York, New York 10014, U.S.A.
Penguin Group (Canada), 90 Eglinton Avenue East, Suite 700, Toronto, Ontario,
Canada M4P 2Y3 (a division of Pearson Penguin Canada Inc.)
Penguin Books Ltd, 80 Strand, London WC2R 0RL, England
Penguin Ireland, 25 St Stephen's Green, Dublin 2, Ireland
(a division of Penguin Books Ltd)
Penguin Group (Australia), 250 Camberwell Road, Camberwell, Victoria 3124,
Australia (a division of Pearson Australia Group Pty Ltd)
Penguin Books India Pvt Ltd, 11 Community Centre, Panchsheel Park,
New Delhi – 110 017, India
Penguin Group (NZ), Cnr Airborne and Rosedale Roads, Albany, Auckland 1310,
New Zealand (a division of Pearson New Zealand Ltd)
Penguin Books (South Africa) (Pty) Ltd, 24 Sturdee Avenue, Rosebank,
Johannesburg 2196, South Africa

Penguin Books Ltd, Registered Offices: 80 Strand, London WC2R 0RL, England

First published in 2006 by Viking, a member of Penguin Group (USA) Inc.

1 3 5 7 9 10 8 6 4 2

Copyright © Nina Kiriki Hoffman, 2006
All rights reserved

Library of Congress cataloging-in-publication data is available
ISBN: 0-670-06071-2

Printed in the U.S.A.
Set in Berling
Book design by Kelley McIntyre

This one is for Sharyn,
for cuts, capers, and encouragement.

It's also for my nephew Connor,
who reads my books to pieces.

spirits that walk in shadow

PROLOGUE: Kim

When I was small, my thoughts and feelings were all visual. The taste of chocolate might be a smear of deep, warm yellow, with gold sparkles. Hot water was a warm, blue blanket, but really hot water had prickles and spikes like shiny silver needles, and cold water, the kind that froze your hand when you dipped into it, looked like sheets of gray ice with bright light shining through.

Images came all the time. Sometimes the pictures were jumpy, like a slide show, images flashing fast, overlapping; sometimes smooth and fluid, like Chinese calligraphy.

One day after I had learned to read, I had a mental click. I was wandering the playground during recess. I watched kids on swings, scraps of color arcing up and down against the chill blue sky, and I wondered if I could think about this in words.

It wasn't easy. It was the good kind of hard, puzzling

and compelling, with the same pull I got from computer solitaire. I felt like I was solving something, and I didn't want to stop.

Words were slower in lots of ways, more linear. I couldn't just leap from thought to thought.

The better I got at thinking in words, the fewer pictures I saw. My brain was all noises weighted with meaning and hooked together in strings.

One morning after a dream of ocean and sky, swimming and flying melting into each other, I woke up and the pictures faded. I thought, *Time to get up. Better get ready for school.*

I felt like I had lost my native language.

I wanted the pictures back.

My parents kept art supplies in a cupboard where my older brother Don and I could grab them any time we wanted, and they sent us to an art teacher two afternoons a week after school.

Our art teacher always put something on the table in front of me and Don and told us to sketch it, but I wasn't interested in drawing fruit, or a stupid sculpture of a robin, or a vase.

Don did our teacher's assignments. He got good at representational art and branched out into illustration. He drew hot, big-breasted manga girls, which made him popular at school. All the guys wanted him to do notebook covers and pictures for them.

I wasn't interested in drawing an object the way a camera took a photo. I made pictures of how I felt.

After I lost my pictures to words and had to work to get them back, I was less inclined than ever to paint what was in front of me. I laid down colors on paper, dripped and drizzled other colors, mooshed things together, tried different brushes and pressures. My hands could still make pictures, even if my head wouldn't.

In pursuit of my lost language, I used up reams of scratch paper, jars of poster paint, and cakes of watercolors. Brushes lost their bristles, left hairs in my pictures. I made images on paper until I could summon them in my head again. Getting them to flow without defining them in words was another big job. I finally did it, though. I forced the flow until it came back.

Now that I could think in pictures again, I used art to capture them. Once I'd made the pictures, I had them for good, even if I threw the paper version out. In the process of traveling from my head out my hands and onto the paper, the pictures printed themselves in my memory, fixed there so I could summon them at will.

At first Dad didn't get my art at all, but Mom liked it. She used the fridge as my gallery, swapping out paintings every week when I brought them home. Later she convinced Dad to attach corkboard to a whole wall of my room. I tacked up big sheets of paper all across it. Finally, I could paint as large as I wanted.

I had just finished a big piece—*Delight*, a green core streaked with gold, lots of little yellow explosions around the edge, red dots, and blue-green spirals—when Dad knocked and came into my room. He stared at the picture. Then he went and got the digital camera.

After Dad photographed *Delight*, I ripped it down and started on *Sadness*, not deep sadness, but the melancholy of *Nobody really gets what I think*. It had a lot of squiggles like question marks, so it was more puzzled than the melancholy I set out to do, and there was some lavender in it, and orange like the inside of a ripe mango, and light pink. Not depressing enough, but maybe it was a picture of something else. That happened—part of the confusion between words and pictures. I would think I understood my thoughts in words, and the pictures would tell me a different truth.

"Kim," Dad said when I was still working. "Come here a sec."

He took me to his office and showed me how he'd put my artwork on the computer. He'd done it in layers—a yellow layer, a green layer, a layer for the spirals—so he could move the elements around.

At first I hated it. My picture was perfect the way it was. Then I got intrigued. I could make some parts bigger and other parts smaller, change the placement, blow the whole thing up so big I could see the brushstrokes and the paint that had flicked off when I lifted the brush.

Dad put the art program on my laptop and gave me a digital camera. I still painted giant art on my bedroom wall, but then I worked on my pictures in new ways.

I promised Dad I'd photograph all my pictures and store them on the hard drive. He asked permission to use them in the computer games he designed, and I thought, *Why not?* He copied my files once a week and sent them to his graphics guy, Henry.

Henry and Dad came up with great games, but they didn't get along very well. You could see it in their work. Dad's characters destroyed a lot of Henry's scenery, and sometimes Henry's scenery killed or crippled Dad's characters. Dad had given Henry some of Don's manga babes, too, and Henry got rid of them in the first ten seconds. My pictures survived, woven into the fabric of Henry's worlds.

The next year, I discovered science. In biology, what I saw in the microscope astonished and delighted me. After that, I took astronomy. When I saw photographs of galaxies and nebulae, novae and star clusters, I finally got what my art teacher had been trying to do with her fruit and vases; she had just used the wrong objects to inspire me. My bedroom wall teemed with single-celled organisms swimming among stars, ringed planets floating inside amoebae. Dad and Henry designed a game around some of the things I painted: Alice in Macro/Microland.

I never figured out if it was my art that kept me from making friends at school or my lack of friends that made me focus on art. Whatever the reason, I had lots of time to work on art after school because I didn't have anyone to do things with.

Then, a few weeks into tenth grade, Shaina Darnell walked into homeroom.

Shaina had just moved to Oregon from southern California, she said loud enough for everybody to hear. To me, she looked like California: a slender figure in a pale green dress, with a glory of golden hair and tanned skin, gold bangles on her wrists, and strappy gold sandals on her feet. She smiled at us.

The picture in my head had yellow-green streaks of envy along one side, and bubbling delight in pale turquoise and apple green, with silver sparkles. There was something so appealing about Shaina. I added orange for warmth, because her smile seemed to say, "I like you all," and her eyes were amber. I knew Shaina was about to be the popular girl, displacing Amy Singleton, who had been the most popular since fifth grade and was totally mean with it.

Shaina smiled. Boys sat up straight. She looked around the room, and then her gaze stopped at me. Her eyes got wider and so did her smile. She came straight down the aisle toward the back where I sat, and dropped into the desk next to mine.

Everyone was watching. I was sure they were as stunned as I was.

Gold shot into my picture, along with fishhooks of dark purple, the suspicion that my delight was about to be punctured. Nothing this good could last.

"What's your name?" asked the beautiful Californian.

I swallowed and managed to say, "Kim Calloway."

"Shaina Darnell." She held out a hand. Her fingernails were polished sparkly pale pink.

I put my hand in hers. I was interested in the contrast

between her slender, perfect fingers and my paint-stained, calloused ones, but only for a second. Something happened when we touched. Shaina stared at me with wonder. It was almost as if she could see the picture in my head. I added a dusting of golden pollen, and she blinked, smiled, whispered, "Wow. Kim, *please* say you'll be my best friend."

First time somebody asked to be my friend. The picture I saw then was too big and bright to fit on a wall.

Having Shaina changed everything. Everybody wanted her at their parties, and she never went anywhere unless I came, too. We weren't glued to each other, but she made people be nice to me; she made sure I felt safe. At first, I sat in dark corners and watched, but then one or two people talked to me, and then a few more. I learned how to talk to them, how to joke. How to relax.

Shaina talked me out of wearing my paint-spattered overalls all the time, and into wearing regular clothes. She and I went to the earring store and got matching ear-piercings, adding new ones to celebrate major triumphs, like good test scores, my artwork getting into the yearbook, her poem being published in the school newspaper.

After I met Shaina, I stopped working things out on my art wall. I still had my mental picture side—anything could spark a flood of images—but I just let them flow through my head, not through my fingers. Mom got mad when she noticed I wasn't bringing her anything new for the fridge. I slapped down a few of my best moods for her every once in a while, but I had lost the drive to capture everything.

Shaina's arrival started two and a half of the best years I had ever lived. Then, in the middle of senior year, things changed.

If I had still been painting, those spring and summer pictures would have been black, relieved by occasional dark purple splotches and starved faces staring up from the bottom of a dark pit.

I hardly even noticed high school graduation.

In the fall, I ran away to college.

CHAPTER 1: *Jaimie*

"Jaimie, you know how to get in touch with us?" my dad asked. We grabbed satchels from the back of the pickup and headed toward my dorm, Fernald Complex. Other Sitka State freshmen and their parents were milling around or carrying things up the wide steps into the brick building. The leaves on the trees were still green in late September, and the lawns that spread between the buildings were green, too. Looked like fall came later to Spores Ferry, Oregon, than it did to Arcadia, where Dad and I had driven from.

The air was full of hope and fear, dust and sunlight. The other students looked young, but that made sense; I'd decided to go to the university after I'd been out of high school two years.

"*Dad.*" A day and a half on the road, a stopover in my first hotel ever, and he had already asked me six or eight times if I knew how to call home. I never had a good answer.

"*Jaimie,*" he said. Then he smiled. "I know, I know. I should let go of it. But you're my youngest daughter, and you're leaving home. I can't help worrying."

Rugee, the Presence who had decided to come with me, stuck his green-and-orange head out of the open outer pocket of my smaller satchel. At present, he was in the form of a really big salamander. He stuck out his wet, white tongue to taste the air. I took a sniff. Autumn, even though the leaves hadn't changed yet. The air smelled like transition.

"If you guys would just get a phone, everything would be easier," I said. I'd been living away from my family's home complex, Chapel Hollow, for a while—most recently in Arcadia, the nearest town, with Trixie, a normal human being whose house had all kinds of things we didn't have, starting with electricity. Television, radio, a CD player. A computer. An automatic dishwasher, washing machine, and clothes dryer. Water you didn't have to heat using spells.

Trixie had a telephone. Simple, handy! Used by nearly everyone in the world except a bunch of snotty *Ilmonishti*—my family.

"Who needs easy?" said my dad as we climbed the dorm steps.

"It would be nice if *some*thing was easy." I opened one half of the double door, and we went inside.

"Lots of things are easy for you. You're full of talents. You're Sign Air. I don't know why Wordwaft doesn't come easily to you."

I'd learned a lot since I had left home, mostly about the

gaping holes in my magical education. My generation had been taught by someone who, we learned too late, wanted us to grow up warped and ignorant of much of our heritage.

Unlike some of the others, I wanted to change. I knew some of the ways I had been twisted, and I'd worked against those twists in my own fashion, but I also knew I had damage I didn't even know about. I was still learning about right and wrong. That was one of the reasons I wanted to go away to college. Maybe here, Outside, among normal people, I'd find a new perspective.

I glanced around the dorm's entrance. Strong cleansers edged the air, blurred by the scent and presence of unknown humans. To the left, double doors opened into a big room with ragged chairs, couches, a TV, and some vending machines. Straight ahead was a broad hall.

Everywhere I looked, strangers.

We had my dorm and room assignment—Fernald, room 214. Dad had helped me fill out the paperwork for it way back in March, but the university hadn't sent a key or a dorm map.

People were especially thick around something across the hall. I straightened my shoulders under the straps of my satchels and headed over. Dad followed. Rugee ducked back into his pocket. I shifted the satchel so he wouldn't get bumped.

Like me, Dad was Sign Air, only he'd been at it a lot longer and had more effective training. I noticed that people parted in front of us, and when I trelled—a Sign Air sense that combined taste, touch, smell, and something else—I sensed Dad was using air to push people just a little sideways. I wished I knew how to do that! So elegant! So useful!

There was a bulletin board with room assignments listed on it alphabetically by last name. Next to it stood a person wearing a red button that said *R.A.* She was answering anxious parents' questions, handing out brochures, and smiling the kind of smile you get when you have a headache.

I glanced lower on the bulletin board and saw a map of the building, its three stories laid out one above the other. There were two wings branching out from the ends of the front hall, forming a giant U. Each length of building had its own name. The front section was Spangler, the left wing was Ellis, and the right wing was Light. My room, 214, was on the second floor in the center of Spangler.

"Where do we get keys to the rooms?" Dad asked R.A.

"Show picture ID to the woman in room one oh nine, down that way," said R.A., still smiling. She gave Dad a brochure. "Here are the dorm rules. You'll need to sign out a key."

Room 109 had another hive of buzzing people around it. Again, Dad worked his way to the front, with me following.

Picture ID, I thought. Not like I had a driver's license or anything. I'd never needed any kind of identification. Everybody knew who I was . . . until now.

Dad glanced at me and muttered something, rubbed his thumb across his fingers. A white rectangle shimmered there. He handed it to me.

It was a driver's license. The picture showed me, in a green long-sleeved T-shirt, with my thick dark hair pulled back—exactly what I looked like right now. Of course, it was a picture he took two seconds ago without even using a camera—air had the power of image—only with a blue background. I glanced around. Nothing in Fernald Complex was blue. Dad was good. All my vital statistics were on the card, and so were these gold overlay holograms that said OREGON over and over with many copies of the state seal. It looked real.

I held it up and trelled it. Layered, compressed air. I had never seen work like this before. My dad, lawyer and master criminal!

I handed my new license to an old woman behind a half-door. "Jaimie Locke. Room two fourteen," I said. She sniffed, frowned, went to a board covered with hanging keys, came back with one for me, made me sign my name on a form on a clipboard, and handed my license back. Then she dug through a box of blue folders, pulled one out, checked the name on the front, and gave it to me. "Don't lose this," she said. "You'll need to complete the form in there for your student ID."

I tucked the license in my back pocket. I felt it dissolve.

Dad and I eased through the crowd around the door. I nudged him when we hit the open hall. "Why'd you make the license go away? I bet I'll need it to get my student ID. Besides, what am I going to do with it that I wouldn't do anyway?" I opened a pocket on my satchel and shoved the blue folder inside.

Dad slung an arm around my shoulders and kissed the top of my head. I felt like an idiot, him doing that in front of all these strangers, and could only thank the Powers that no one here knew who I was yet. "It's a whole new world," he said. "Who knows. You might even try to drive."

"*Dad.*" Before I got my powers, driving or any kind of transportation that would get me far, far from my two oldest sisters had been all I could think about. After I learned how to fly, I didn't care.

"C'mon, Jaimiala, let's find your new home and set it up."

I didn't tell Dad not to call me by my full name in public. Nobody was listening. I hoped.

Besides, I kind of liked how he was when we were alone together. When I was growing up, Dad had mostly been out of the picture. During the day, he worked in town, away from Chapel Hollow; our lives only intersected at supper, and then in the middle of family.

A whole day and a half on the road was as much time alone with him as I had ever spent. We stopped on the way and looked at things, talked about them. He told me what his college experience had been like. He was one of the few of his generation who actually left home long enough to go to college. He hadn't lied to me about how hard it was for him when he first left the Hollow to live among Outsiders.

I wished we'd talked like this before.

On the second floor, we wandered around, passing stacks of luggage and many more confused people, and located my new room. Dad knocked on the door before I could get out my new key.

"Just a minute," said a voice on the other side.

I looked at Dad. "There's someone in my room?" I whispered.

"Sure. You have a roommate."

"What?"

"You said you wanted to experience Outside life."

"But not—but I need—but Dad—"

The door opened. On the other side was a slender girl with straight dark hair, thin dark brows, and tilted gray eyes with shadow smudges under them. One of her ears had four earrings in it. She was a few inches shorter than my five foot seven, and wore a long-sleeved orange shirt and faded jeans. Her lips and skin were pale. She looked way too young to be so haunted. "Hi. I'm Kim Calloway," she said in a soft voice. "Are you my new roommate?"

CHAPTER 2: *Kim*

M om and Dad dumped me off at the dorm at about ten in the morning a couple of days before orientation. They couldn't wait to get rid of me. "Do your best, sweetie," Mom said. "Call us every Sunday. Send me a painting if you ever do another one. Let us know if you need anything. It's not such a far drive."

"We love you, Kimmie," Dad said. "Play some Intergalactic Agent X. Maybe it'll get your mind off your troubles. On Level Five you might recognize some of the backdrops."

I could have cried. I hadn't given Dad any new art in three years.

They kept their hugs short. Probably afraid I'd drown them with tears if they stuck around. One of the psychiatrists I saw over the summer had looked into chemical imbalances, but nothing she prescribed had stopped the tears or put a dent in my misery. Maybe the medical department at Sitka was running clinical trials I could be part of, research on the terminally weepy.

My parents left me in the dorm room—well, after Mom got out the Formula 409 and a roll of paper towels and wiped down all the surfaces—and I curled up on the bed and cried.

Eventually I ran out of tears. So I unpacked.

Mom had slipped a big sketchbook and a giant box of markers into my suitcase, with a little note—"Hope you'll send me something new for the fridge."

That was worth a half-hour sobfest.

I found my old teddy bear in the bottom of one of my suitcases and sat around hugging it and cried some more.

I cried as I made my bed. I put my books on the built-in shelf above my bed. I set up my desk, with my laptop, printer, phone, and the big Webster's *Encyclopedic Dictionary* Aunt Molly gave me for a graduation present. She lived in Indiana and hadn't known how much disgrace I was in.

I glanced at the inscription: "To Kimmie, for a bright and definable future. Love, Molly."

I cried as I put my school supplies in the desk drawers and hung clothes in the closet and stowed other clothes in the dresser. Mom had tucked some boxes of Kleenex in one of my bags, and that made me cry, too.

I set a photo of Mom, Dad, and Don on my desk where I could see it from my bed. More tears. I stuck the photo in a drawer.

I studied the other furniture in the room, the second bed, dresser, and desk that would belong to a stranger. I knew her name: Jaimie Locke. I'd tried to find out about her in the roommate database, but there wasn't much information, and no way to contact her by phone or e-mail.

Jaimie Locke came from some northeastern Oregon town called Arcadia on the Columbia River. Its circle on the map was tiny, and so was the type. She was a small-town girl, like me. Maybe she wouldn't know enough to hate me.

I had turned into such a crybaby *I'd* hate me now if I was meeting me for the first time. My mistakes back home might not be branded on my forehead, but I wasn't hiding them very well.

I blew my nose, locked the room, and ran downstairs to check the schedule for orientation. It still didn't start until Wednesday, and this was only Monday. I scoped out the vending machines on all three floors. Pepsi instead of Coke. Baby Ruths, no Snickers. Nothing I liked.

The floor in my room was ugly gray carpet with scattered cigarette burns from before the hall went nonsmoking, mysterious stains, and shaved spots.

I got out my checkbook and looked at the balance, wondering if it would cover a throw rug. There was a big bunch of money in there Mom and Dad had given me for textbooks, but the money I'd earned myself was minuscule. I had been too miserable all summer to line up any part-time jobs.

Midway through the soggy afternoon, someone knocked on the door. I managed to drive the tears deep inside myself. We were going to live together for a year. I didn't want her to think I did nothing but cry.

Jaimie was tall, with lots of long dark curly hair tied back. She had a jaw like a superhero, and wide green eyes under slanting black brows. She looked like she came from some country where people spoke with Russian accents. She wore a green sweatshirt, black jeans, and black boots, and she was carrying this luggage like nothing I'd ever seen before—tapestry cloth bundles tied up in string.

The guy she was with? GQ gorgeous. Expensive haircut, green eyes. He wore an olive crewneck sweater and khaki slacks and dark leather slip-on shoes. He was carrying more weird luggage. He gave me a smile that made me feel warm.

I swallowed, held out my hand, introduced myself, and of course managed to ask the dumbest question possible: "Are you my new roommate?"

CHAPTER 3: *Jaimie*

I slugged Dad in the shoulder—how could he not have told me I'd be living with someone?—and said, "I guess I am. Jaimie Locke. Hi there."

Kim shook my hand. Her hand was small and cool, her grip stronger than she looked. "You brought your boyfriend? I think there are rules against that. The halls alternate boy and girl floors. There are no co-ed rooms in Fernald."

"This isn't my boyfriend. It's my dad."

Her mouth dropped open. Red washed her pale cheeks. "Sorry, Mr. Locke. You just look—"

"That's all right, Kim." He smiled.

I took a good look at Dad. Well, okay, so he was really handsome and you couldn't tell how old he was. There were lots of ways to alter your appearance. Sign Air had access to more ways than most, since light is part of air, and light is what people use to see. As a lawyer, Dad needed an appealing surface. I'd never thought about how young he looked, though.

"Lucky genes," Dad said.

Kim glanced from Dad's face to mine. Did I have lucky genes? She didn't seem to think so. "Well, please come in," she said, standing back. "I got here first, so I went ahead and picked my furniture. I hope that's all right."

The room smelled of despair.

The bed nearest the window was already made up with a blue bedspread. A scruffy stuffed animal lay on the pillow. The desk under the window had a dictionary, a phone with big buttons, a laptop, and a printer on it, leaving me the bed, desk, and dresser against the near wall. I set my satchels down on the unmade bed and turned to face Kim, my hands on my hips. "You mean you get everything with a view?" It was the sort of move I'd expect from my older sisters, but not from someone I wanted to get along with.

Spots of color showed in her cheeks. "I—I could trade if you want."

"Maybe we can change things around a little," said Dad. He put the two satchels he had brought from the car on my bed. We still had a few more things to collect, but it would be good to know which furniture was supposed to be mine before we went for them. "If we move your bed over by the wall and put the desks next to each other, both of you can look outside while you study. How would that be?"

"Fine with me," said Kim.

"Thank you. Jaimie, let's move some furniture, shall we?"

Already, things were odd. At home, if we wanted to move something, we used skills and persuasions—convinced air to lift objects for us and wind to direct where they went.

Dad stooped and gave Kim's bed a shove. It was on wheels. Kim and I went with him, and we pushed the bed over to the left side of the room.

The desks were different: no wheels. They required lifting. Dad put his bare hands on Kim's desk. I went over and put my hands on it, too. We exchanged glances. How did this work? Maybe we could use air and just act as though we were lifting? Dad whispered a word and the desk rose.

Kim helped us. She gave us visual clues about how to lift heavy things. Dad and I watched her and imitated, with subtle help from air. We changed the whole room around until we had beds against opposite walls with dressers at their feet, and side-by-side desks with half a window each to look through. I checked the view: our window overlooked the building's courtyard, which contained a cement patio and some white paths winding across summer lawns toward other buildings. Down below, people threw round disks to each other, or stood in clumps talking, or sprawled on the lawn with books in front of them.

Kim took the dresser and the closet on the left, the side where her bed was, and I got the dresser and the closet on the right.

When we'd finished shifting furniture, Dad said to Kim, "Our religion requires us to consecrate any space where we live. Is that all right with you?"

"Huh?"

"We need to do a ritual in the room. Could you please leave us alone for half an hour, Kim?"

"My stuff," she whispered.

"It will be safe with us."

"But—" She went to her desk and grabbed her laptop.

"*Faskish*, Kim," I said. "What are you going to do when it's time for class if you can't even trust me alone in the room with your stuff?"

"But I don't know you yet." A tear beaded in the corner of her eye. She wiped it before it fell, shook her head. "I'm sorry. I know that's dumb. I just—"

I looked at Dad. Persuasion was one of his strongest gifts, and not part of my repertoire yet. I liked Transformation more, and hadn't practiced Voice. Dad smiled at me and said, "Outside, Jaimie."

Meaning, *This is what you came here to learn, how to operate like an Outsider. I'm not going to help you with this.*

Kim rubbed her eyes. "I know this is stupid. I know I have to get over it. I'm sorry. I just had the worst six months of my entire life. This is supposed to be my new start. I've never been so far from home and alone—God, I'm acting like a baby." She let go of her laptop and stood up. She took her purse, a green leather sack, from the foot of her bed and slung it over her shoulder. "I'll be just outside." She took three steps away from her desk, then returned, grabbed the laptop, unplugged it from a couple of cords, and headed for the door.

On the threshold she whirled, the laptop hugged to her chest. "Why can't I stay? I won't say anything. I'll just sit on the bed and watch. Besides, I'm not sure how I feel about some religion being practiced in my room. I think there might be laws about that. Can't you go to church?"

"It's just—" I didn't know how to explain. I couldn't remember if Outsiders did anything like this. Was this one of the forbidden topics? I had a piece of paper somewhere in my luggage labeled LIST OF FORBIDDEN TOPICS. Aunt Agatha, our *Arkhos*, the community leader, had written it out for me. I was trying to memorize it, but it was long.

"Never mind," Kim said. She stepped out of the room and closed the door behind her.

CHAPTER 4:  Kim

Miraculously, I managed not to cry about getting kicked out of my own room. I sat in the hall and watched other people moving in.

A red-headed, green-eyed boy in jeans and a Floater T-shirt stopped near me. "Hey," he said. "That your room?" He nodded toward the door.

"Yeah." A guy was talking to me. A cute guy.

"What happened? Bad fight with the new roommate?" He dropped beside me.

"Um, I don't think so. She wanted privacy."

"This your first day?"

"Yeah."

"And she already booted you?"

"Yeah."

"Bad precedent. Don't let her push you around so early on, or she'll just keep doing it."

I tried to relax my death grip on the laptop, but I couldn't. "How do you know so much about it?"

"Older sister. Also, I know from experience. Here I am, running around on the women's floor, while *my* roommate's alone in *my* room, doing God knows what. Hi. I'm Casey Galvin."

"Kim Calloway." I managed to unhook a hand and shake. His hand was a little sweaty, but not too clammy.

He scooted his back against the wall. "You were smarter than I was. At least you brought something to do."

"Huh? Oh." I glanced at my computer. "Guess I could play solitaire."

"I could help you. What excuse did your roommate give for getting rid of you?"

"She and her father are conducting a religious rite to consecrate the room."

"Whoa. Loads better than mine. He said he's a CIA spy, and he has to secure hiding places in the room for the tapes he's going to make of budding terrorists. My guess is he's figuring out where to stash his dope."

"Yikes."

"What he doesn't know is that I have years of experience in uncovering other peoples' secrets. Suppose I find his stash, would you be interested in sharing any of it with me?"

I licked my lip. This was new. In my whole previous school career, I'd never had an offer like it. The wages of being labeled a geek. A few hours at college, and already opportunities were multiplying. "Ask me again when you know what it is," I said.

"Okay."

I flipped open my laptop and showed Casey my current game of La Belle Lucie. We played, me running the trackpad, Casey pointing to cards and where to move them.

My picture side blossomed: warm orange for a new friendship and the comfort of collaborating—Casey didn't always jump in and tell me what to do, he waited until I had a chance to see what was available; small green tips rising for the hope building inside me; a purple wash of apprehension; freckles of silver and blue; hints of red because Casey smelled good: chocolate, soap, boy.

I didn't notice right away what was going on in my head. It had been a long time since I'd built a picture with so many hopeful colors.

When I realized, I savored. I hadn't lost everything good. College could help me.

We played three games before Casey scrambled to his feet. "I'm going to go knock on the door, see if Flax will let me in. Will I see you at dinner? You going to eat in the dining hall?"

"I hope so."

After he left, I put the computer to sleep and sat there basking in the glow of having made a new friend and reconnecting to my picture side, until Jaimie peeked out the door and invited me back in.

CHAPTER 5: *Jaimie*

Dad waited half a minute after Kim left the room, his gaze on the door. "There's an appeals process, I think, if you want to change roommates."

"Maybe she'll settle down. Maybe she's homesick or something, and she'll get over it. The next one could be worse." Maybe this whole college idea was nuts and I'd give up and head home tomorrow. I went to my satchels on the bed and opened Rugee's pocket. "Please, Presence, bless and guard my new place." He climbed out of the pocket and up the wall, tasting the surface every few steps. He reached the ceiling and went invisible.

"Where do you want to set up your altar?" Dad asked.

At home, we had tools of worship on the mantel above the fireplace, where anybody could address Powers and Presences as need or ritual dictated. When I'd lived with Trixie in Arcadia, I hadn't set up an altar; I was close enough to go home when I needed to. Now I was going to be away from my homeplace for a long time, and I needed an altar. If Kim was nervous about this stuff, though—

"Do you think it's okay in one of the desk drawers?" I had never had to hide my faith before.

"Sure," said Dad. "That's where I kept mine."

I pulled out the lowest drawer in my new desk. It was sectioned into two compartments. I got out my devotions pouch and sat on the floor. "Power of air, help prepare." I stroked my hand over the surface of the back compartment in the drawer. Air pulled out the stains, physical and psychic, left by who knew how many other people.

I took a piece of midnight-blue velvet and laid it on the bottom of the drawer. "Let the nest be blessed," I murmured, smoothing it, "safe and comforting, restoring and restful."

Dad squatted across from me, quiet.

I opened my devotions pouch, pulled out the set of four small celadon pottery jars and the tiny herb bowl my cousin Forrest Bolte had made especially for me in my travels. The clear overglaze had crackled into webworks that almost formed symbols. I set the jars on the velvet.

I took out the wrapped green silk that held a sliver of our snow crystal, a part broken off of the whole that everyone in the Family had touched down through generations. Each had left a frozen shade of self there. A gifted Deadspeaker would have been able to summon them for conversation. Nobody in my branch of the Family had been able to speak to the dead in a long time, but we could all sense them a little. The snow crystal was a way to carry Family with me wherever I went.

I placed the crystal on the velvet, and added the carved and polished willow whistle my *miksash*, my godfather and personal teacher, Uncle Trevor, had given me as a farewell present. I let my fingers rest on the whistle, sensed that there were secrets in it. I hadn't tried it yet, and now I didn't know when I would. Maybe it was a summoning whistle, and it would call up something I didn't know how to deal with. Trevor set me teaching tests sometimes.

Rugee turned visible, scuttled down from the ceiling, dropped onto the desk, and hung his head down just above the nest compartment of the bottom drawer. He stuck his tongue out.

"Powers and Presences, aid me and guide me. Help to protect me so far from my home. Please bless my sleeping place, keep me in comfort, answer my summons wherever I roam."

I opened the first jar, dipped a finger into water from our home well. I touched my wet finger to my tongue, to Rugee's tongue, to Dad's tongue, to the drawer, and then the floor. "Water be with us."

I opened the second jar, dipped a finger into salt, touched it to our tongues, drawer, and floor. "Salt be our savor, our purifier, our covenant of truce."

The third jar held earth from the amphitheater at home, where we practiced most of our rites. I took out a pinch, dusted the velvet with it. "Earth of the homeplace, make this place, too, home earth for as long as I live here."

The fourth jar held herbs dried in our kitchen. I took out a bay leaf and a sprig of sage, touched flame to them, set them in the little bowl to burn. "Smoke, bear our prayers to the Powers and Presences. Thanks for all blessings. Thanks for your listening. Thanks for our present, our future, our past."

I unwrapped my snow crystal sliver, passed it through the smoke, and set it naked on the velvet. "I am distant but I have brought my family here. No place is far from Family."

Dad and I kissed our fingers and touched them to the crystal. I felt the shivery tingle I always felt.

"Thanks," Dad and I said together. We sat to think and savor. The herbs burned to ash. I put the lids back on my jars, rewrapped the snow crystal, asked air to hold everything in the compartment steady so it wouldn't tip, and pushed the drawer shut on my sacred things.

I got up and went to the door.

Kim sat on the floor just outside, knees up, the laptop tight to her chest, purse at her side. She was smiling and staring down the hall. She looked nice when she smiled. She glanced up at me.

"You can come in again. Thanks for giving us a little space."

She rose and stepped over the threshold. "What's that smell? Did you burn incense?"

I shook my head. "Just a couple of herbs."

"It smells nice. Kind of like food." She licked her lip. "It wasn't some controlled substance, was it?"

"Nope, bay leaf and sage."

"It's making me hungry." Her voice changed. "Um, what's that?"

I looked where she was looking, and saw Rugee, gleaming green and orange, still hanging on the front of the desk, his white tongue extended, probably to sip prayer smoke, which had been meant for him, among others. "Oh, dear."

Kim shut the door quickly. "There's a dorm policy about pets," she said.

"He's not exactly a pet."

She put her laptop on her desk and knelt next to Rugee. "Is he real?"

Rugee turned his head toward her. She held out a hand, hesitant. He tasted the tip of her finger, bobbed his head three times. "Hi," she said. "I thought I knew all types of salamanders and geckos. Reptiles and amphibians are some of my favorite animals. I've never seen anything like you before."

I glanced at Dad, who leaned against the wall, arms crossed over his chest. He cocked his head and watched Kim.

She stared up at me. "If he's not exactly a pet, what is he?"

"Um," I said. "A household god."

She sat back on her heels. "Are you making fun of me?"

"No."

"What kind of religion *is* this?"

"A family religion." I knelt next to her and held out my hand to Rugee. He was about ten inches long at the moment. He condescended to step onto my forearm. "Rugee, this is Kim, my new roommate. Kim, this is Rugee. He came to help and protect me. Since we're living together, he'll probably help and protect you, too, if you want. What do you think?"

"I think my mom would think this was crazy." She stroked Rugee's head with an index finger, something I wouldn't dare do without asking. He closed his golden eyes, then blinked at her. "But she's not here, is she? I think it's lovely to have a god living in our room. It's nice to meet you, Rugee. Please take care of me, too, if you can."

He touched his tonguetip to her finger again, bobbed his head at her, then leapt from my arm to the desk. He ran up the wall onto the ceiling and vanished.

Kim gasped. She turned her crystal-gray eyes to me.

"He's still there. Just invisible."

"He's a chameleon," she said.

"Sort of." I dusted my hands on my jeans and stood up. "I have to get the rest of my luggage."

"And then I need to say good-bye," said Dad.

"You do?"

"I have a couple of cases pending at home, Jaimie. You know that."

Of course I knew that. I just didn't want to lose him.

"Annis and Barney are just across town," he said.

My favorite sister, the only one I could stand, had moved here with her husband and baby son a month before. I had their phone number and address, but I didn't know where the dorm phones were, or how to find Annis and Barney's house.

I wondered about cell phones. I'd seen ads for them on

Trixie's TV, but Arcadia was too rural to have a signal tower; I'd never used one, nor known anybody who had.

Dad patted my shoulder. "Let's go, Jay."

"We'll be back," I told Kim, who nodded. As we left the room, I felt a pang. I was leaving my things with a stranger. Why hadn't I warded the drawer against intruders?

She must have felt like this while Dad and I consecrated my new place.

We needed to talk. If she didn't follow the rules, I would have to force her to, even though here at college I planned to try to live like a normal person, a person who couldn't use Voice to make others do her bidding.

How did normal people stand each other?

I had a lot to learn.

Dad and I headed back to the car, passing other students and parents again, some hugging each other good-bye. Students stood in clumps, talking to one another; there were a couple of people yelling at each other in the lounge downstairs. Dad smiled and shook his head. "What a time you're going to have."

One of my satchels had my favorite books in it. I tried lifting it with no help from air and hurt myself. "I can use my skills if I'm stealthy, right, Dad?"

"Yeah," he said. "Watch how other people are watching you, though. Tune in to what's around you. The minute people think what you're doing is too weird—you'll need to take steps."

"Like what?"

"Memory wash."

"Ick." Some people at home loved memory wash. I hated it. I had the feeling my older sisters Sarah and Gwen had used it a few times too often on me. The rule at home was you could do anything you liked to someone as long as it didn't scar them. Memory wash gave a person a lot of latitude. I had lost days here and there; no one would tell me what had happened. Sometimes I found bruises, though. Sometimes people looked at me with the wrong kinds of smiles.

I knew what memory wash tasted like—so delicious you wanted more. So lovely it was all you remembered later.

I knew how to make it and how to administer it. There had been a few times when *I'd* gone overboard, back in the days when I wanted to be my dark teacher's best pupil, because when she loved you, she made you feel wonderful and special, especially when you did terrible things to other people. I had memories of things I'd done to my cousins, even to my favorite sister Annis, that I was glad they no longer shared.

"You can avoid it by not using skills and persuasions," Dad said. "But stealth is good, too."

"Okay." I asked air's aid to lift my satchel of books and my second satchel of clothes. I acted as though my bags were heavy and I was having trouble managing them.

Kim was at her desk, staring at her laptop's screen when we got back.

After we dumped the last of my things on my bed, Dad gave me a big hug. I held on to him hard, pretending I didn't have to let go. Eventually he eased out of my embrace. He gripped my shoulders and stared into my eyes. "I've really enjoyed our journey together. You'll come home for Christmas break, right? Will you be home Thanksgiving weekend?"

"If I have to take the bus? I'd spend all my time on the road."

"You could get a ride with Barney and Annis, but that's true, it's a long drive. You could fly."

I smiled. "Oh, yeah!" I hadn't had much practice, but I knew I could turn myself into a dragon. Maybe on the weekends I could find somewhere to practice.

"Good," said Dad. "Work on Wordwaft. I'd like to be able to talk to you."

I shook my head. "I'd need a teacher."

"Maybe you'll find one here. Some of your Southwater cousins go here, too, you know."

"What?" I stared at him.

"Joshua Keye, Harrison Locke, Zilla Seale—you know them from the Gathers."

"They're *here*?" Josh was a year younger than I was, and Harrison was my age; they were upperclassmen. Zilla was two years younger than I was. That would make her a freshman, too.

I liked Zilla, as much as I knew of her; at our biannual family gatherings, she disappeared into the woodwork, and I had been pretty nasty for a couple years, so my nice cousins had learned to avoid me. Then I had gotten banned from the Gathers. I hadn't seen these cousins in five years. Joshua struck me as a cipher. Harrison, on the other hand, I pretty much hated. Sanctimonious know-it-all. Bossy. Unfortunately, way smart and talented, better at many skills than I was, not easy to intimidate or overmaster.

Possibly a teacher. Just lovely.

"They're here, and so's Annis. Well, she can't Wordwaft either. Worse comes to worst, call Trixie."

"Okay."

He kissed my cheek. "Bye, honey. Study hard."

"I will."

A heartbreaker of a smile, and he was heading for the door. "Bye, Kim."

"Bye, Mr. Locke."

The latch bolt clicked shut. I shoved my satchels to one side and slumped on the unmade bed. I trelled for Dad, felt him moving down the hall, down the stairs, down the hall downstairs, out the door, off to the car, and out of range unless I wanted to exhaust myself.

Dad took off and left me here all by myself, away from Family. For half a minute I let myself wallow in that despair.

Kim turned to me. "What's Wordwaft?"

Faskish, where was my list of forbidden topics? I was sure this was on it, but I hadn't even mentioned it! Dad was the one who brought it up in front of an Outsider. "It's a form of communication," I said.

"How does it work?"

I sat up. "Kim, there's some stuff I just can't tell you, okay?"

She cindered. It was weird. She was still sitting there at her desk with the computer in front of her, and she was still physically the same size, but something happened inside: she collapsed and withered.

I jumped up. "What? What?" Already I'd made a giant mistake. I hadn't even used skills to do it. Was I going to have to mix up memory wash already?

"Um, nothing." She stared at her laptop screen. It was dark.

"Don't do that," I said. "Don't zone out and pretend nothing happened. I hurt you. I didn't mean to. I don't even know what I did."

She bit her lower lip and looked at me. "It's not you. It's me. I'm a mess. God, I thought I'd be able to get beyond this."

I didn't even know if I liked Kim. I liked how she had responded to Rugee. Was she always such a whiffleball, though?

"How do I do this?" I asked. "I'm used to dealing with my family. I don't know what to do about you. What do you need from me?"

Tears spilled from her eyes. "God. I'm sorry, Jaimie. Want to go on a walk? Sometimes that helps."

"All right."

She grabbed her purse. I glanced at the ceiling, where Rugee hung, invisible; I trelled him. I knew he'd watch over our room, so I decided not to take anything. Kim locked the door and strode off down the hall as though if she walked fast enough she could leave her sadness behind. It clung to her, though, a sour gray surround of mood that nudged at my trell.

How was I going to live in a room with that? It would be like being stuck in a rainstorm for months on end. I hadn't met anybody in Arcadia who gave off such a strong cloud of feelings.

I could wall myself off, make an air envelope around me to keep Kim's atmosphere from brushing up against me. That would take only a little effort. I worked up a test version, a shield that would form if someone else's aura tried to swamp me. Okay: there. An invisible shield just under my skin that would spring out with a thought and form a bubble around me, keeping other people's moods at bay. I dropped it into a dormant state. I walked faster, caught up with Kim.

"Did you know this campus is an arboretum?" Kim said, her voice steady.

"What's that?" We were outside. I hadn't even noticed leaving the building. I glanced around. We were walking on a concrete path across a lawn. Big trees grew here and there. The light had yellowed as the world eased toward evening. A couple leaned against the trunk of a giant maple and kissed, her hands gripping his head, his hands on her butt.

Normal boys. People from my family were supposed to marry other people from my family, but I hadn't warmed to any of the appropriate Southwater cousins. One of my college goals: an intimate study of normal boys.

"An arboretum is a place where people study trees," Kim

said. "There are trees on this campus from all over the world."
Her step quickened. She led the way under a building arch
into a little courtyard where water ran over a tilted, textured
wall to drip, a fringe of plinkings, into a cup-shaped pool.

"Whoa. That's ugly," I said.

"Close your eyes."

I closed my eyes, wondering what she was up to.

"Listen," she whispered.

The water was talking, a whole conversation of voices as
it flowed over dips and gaps and obstructions on the wall.

I listened, memorizing the song. Water wasn't one of my
natural elements, but the sound of water strengthened water
workings. I wanted to be able to summon this again.

"A blind woman designed the fountain," Kim whispered.

My trell reached out to her and found her mood had
shifted. It seethed with spicy delight.

She touched my arm. "Come on." We went up stone stairs
to the top of the fountain wall and then down the other side
into another courtyard. At the far end, the building curved to
cup a grove of tall, lacy conifers with rough, orange-brown
trunks. Their tops reached higher than the four-story building; their branches interwove on the way down. The ground
beneath them was carpeted with ginger-colored needles.

I stopped. This was a power place. The trees gave off an
aura of ancient calm, a sense that their roots reached down
into the spirit core of the planet. Something vast and smiling
slept here.

Kim responded to it. Her mood steadied. We stood beside

the trees, breathing their spicy scent. "These are dawn red-woods," Kim said. "Everybody thought they were extinct, but then someone found a grove of them in a remote part of China."

"How do you know this stuff?"

"My parents brought me here on a university tour in August." She sighed and opened her eyes. "I don't know if you noticed, but I've been really depressed lately."

"No duh."

"The only way I could get out of it was to obsess about something else." She touched a sheaf of feathery needles. "I decided to obsess about the university. I studied everything they sent us and went online and read everything on the Web site. Okay? Scary fact number two or three about me: I'm hyper-prepared."

"Okay, good, because I'm not. Dad tried to explain how college works to me on the drive over, but I still don't under-stand. I thought I'd figure it out as we went along. If I can't, I'm prepared to ditch it and head home."

"You *are*?"

"Sure. Almost nobody in my family goes away to college. They think I'm weird."

"What about those cousins your dad mentioned?"

"They're all from the other part of the family, the south-ern branch, and they're weird, for sure. They're not as clan-nish as the northern branch. They live much closer to the *Domishti*."

"The *Domishti*."

I swallowed. Probably on my list of forbidden topics. "That's what we call normal people."

"As opposed to what?"

"The *Ilmonishti*, members of my family."

"What's the difference?"

"Um." I checked her mood again. Calm, not depressed. She had lost the earlier delight from the sound fountain, but she seemed stable. "Kim, don't fall over a cliff again, okay?"

"What?"

"There's a bunch of stuff I'm not supposed to talk about with—with *Domishti*. It's got nothing to do with you in particular. I'm not saying it to be mean, all right? I just—have my orders."

The gray swooped up and enfolded her like a giant pair of wings. I activated my aura shield. Air gave me the power to stand beside her without getting rained on by her depression.

"Don't do that!" I said.

She swiped at tears. "Do what?"

"Don't keep falling in a pit!"

"I'm sorry, Jaimie. I can't seem to stop."

I dropped my shield. I reached out and grasped a handful of redwood needles. The ancient spirit of the trees hummed in them and let me connect. I gripped Kim's hand and channeled a flow toward her. It was easier to transfer through touch; it wasn't exactly an Air matter. She blinked, stared at me as the sour, aching smoke slowly faded from her aura. "What are you doing?" she whispered.

"Something I can't talk about. How do you feel?"

"Better." She straightened. "Wow. So you can't talk about it. But I could guess, right? And you could tell me whether I guessed correctly."

"No, I can't. I shouldn't."

"Oh." The gray tried to creep back, so I kept up the tree-spirit flow and diluted it. "I can guess anyway."

"Yeah."

She was silent. I might have felt embarrassed, standing there with one hand around a bunch of plant matter and the other gripping my roommate's hand, except the tree-spirit calmed me, too. Finally Kim said, "Trees take a longer view, don't they? The minute's not that important."

"Kind of depends on the minute," I said. "I've never talked to a tree while it was on fire."

She swallowed. "What do you want to major in?"

"Psychology."

"And you talk to trees?"

"Not usually."

"But right now—it feels like—" Savory flavors seeped into her moodscape as the despair washed out. She smiled. "Well, this is definitely weird, but wonderful. Thanks, Jaimie."

"You're welcome. You okay?"

"Yeah."

I let go of her hand and channeled some of the tree's quiet and calm into my power reservoir. I might need it later. I let the needles slide out of my hand, extending my thanks to the tree, which might or might not have noticed. "What else do you know about campus?"

"It would take hours to tell. I want to show you one more tree." She checked her pink Powerpuff Girls watch. "Supper's already started, but it lasts an hour and a half, so we can be late."

She led me out of the tree courtyard by a different exit, between two wings of what she said was the Art and Architecture Building. We walked past some sixties-era dorms, which looked like hives—stories and stories of glass cubicles. I was glad I hadn't ended up in one of those. On a corner where two streets intersected, a pine tree stood, half surrounded by a low burnt-brick wall. The tree looked healthy and young, but it was just a Doug fir, same as lots of other trees in Oregon. I glanced at Kim, wondering what the big deal was.

"Can you tell what's different about it?" she asked.

I stepped closer to the tree, closed my hand around a needle-furred branch. Tree spirit, vigorous as trees I'd known at home. A tiny touch of otherness beneath it, though; a sense of lost-and-found I couldn't understand. "There's something. What is it?" I asked.

"It's a moon tree," she said. She lifted a concealing branch and pointed to a plaque on the brick wall.

THIS TREE GROWN FROM A SEED THAT ORBITED THE MOON IN THE APOLLO XIV CAPSULE IN 1971. PLANTED HERE IN HONOR OF THE NATION'S BICENTENNIAL. APRIL 30, 1976.

I shivered and felt strange then. The seed had left Earth. It had gone beyond Air, Water, and Fire. Then it came back. Had it lost touch with home during its trip? It felt almost like a normal tree. Almost.

"Let's go see what horrible food the cafeteria has," Kim said. "Don said it's legendary."

"Who's Don?"

"My extremely irritating older brother, who graduated from here last spring. He told me lots of things about campus life. I hope he was lying about some of it."

When I released the moon tree, an inch-long needle fell into my hand. I tucked it into my pocket. I love gifts.

CHAPTER 6: Kim

As we walked back, Jaimie said, "What do you know about normal boys?"

I heard her, but I was lost in a flood of pictures. Images of green fossil needles, Jaimie's long slender hand touching them, our hands clasped, a green river superimposed over the transaction, a silhouette of the whole tree with a deep root leading—I didn't know where—to one side. My fingers itched for those marking pens Mom had sneaked into my luggage.

"Kim?"

I savored the collage in my head long enough to memorize it—I hoped—then abandoned it, shifted into wordthought, and considered Jaimie's question. "Boys? I don't have a lot of experience. I dated a few times in high school, but just so I could double date with my best friend." Shaina. Just thinking her name turned my picture side to shadows.

"Quit it," Jaimie said, shaking me.

"What?"

"You're falling into a pit again!"

"How can you tell?"

"Never mind. Just stop it."

"Don't you think I would if I could?" I cried.

"I don't know what you do for entertainment. Maybe this is your idea of fun."

"I hate it!" I yelled. "I absolutely hate it! I want it to stop!"

"Oh, okay. We can work on that, then."

"I've tried everything. Herbs. Psychiatrists. Drugs."

She said, "That's not everything." She gripped my hand again, and even though she wasn't touching the dawn redwoods, I had that feeling of timelessness again. Emotions were momentary; it was the long run that counted.

"Oh, God," I said. "Thanks." This was no normal thing. My picture side understood immediately: a silhouette of Jaimie with a corona of colored light around her. Words put it together, too, but took a little longer: Strange religion. Forbidden topics, including something called Wordwaft. Talks to trees. Can put a spell on me. So far, benign. Fingers crossed it stays that way.

My roommate was a witch.

I pictured Jaimie in black, with a rippling cape and a tall pointed hat. No. That was ridiculous. Maybe I was getting better all by myself, or maybe spending time with someone my own age who didn't hate me was what I needed to get out of my depression.

I blinked Jaimie back to herself. She looked anxious.

She gripped my hand. "You're welcome. I won't ask you about boys anymore."

Inside the dorm, I headed for the dining hall. People were talking, and silverware scraped on plates. We paused in the hall. I said, "It's not talking about boys that bothers me. It's the other part. The best friend part. I'm not the person to ask about boys, anyway." Now that I was calm, I could talk about it. "I never had anyone special, just guys who would settle for me temporarily because it put them close to my best friend." I stopped, waited for the misery that swamped me every time I said "best friend."

Nothing. *Nothing!*

Maybe my roommate *was* a witch! She was better than therapy or antidepressants, anyway.

"Do you want to find out more about boys?" Jaimie asked.

A bright red spiral of interest, outlined with yellow, shot up through my picturescape. "Yeah." I smiled. I couldn't help it. I couldn't remember the last time I had smiled because I couldn't stop myself.

"Good. Let's eat," said Jaimie.

I followed her into the noisy dining hall.

CHAPTER 7: *Jaimie*

A room full of strangers! So many I couldn't have turned them all into toads at once if I tried. They were eating and talking and throwing food—well, some of them threw food. The room was smoky with anxiety and hope, small puffs of happiness and apprehension, and a thin, pervasive sweet-and-sour homesickness.

I'd been seeing strangers all day, but this was my first concentrated dose. These were the people I was going to live with. I had no clout with them yet; none of them knew me well enough to be scared of me.

I wanted to go home.

"Did you bring your wallet?" Kim asked.

Kim! Okay. I knew somebody. "No." All I had in my pocket was a fir needle.

"I'll loan you money for supper. Once you get your student ID, that's your meal card, but until then, we have to pay."

"Thanks. How do we get food?"

"It's a buffet. Just take what you like." She headed over to a stack of turquoise trays by a rail that ran alongside glass-fronted displays. Nobody was there except some people in white hats behind the counter; everyone else already had food. Kim took a tray, napkins, and silverware, and set it on the rail.

I got it. We'd had a buffet in the Arcadia High School cafeteria, but I'd always brought my lunch from home, like all the other Hollow kids. I was hungry. It had been a long time since lunch, and despite Kim's brother's dire prediction about cafeteria food, everything looked good. I grabbed lots.

All Kim bought was an empty plate, which I didn't understand. Why should an empty plate cost $5.95?

We stood there with our trays and looked around. I trelled Kim's mood as it darkened. I felt the same way. None of the tables were empty. They were all occupied by people neither of us knew. Empty seats were scattered here and there, but how were we supposed to go up to strangers and sit with them?

A haze of shifty dark gray depression surrounded Kim, only this time something odd happened; it thinned and threaded across the room, a smoky river, toward the windows, where I lost track of it.

As I trelled the flow, a girl at one of the four-person window tables waved lazily at us. "Come on," I said, and headed for the girl, who had short spiky black hair and looked skinny and extra-pale. Kim's bad mood dissolved as soon as we had a direction.

The girl who had waved wore a knit top with wide black-and-white stripes. Not a hiding outfit, unless she was hiding out in a zebra herd. The other girl at her table had a lot of dirt-brown hair in an undisciplined snaggle above a dark baggy shirt. She was staring at a book and eating soup.

"Hey," said the spike-haired girl. "Have a seat. I'm Nan Quinn, and this is my roommate, Lydia Polydorus, who, as you can see, is a barrel of conversational laughs."

Lydia parted her hair long enough to peer at us through round, horn-rimmed glasses. Her gaze dropped back to her book. I trelled. She had a slick, don't-touch-me surface, but underneath surged a high tide of wild dreams. Nan was bright, with spikes in her aura as well as her hair. Her curiosity trelled sweet and acid, like a mandarin orange. I wondered if anybody else in the room had a pit of misery like Kim's. The dining hall was too bright and chaotic to sort, too many people's auras melding with one another. I'd have to explore when I was in smaller groups.

Kim held out her hand to Nan. "Hi. Kim Calloway," she said. "Spangler two fourteen."

"Spangler two twenty-five," Nan said. She shook Kim's hand and looked at me.

I stuck out my hand, too. "I'm Kim's roommate, Jaimie Locke." My voice always deepened when I shook hands with people, partly because I thought it was a funny custom, and partly because it made me nervous to touch strangers. In my family, a touch could be coercion; you could set up a spell or curse to activate the moment you touched someone.

Nan didn't do that. She just smiled as we sat down and asked if we knew about the Fernald ice-cream social and movie Thursday night.

"Sure," said Kim. "Part of orientation. Every residence throws a party so we can meet each other."

"Are we really supposed to wear pajamas?"

Kim made a face. "That's what it said in the Welcome Handbook."

"Way to make us feel like grown-ups," said Nan.

Kim laughed. First time I'd heard her do that. I liked it.

CHAPTER 8:  Kim

I wondered how Jaimie was at making friends. She could tell things about my moods just by watching me. Maybe she had secret knowledge. I wanted to think about the witch thing and collect data.

Was hanging out with Jaimie going to be anything like hanging out with Shaina? I wondered if she would be light to my shadow.

Jaimie smiled at me, smiled at Nan, and wolfed her food as though she expected someone to steal it if she left it on her tray too long. Nan and I talked for ten minutes before Jaimie said anything.

She started by embarrassing me. "Kim, why'd you pay five dollars and ninety-five cents for a plate of air?"

"What?" I looked at the plate on the tray in front of me. "Oh. D'oh! 'Scuse me." I went to the salad bar. I wished I'd looked before I paid, because there wasn't much of a selection.

"Are there bathrooms on every floor?" Jaimie asked as I

sat back down. "I haven't seen any yet, and I'm going to need one soon."

"Well, sure, but you shouldn't use the ones on the men's floors unless you give plenty of warning," Nan said.

"Why not?"

"Have you ever been in a men's bathroom?" Nan was grinning, the joke on Jaimie, and it made me a little mad.

"No," Jaimie said. "Are they different?"

"There's restrooms off the front hall next to the lounge," I broke in. "You're not supposed to use the residents' restrooms on the men's floors, which are first and third, Jaimie."

"Oh. Too bad." She smiled at me. "Sounds like a good place for boy research, but okay."

"Boy research?" Nan asked. One side of her grin rose higher than the other. Again, I suspected she was making fun of Jaimie, and I didn't like it. I'd never felt protective toward anyone before. Shaina had protected me from other people's spite until people fell out of the habit of teasing me.

I didn't want Jaimie to start out like I had.

Like I could do anything to stop it, when I was on shaky ground myself.

Before I could figure out what to say to deflect Nan, Lydia parted her hair to peek at us, mostly at Jaimie. She had finished her soup and sat there with her book open. If I was a hermit, I would have left the table and gone where no other people were, but she stayed. My picture of her, overlapping layers of brown, brightened, with a magenta question squiggle in it.

"I want to know more about normal boys," Jaimie said. "Are you a good person to ask?"

Nan laughed, but her answer was serious. "I don't claim to be an authority. I think they're just as confused as we are. My high school boyfriend went to college somewhere else, and he said he thought we should see other people. Sort of makes me want to dump him. I decided to try a new look and see if I *could* hook up with somebody else." She ran her fingers through her hair, making the spikes stand up straighter. Her fingernails were polished black, with white moons. "College is my lab. Sign me up for your research project."

I relaxed. Maybe this would be all right.

"Okay." Jaimie frowned, then looked at people at other tables. Fernald was a co-ed dorm; half of them were boys. I saw Casey about four tables away, sitting with a giant guy who had long dark hair. Casey smiled at me. Red flared through my picturescape, along with orange sparks of surprise. I smiled back and wondered whether I should tell Jaimie I already knew a boy. "Kim's in it, too," Jaimie said. "Lydia?"

Lydia shook her head without looking up.

"What kind of research did you have in mind?" Nan asked.

"Don't say anything until I have a notebook or a laptop in front of me," I said. "Any scientific endeavor needs documentation."

Jaimie grinned. "I realize it's a radical idea . . . but maybe we could just talk to some of them."

"Genius," said Nan.

They were still plotting after I'd finished. Most of the other people in the dining hall had left. Jaimie was happy and shiny enough to remind me of Shaina before things changed; I felt oddly at home. Lydia was like a bad reflection of me, Nan's shadow companion.

Nan had reinvented herself. I wanted to start over, too, but I wasn't sure how. Maybe fate cast me as a companion. Maybe I would betray Jaimie, too. That was who I was, after all. A betrayer. I deserved what I got.

"Kim!" Jaimie shook my shoulder.

I stared down at my empty plate without seeing it. Shadows darkened my vision.

"What's wrong with her?" Nan asked.

"Homesick," Jaimie said, with a catch in her voice. "Kim, come upstairs. You can call your family, huh?"

"I'll bus your trays," Nan said as Jaimie dragged me away.

Lydia parted her hair and stared after us until the cafeteria doors swung shut.

CHAPTER 9: *Jaimie*

Kim had slipped into depression again. I was going to run out of calm, maybe before I pulled her back. The dawn redwoods weren't too far, so I knew I could go outside and pick up a new supply of equilibrium without too much trouble, but if this kept happening—

In the hall, I stopped and gripped Kim's shoulders, sent her all the calm I had on reserve, though it didn't work very well. I couldn't believe she could go from relaxed to this in no time flat. What had triggered it? I trelled. Something was tugging on her, something still in the dining hall; my trell followed a trail of gray through the doors, but it diffused too much for me to track it to its end point.

Rugee might be able to help. I grabbed Kim's wrist and dragged her upstairs.

"Where's your key?" I asked Kim when we got to our door.

She rummaged in her purse. Tears flowed down her cheeks,

dripped off her chin onto her shirt. She handed a key to me.

A home feeling embraced me as I pulled Kim into our room. I felt the glow from the drawer that held my altar, and the shift in atmosphere near the ceiling where I trelled Rugee's presence. I closed and locked the door, then walked Kim to her bed and sat her down.

"Help," I said.

Rugee walked down the wall behind Kim, shifting from invisible Presence to his green-and-orange salamander manifestation. He scuttled across the bed, climbed onto her thigh, and stared up at her lowered face with golden eyes.

This mood isn't a natural thing, Rugee told me.

"Do you know enough about normal people to be able to tell?" I asked.

Use your senses, Jaimiala. A substance comes off the girl; something summons it.

He confirmed what I had already noticed, but I didn't know what it meant.

Kim sniffed and scrubbed the tears off her face. "Do I know enough about normal people to tell what?"

"I think there's something seriously wrong with you," I said.

She picked up a plastic water bottle from her desk and drank, then laughed shakily. The sobs had stopped. "Sure," she said. "What was your first clue?"

"Something that's not your fault."

"But it *is* my fault. I did something awful. I deserve the guilt."

"You feel this way because of something you did?" I asked.

She nodded. She ran an idle finger down Rugee's back. I shuddered. There she went again, treating him like a pet instead of a god. If I had done anything like that, I would have expected to lose my shape or my luck for at least a week.

"I betrayed my best friend," Kim said to her lap. "That's when it started." She glanced at me. "I'd like you for a friend, Jaimie, but I don't know if I deserve you. I might do it to you, too. Maybe I'd better tell you, so you'll be able to make up your mind. I came here to get away from all this, but . . ."

I waited for the end of the sentence. She stroked Rugee again.

"I brought myself with me," she said.

I sat on the swivel chair by Kim's desk, rolled it over to face her. "Tell me the rest."

CHAPTER 10: *Kim*

I sniffed a couple of times, got a Kleenex out of my pocket, and blew my nose. I took a deep breath, released it. "My most important relationship used to be with paper and paints. Everybody ignored me, and I returned the favor. Then Shaina transferred to my high school when I was in tenth grade. She really *saw* me somehow. For the first time in my life, I had a best friend. *And* she was the coolest person in school. It was magical. You ever felt like that?"

"The friend part, or the magic part?"

"Either."

Jaimie pressed a fist to her chin. "The friend part, not so much. I was kind of a juvenile delinquent, and I scared the town kids. I did mean things to them. I have a big family, and we were pretty mean to each other, too. I finally figured out I really like my sister Annis. She's my best friend."

"Annis, the one who lives across town?"

"Yeah."

"Lucky!"

"Yeah," she said, sounding surprised. "As for the magic part—what do you mean?"

"Like nothing bad could happen. Like everything was going so well it was spooky. Like I was living in a dream."

She shook her head, smiling. "With *my* family? Naw. Never felt like that."

I studied her. "My older brother is an asshole, too. But you get along with your dad?"

"Yeah. I guess. So what happened with you and Shaina?"

"For a year and a half, we were golden. But she got a boyfriend senior year, and then she didn't want to be with me all the time. She'd say, 'Come on, Kimmie, you know other people.' When I wasn't with her, I didn't feel special or interesting. I'd forgotten how to be alone and happy. I'd stopped doing art when I met Shaina, and I couldn't get myself to pick up a brush again, so I was confused.

"I still did one best-friend thing for Shaina. She often stayed out all night with Peter and used me as an alibi with her mom. Her mom didn't even know Shaina had a boy-friend; I'd pick Shaina up and drop her off at Peter's. So I always knew when to lie about where Shaina was.

"One night when I hadn't picked Shaina up, her mom called and said, 'Could you put Shaina on? I need to talk to her.' And like an idiot, I said, 'Shaina's not here.' And she said, 'Where is she? She told me she was spending the night with you.' And I said, 'She walked down to the corner to mail a letter.' That was the only thing I could think of. And she said, 'It's eleven o'clock at night.' And I said, 'She just finished writing it.' And she said, 'Shaina's father had a heart attack. Please go get Shaina.' And like a dope I said, 'Oh, God. I don't know where she is. She never called me.' And she said, 'What?' And I said, 'I'll go find her.'"

This was the place where I always walked down into darkness and couldn't remember what light was.

"So then what?" Jaimie asked quietly.

I took a deep breath. "So I called every place I could think of, found out Shaina wasn't there, then drove around looking for her. I was insane with panic the whole time. It was amazing I didn't crash the car. It took me a couple of hours to find her. She and Peter were parking. They were furious." I had never seen Shaina angry before. Even after she hooked up with Peter and pretty much dropped me, whenever I saw her, her eyes were full of tenderness, and her smiles told me she remembered all the things we had done together. I hadn't known she could host such a storm inside, or that she would unleash all that scorn and anger on me.

I pulled myself together, made myself look into Jaimie's green eyes, so different from the amber of Shaina's. "It turned out her dad had a heart *event*, not a heart *attack*. It wasn't even serious. So because I was an idiot, Shaina's mom found out I had been covering for her, and both of us were grounded for the rest of the year, and Shaina wasn't supposed to be Peter's girlfriend anymore.

"Shaina hated me. She despised me. She told everybody

at school what a horrible friend I was, and I went home every day and cried. I don't know how I managed to finish school and get good enough grades to go to college. I couldn't think about anything except what an idiot I had been." My hands were fists on the bedspread. In the sessions with Dr. Fredericks I'd had during the summer, I hadn't been able to get this story out in one piece. I had just told him what happened at school every day, and that was enough to sink me into tears for the rest of the hour.

"That's stupid," Jaimie said.

"What?"

"Maybe I just don't understand this stuff. My parents couldn't control me. I always did whatever I wanted. But, I mean, *she's* the one who was trying to fool her mom. It wasn't your fault. You didn't offer to cover for her, did you?"

"Well—I think I did offer." I stared at the top of my desk. I couldn't remember how my alibi service started. Shaina told me friends did things like that, but was it before or after I offered? She accepted, and I had felt the connection between us again. "No, it was her idea, but how could I refuse? She was my best friend."

"Then it was a failure of planning on her part. She should have told you she'd need you to cover for her that night, if that was the way you had it set up. Besides, the whole heart attack thing would throw anybody off, wouldn't it?"

"Well, sure," I said, a little surprised.

"So maybe you made a mistake—if you could call it that

when she didn't brief you ahead of time and the circumstances were so extreme." She shrugged. "So what? You made a mistake. If I made a mistake like that, my sister might turn me into a rock for an afternoon, but she wouldn't stay mad."

"Your sister might turn you into a *rock*?" I blinked a couple times, trying to process this.

"Um. Or more like a statue? When we're really mad at each other?"

"How does that work?" I asked. She was backpedaling. Fascinating!

She looked alarmed. "Like, if I'm mad at you, um, you're a statue. I don't see you move, hear you talk, or talk to you. I ignore you."

"For an afternoon."

"It depends on what you do. It might last longer." She shrugged again. "So you're crying because of some dumb mistake you made?"

I hugged myself. "I guess I am. It sounds so stupid when you say it. I don't know what's wrong with me. I really like what you said. It was Shaina's stupid mistake." I smiled, felt a surprising glow of happiness in my chest for about two seconds.

Despair tackled me again. I couldn't figure out why.

I'd made some dumb mistake months ago and had a hard time at school, sure—but Shaina wasn't here anymore to torture me about it. What was wrong with me?

CHAPTER 11: *Jaimie*

Rugee touched his tongue to the back of Kim's hand. Then he looked at me with wide golden eyes.

Jaimie, there is a taste to her. I sensed it before. The story explains it a little.

"What kind of taste?" I asked.

Kim raised her eyebrows, her gaze on me.

Something has trained her to be miserable. Something feeds off her misery.

"What does that even mean?" I asked. "Vampires? There were vampires in that story?"

Viri.

"Am I supposed to know what that is?"

"Are you talking to me or Rugee?" Kim asked.

"Rugee," I said.

"Huh?" She stared down at Rugee. "You think he can talk?"

"Of course. He says some viri thing is feeding off you."

"What?"

"Damn! I probably wasn't supposed to say that." I pressed my fingertips into my forehead, my thumbs into my cheeks, as though I could drill some sense into my head. "Rugee, how am I going to not talk about this stuff to Kim? I don't know how to watch my tongue yet. I thought I'd have private space to decompress every day. I didn't know I'd have a roommate."

She has accepted my protection. She needs it. I give you dispensation to speak with her.

"You didn't know you'd have a roommate?" Kim asked.

"Dad didn't tell me until he was knocking on the door."

"Oh, God." She drooped again, the haze rising off her. She dragged out another Kleenex.

"Stop that. Quit dripping."

She can't control it. Something outside her desires her tears, has taught her to suffer.

"What do we do?" I asked Rugee.

Talk to her.

"Kim? Rugee says I can talk to you. Even about all the stuff I'm forbidden to talk about."

She smiled, though her eyes were still blurry. "I'm glad." She stroked Rugee's head.

I winced again. Then I searched my satchels. After I'd dumped most of my things out on the bed, I found the list of forbidden topics. "Look. Here's all the things I'm not supposed to talk about." *Wordwaft* was number sixteen. I handed the paper to Kim.

Her despair haze lightened as she read the list. I trelled

cinnamon for curiosity, and granite skepticism. Her brow furrowed. "Wow," she said. "Wow. This is—I mean—Jaimie, are you a—? Transformation? Spiritspeak? Deadwalk? Othersight? Krifting? What's Krifting?"

"Uh, it's a little hard to explain. I don't know any good krifters, but it's sort of a fortunetelling or figuring-out art."

"An art. A dark art?" she asked. A faint ammonia smell of fear.

"Depends on who's doing it and why. All these things can be used for good or ill."

"And you can use them?" Her face was pale, but at least her eyes weren't leaking anymore.

"Well, I'm Sign Air."

"What does that mean?"

"It's my orientation, where my strengths lie. I can work with the powers of air more easily than with the powers of earth or fire or water. My people, the *Ilmonishti*, usually have stronger skills in one direction or another. Air's good for vision and hearing, flying, a bunch of other stuff—" Kim looked a little shell-shocked, so I stopped. "You okay?"

"I thought you might be a witch," she said, "but I also thought I was making that up." She frowned down at Rugee, her hand stroking along his spine over and over. He looked up at her. His eyes glowed with golden fire. "You're really not a gecko, are you?"

He shook his head.

She grabbed her purse, pulled out a plastic case with bright artwork on the cover. Graffiti-like letters spelled out Alice in

Macro/Microland. "My dad writes games for a living," she said. "Some of these games, you drop right down into them and believe the world is different as long as you're playing. This one's my favorite." She could have been talking to herself. She handed me the case, and I saw a sketch of a blonde girl. She held up hands with powerglow around them. Above one hand spun a galaxy, and above the other was a paramecium with a face.

I guessed this was a computer game. My friend Trixie didn't have a game-playing system, but I'd seen ads on TV.

"In some of these games, I have magic weapons, spells that shoot from my hands and fry things at a distance, and in some I have other powers, power kicks, special attacks."

"What I am is not a game," I said.

She tilted her head and studied me.

"Seriously."

Kim sighed. "Well, at least let me *pretend* it's a game for now, all right? Sign Air, eh?" She studied the list. "Which things on here can you do?"

"I'm *really* good at Transformation. Most of the rest of them . . . I have a lot to learn."

She consulted the list again. "Voice? You're not supposed to talk about voice?"

"Not the way we use it."

"There's nothing on here about vampires."

I took the list and read it. No vampires, no viri, whatever that was. "Heh. Cool. Except I don't know anything about vampires or viri yet, so there's not much I can tell you. Rugee said I can tell you about the other things because you've accepted his protection, and it turns out you need it."

She grabbed the list, read it, and stared past me. Then her eyes narrowed. "Is this some kind of elaborate joke? Are you getting back at me for being pathetic?"

I looked at Rugee.

He bit Kim's index finger.

"Ow!" Kim lifted her hand to shake him off, but I leaned forward, pressed down on her wrist, held her hand still. Rugee chewed on her finger. He drew blood. He didn't have teeth, but his mouth had hard edges, and his tongue could produce a whole array of venoms.

"What are you doing?" she asked me, tears spilling from her eyes. She tried to jerk her hand free of my hold. "It hurts! Let go!"

"He's a god, Kim. He must have his reasons."

Rugee released Kim's finger, raised his head, and glared into her eyes. *Kim.*

She gasped.

Do you accept my aid?

"It hurts," she said in a small voice.

Yes. To give you my language, I had to hurt you.

"Oh, God. You *can* talk." She closed her eyes, drew a ragged breath. She shook her head no. Then she stared at Rugee. "I don't believe this. I can't believe this. I'm dreaming. I'm down the rabbit hole."

Before, you accepted my aid unknowing. Do you knowingly accept it now?

She shook her head again, then reconsidered. "Okay, I think I hear you talking. I'm going to pretend this is really happening. You really want to help me?"

He bobbed his head.

"Oh, God. I can use all the help I can get. Yes, Rugee. I do accept your aid."

Good. Someone has trained you in misery. Someone feeds off your misery. Jaimie, release her.

"Huh? Oh." I let go of Kim's wrist.

Taste your own blood. Taste my saliva.

Bewildered, she considered her bloody finger. It had a slick of clear venom mixed with the bright red. "Why?"

It will strengthen my presence within you and bind us better together.

She licked her upper lip then slowly put her finger in her mouth. "Tastes sort of like peppermint hot sauce," she said in a choked voice. "I can't believe this is what my first day of college is about." She clutched her stomach. "Confessing my sins, talking to geckos, taking drugs. My mom will be so proud."

I grinned. I liked this Kim. Then I sobered. "He says there's something called a viri that's using you. Making you miserable."

"Oh, great."

"But maybe we can do something about it."

She looked at the ring of red on her bitten finger. Cinnamon and the smell of fresh glue—the scent of confusion. "When you were talking about your sister turning you into a rock, you weren't kidding, were you?"

I shook my head.

"That statue stuff was secondary lying, huh?"

"Hey. I'm an Air Sign. I'm supposed to be good at lying. Guess I need more practice."

She licked her finger once more, then wrapped it in a Kleenex. "A rock. Your sister can turn you into a rock, but she doesn't leave you that way for longer than an afternoon. Is this your sister Annis, your best friend?"

"Yeah. My other sisters, Gwen and Sarah, they're nightmare people. You can't trust them to take care of you. Annis is never mean, just kind of strict."

Kim shook her head. "This is going to take some getting used to, Jaimie."

"For me, too. I've never explained my family and what we do, so I might not be doing it right."

"You said you're good at transformation. Could *you* turn someone into a rock?"

"Sure."

"Or something else?"

"Oh, sure. Annis does rocks because she's Sign Earth. I like animals better."

"Wow." She went back to the list. "Lifeskin. Tangles. Beguiling. What *is* Wordwaft?"

"Wordwaft is when I say something in this room and waft it to my father's room at home three hundred miles away. Then he says something, and his words waft back to me."

"This is different from a telephone how?"

"Home isn't wired for electricity or telephone service. We do it using skills."

"Oh." She set the list down on the desk. "Are you a good witch or a bad witch?"

"Um, well, that depends. I'm very good at the skills I've mastered. Is that what you mean?"

"No." She crossed her arms. "When you use these powers, are you doing things to help people or to hurt them?"

"I can go either way."

Gray eyes met my gaze. "Are you going to cast spells on me to hurt me?"

"You're under Rugee's protection now. He can protect you, even from me. I don't intend to hurt you, Kim. I hope I can help you."

She swallowed. "Okay. Good. Thanks. Hey. You hungry?"

"After that dinner?" I unloaded the oranges I'd stuffed into my pockets and set them on my desk. "Maybe."

"Me, too." She opened her desk drawer and got out a cookie tin. "Mom made these for me yesterday." She lifted the lid, took out some chocolate chip cookies. She gave me three, took one for herself, then broke one in half for Rugee.

"Thanks, Kim." I chomped two cookies at once. Not as good as the cookies Delia made at home, but decent.

Thank you, Kim. Rugee lowered his head and bit the cookie. He chewed slowly, his mouth opening and shutting. I had never seen a Presence eat before, had somehow assumed they either didn't eat or did it in secret.

"You're welcome." She bit a cookie. "Oh. Okay. Tastes

almost normal. I thought maybe I burned out my taste buds. Rugee, am I going to get infected from your bite?"

No. That wouldn't qualify as protection.

I laughed. I had never heard a Presence make a joke before. Or maybe it wasn't a joke?

"Did you bite Jaimie?" Kim asked.

Yes. When she was just a baby.

I hadn't known. I had just felt lucky that a Presence agreed to come with me. Few of my family had ventured away from home in any direction but Southwater. Only now were some of us leaving for the wider world, and I didn't know anybody else who'd been accompanied by a Presence. "You *bit* me?"

You were a charming baby. I wanted to claim you.

"Whoa. I never knew."

Later I wasn't so sure of you. Now I have hope.

Kim put her cookie down. She blinked at me. "See, this is totally not what I was expecting from my college career. And I—" A tear spilled down her cheek. "Damn it."

"Kim? I can make you forget everything I've told you so far, and we can start over if you want."

She frowned. "Let me think about it."

I ate my other cookie and wished I had more. If Dad were here, he'd be able to get Kim to offer him another cookie with just a look, but I didn't want to use power on Kim for things like that. I let my silent wish go without enforcing it.

Kim opened the tin. "Help yourself." She crossed her arms and leaned against the wall.

I ate three more cookies and then figured I'd better stop.

I already owed her for supper—where was my wallet? I was about to look for it when Kim said, "Something's sucking on my misery."

"Yeah, according to Rugee. I saw something happening with your mood I didn't understand, and that explains it a little."

"If I forget everything I've already found out about you guys, it'll still keep happening, right?"

"Rugee agreed to protect you. I think he'll work on stopping it, even if you don't remember he's protecting you."

While you are in this room, I can protect you, he said. *I am a local god. Unless you invite me to accompany you, I cannot protect you outside my sphere.*

Kim sighed. "See, I don't even know if I believe any of this. I could be way over the edge already, totally high on lizard spit and making up my own world. But on the off chance I'm not . . ." She shook her head. "I don't want to forget. I just wish I'd stop bursting into stupid tears. Way to make a first impression."

"Let's work on it. Maybe we can get you off the tears."

"That would be great," she said, and sobbed.

"Is there anything we can do right now to help her?" I asked Rugee.

I need to study this. Let me taste your tears, Kim.

"Oh, God! How creepy is that?" She set her hand down in front of him, though, and he climbed onto her forearm. She held him near her face. He licked a tear from her cheek, then another.

She lowered her arm and let her hand rest on the desk. He backed off of her and sprawled across her big dictionary.

He meditated. *The power is not in the tears, but in the feelings. Jaimie, trell what comes off Kim.*

I trelled Kim. Her haze was sweet and sour, smoky, and more concentrated than any personal atmosphere I'd sensed before. Most people's auras were lighter; they kept most of their feelings inside.

"You getting anything?" Kim asked.

"Yeah. You do give off something special, Kim. I've been noticing it since we met."

"Okay. Weirded out. Can't figure out how much more weirded out I could get, but I suppose there's lots of room for weird with you guys."

Kim.

"What, Rugee?"

Let me place my mark on you.

"Why?"

It is not much protection, but it is a little. It will alert those who can sense it that you are not alone, that if they harm you, they will have to deal with me.

She turned to me. "What is this—now he wants to *mark* me? How's that going to look?"

"I don't know. I've never heard of this before."

"Rugee? What kind of mark is it?"

Only sensitive people will see it. It will not disfigure you.

"Will it hurt?"

Yes.

"Like I need another reason to cry?" Kim stood. "Not right now, Rugee. Let me think about it."

He scuttled to the edge of the desk and stared at her. He swelled to twice his size. His mouth opened; his white tongue extended. Kim gasped and scooted back.

I knelt by Kim's desk. I had never seen a Presence change its form before. They kept to themselves, had their own culture on our ceilings, wove in and out amongst one another and mostly stayed out of sight; I didn't know much about them except we revered them, and if they spoke, we should listen. If we asked, they could advise.

"Please. Let her choose." I stared toward the floor, watched him out of the corner of my eye.

He bobbed his head, once, twice, twice more. He turned, ran up the wall with a patter of round-toed feet, and vanished.

Kim stared, trembling, at the ceiling. "Are you going to mark to me whether I want you to or not?"

No.

"*Were* you going to?"

I am frustrated by how little ability I actually have to care for you.

"While I'm asleep, are you going to mark me?" Tears leaked from her eyes again. Smoky sweet-and-sour flavor surrounded her.

No. No, Kim. I promise I won't.

She stood, wrapped in clouds of misery. At last she said, "Oh, hell, let's get it over with."

Rugee landed on her desk with a thump, visible again. He was still larger than he had been.

Kim startled. "What do I do?"

Put your head down on the desk.

She glanced at me. I jumped out of her chair and backed away. She sat and laid her head on the desk.

Now I'm going to kiss you. It will burn.

She closed her eyes. Rugee walked gently to her, lowered his head, and licked her forehead just above the nose. Kim jerked, sucked breath between her teeth.

Thank you.

"Sure." Kim's voice came out higher than normal. "That hurts more than a piercing. After this, all those tattoos I planned to get should be a cinch." She sighed and sat up, fingered her forehead, lowered her hand, and turned to me. "So what does it look like?"

I swallowed. "A tiny golden flame."

"That doesn't sound too bad. Thanks, I guess, Rugee."

Thank you, Kim.

She opened her closet door and stared at her image in the full-length mirror on the door's inside surface. "Nothing. Hurts like a son of a bitch, but there's nothing there, not even a blister." She closed the door, sighed, and flumped down on her back on her bed. "I had this movie image of roommates," she said. "It was going to be like sleeping over at Shaina's. We change into nightgowns and streak each other's hair. We turn out the lights and talk for hours. But you know? I'm tired enough right now to call it a night, except I have to

brush my teeth. I wonder if toothpaste trumps lizard spit."
Her voice was fading. The misery had drifted off, too.

I put away all the scattered belongings I'd spilled out of
my satchels when I was looking for the list. I made my bed
while Kim fell asleep.

CHAPTER 12:

I woke up with a warm lump on my stomach and the taste of burnt toast on my tongue. I didn't know where I was. It was pretty dark and it didn't smell right. I struggled up, fighting the quilt over me. Something heavy slid down into my lap. It was smooth, breathing, and very hot. I screeched, and someone else switched on a light.

Oh, yeah. College.

Oh, yeah. My roommate. The witch.

The lizard in my lap was a god.

I was wearing the same clothes I'd spent the day in. I felt itchy and sweaty, my mouth tasted awful, and I *so* needed to pee. "'Scuse me." I raced out.

When I got back, Jaimie was sitting up. Rugee was gone. I glanced up at the ceiling, but saw nothing. "Um," I said.

"Good morning," said Jaimie.

I looked at the digital clock on my desk. Four forty-five

A.M. "Barely." I didn't quite know what to say, so I just said, "I'm going to take a shower. You can go back to sleep if you like."

"What time does breakfast start?" she asked.

"Dining hall opens at seven."

Jaimie groaned and flopped down, pulled the covers up over her head. "See you later."

After my shower, I went back to bed. The alarm went off at a quarter to seven. Jaimie grouched at it before she dragged herself out of bed, muttering curses in some other language.

I got the feeling she wasn't a morning person.

I pulled out the pad and markers Mom had slipped me and drew while Jaimie yawned and brushed her hair. I hadn't done any art in three years, and now my hand was practically sketching by itself. Odd. What took shape was a woman defined only by what you couldn't see, the parts in shadow; and that was odd, too. I'd never drawn a human being before.

"Whatcha doin'?" Jaimie asked.

"Nothing." I shut the book and put it away.

Her eyebrows rose. She opened the bottom drawer of her desk, leaned over the shadowed back compartment, whispered something, kissed her fingertips, and shut the drawer again.

"What was that about?"

"I'll tell if you will."

I shrugged.

We dressed without talking.

"How's your forehead?" Jaimie asked as she locked the door behind us.

"My forehead?" I put a hand to it. It didn't feel fevered or weird in any detectable way. "Something wrong with it?"

"Rugee's kiss."

"Oh." I touched the spot where Rugee had marked me the night before. It didn't hurt anymore. I still wasn't sure it had happened. "Is it still there?"

"Oh, yeah," she said.

There were people in the hall, heading toward the stairwell. Jaimie and I joined them.

"Kim!" cried a voice. I turned. Casey.

Jaimie stopped beside me and looked at him. "You know a guy?" she whispered.

"Not very well, but yeah."

She gave me a light sock in the arm. "And you didn't tell me?"

"Shut up," I whispered, and smiled.

Casey laughed as he came down the stairs to where we stood, even though he couldn't have heard what we were talking about. A tall, black-haired guy with brown eyes, a dark tan, and really built shoulders joined us. He wore an oversized pink T-shirt, baggy cargo shorts, and blue Vans. His calves had muscles on his muscles. Casey's roommate? CIA? Oh, sure. Perfect low profile.

"Hi, Casey," I said. "This is my roommate, Jaimie. Jaimie, this is Casey. I met him in the hall yesterday right after you got here."

Casey stuck out his hand, and Jaimie shook it. She looked perplexed.

"Pleased to meet you, Jaimie," said Casey. "This is *my* roommate, Flax Dennison. He also kicks his roommate out of the room on occasion. Flax, Jaimie, Kim."

"Hi," rumbled Flax in a deep, deep voice.

"Way to break the ice, Casey," I said.

"What? I should lie, not say we related to each other because we were fellow kickees?"

"Well, yeah."

"Why bother?" He glanced at Jaimie. "Right?"

She smiled. "Um, because Kim asked you to?"

It didn't seem to bother him, even though he said, "Ow! Oo! Winged me. So can we eat with you?"

"Hey," rumbled Flax.

"What, you have other plans?" asked Casey. "Here I lined up two gorgeous women to eat with, and you have other plans?"

"Well, no."

I glanced at Jaimie. She was still smiling. We all headed downstairs and made our way through the buffet.

All the four-person tables were taken—I saw Nan and Lydia sitting with two other girls—so we snagged a table for six. Jaimie and Flax sat on one side, and Casey and I sat on the other. I leaned back, ate my yogurt, and watched to see how Jaimie's boy research would start.

Before she could start researching Casey and Flax, though, two guys marched up to our table. One was tall, black, and nice-shaped, with muscular arms crossed over his chest; the other was white and thin, with straight brown hair that hid his eyes. The second guy hunched his shoulders and buried his hands in his pockets. They both focused on Jaimie.

She stopped trying to steal a Danish from Flax and looked up.

"So you're here now, idiot?" asked the black guy.

"That's right, jerk," Jaimie said. They stared at each other with varying degrees of evil smile. The two guys sat down with us.

"Uh, who's your friend, Jaimie?" Casey asked.

"That's not my friend, it's my evil cousin Harrison. And my not-so-evil cousin Joshua."

Her evil cousin Harrison. Her other cousin Joshua. The cousins her father had mentioned who might be able to teach her Wordwaft and other skills.

Witches.

I set my spoon down. My stomach clenched like a fist.

Jaimie sighed. "Harrison, Josh, this is my roommate Kim. These are some guys she met, Flax and Casey. You guys, this is Harrison and Josh."

"Hi, there," said Casey, smiling wide. "You guys live in Fernald?"

"You kidding?" said Harrison. "I'm a junior. I moved to off-campus housing six months after I started college. This place is the pits."

"Oh." Casey's smile dimmed.

"Josh is a sophomore," Harrison said. "I got him a room

in my building last year, before he even registered. He never had to do dorm time at all."

I leaned toward Joshua, trying to peek under his bangs. He pushed his hair back to look at me. Okay, one question answered: His eyes were gray. They narrowed as he stared into my face. Specifically, at my forehead.

He smiled with half his mouth.

I straightened. Joshua could see Rugee's kiss. Could Harrison see it, too?

My fingers itched for a pencil. I wondered how I would draw those pale eyes of Josh's, that half smile. I dipped my straw into orange juice, then let the liquid dribble out onto my napkin in shapes like the shadowed underside of his nose, the line of his jaw, the shadows below his brows. The napkin sucked everything sideways, collaborating to turn my art random.

"So you guys aren't, like, kissing cousins or something?" Casey asked Harrison. "You actually *do* dislike each other? You wouldn't help Jaimie find an apartment?"

Harrison frowned. "She didn't ask. She didn't even let us know she was coming. I had to hear it from her dad."

"Dad called you?" Jaimie said. "*Faskish.*"

"Last night. He asked me to watch out for you."

"*Faskish!*" She muttered, "Dad. *Sirella.* Asking a guy my own age to keep an eye on me!"

"No way we could get you an apartment now. Everything's already booked."

"Hey. I signed a year's agreement for my room," Jaimie

said. "I've got a nice roommate, and I'm happy."

"Are you *ever* happy?" Harrison asked with a sneer.

"Shut. Up." She sounded more exasperated than angry.

"She didn't know you guys were here until Mr. Locke told her," I said, backing her up.

Harrison shrugged and fished out a piece of paper. "Missed connections, I guess. Well, anyway, Jay, here's where Josh and I live, and here's Zilla's phone number. She's got an apartment on Fifteenth Street. Call if you have questions or if we can help."

She sighed. "Thanks." She tucked the paper into her pocket. "May I talk to you after breakfast?"

"Um." Harrison eyed my forehead, raised his eyebrows. "I think you'd better." He leaned back in his chair and smiled at me. When he wasn't sneering, he was really handsome. Maybe even when he *was* sneering. "Hey, Kim," he said in a much gentler voice. "Go ahead and eat. We don't bite."

Some of them did. I glanced at my Rugee-chewed finger. I decided to withhold judgment about Harrison, and went back to my yogurt.

"What are you guys majoring in?" Casey asked.

"Biochemistry," said Harrison, "with a minor in environmental studies. Josh is majoring in theater."

"Can Josh . . . talk?"

Harrison glared at Casey. "Of course he can talk. What's your point?"

"Just wondering. He hasn't said anything yet."

"Harrison is better with words," said Josh. His voice was

mellow, deeper than I expected. "What about Flax? He's not much of a talker either."

"Flax is busy eating," said Flax.

"And stealing my food," Jaimie said.

"You started it."

"Oh, yeah?" She thumped his arm. "Where's my bacon?"

Flax pulled out a plate of bacon from where it had been lying in his lap. "Took you long enough to notice."

"Hah. I knew you had it. I wanted to eat my other food before you made anything else disappear." She picked up a piece.

"So, Casey, what are *you* majoring in?" Harrison asked.

"I don't know yet." He finished his oatmeal. "First job was to get here. Now that that's done, I'll figure it out later."

"Huh. Jaimie, you know yours yet?"

"Psychology. I want to find out how people work."

"Kim?"

"Biology."

"Flax?"

"Football." He grabbed Jaimie's blueberry muffin, shoved it all into his mouth at once.

"Eee!" Jaimie yelled, and thumped his arm again. "Go get me another one!"

He swallowed and laughed, spewing crumbs, then climbed to his feet and headed back to the food counter.

"Actually, he's majoring in physics," Casey said. "He's here on a combined science and athletic scholarship. He won some kind of science prize in high school."

I wanted a pencil again, but this time so I could take notes. No more leaving the room without a notebook and a writing tool.

Flax came back with more muffins and gave one to Jaimie. "Want some?" he asked Harrison and Josh, who shook their heads.

"We're not allowed to eat in here unless we pay for it. We're technically not even supposed to sit with you guys," Harrison said.

"What? They have dining hall police?"

"Yep." In fact, someone was heading toward our table. She had long gray hair and wore conservative clothes and glasses, and she looked mad. I held my breath. She walked on by and went to another table, where she started an argument with some kids who were smoking.

Harrison watched her. "They can be bought," he said.

"Wouldn't it be cheaper to just buy a meal?"

"This food? Forget it," said Harrison.

"Tastes pretty good," Casey said.

"That's because it's the first day of term. You just wait. They'll keep bringing the same food out until it's gone."

"Hey," said Flax, "they keep bringing it out after it goes bad, we can take it and toss it and force them to get more."

Harrison smiled at him. "Glad you have a plan."

Flax finished off another muffin and offered the last one to Jaimie, who shook her head but smiled.

We bussed our dishes, then stood around looking at each other. Harrison and Jaimie made eye contact. "Excuse me, you guys," Jaimie said. "I need to talk to my evil cousin."

"Oh, hey," said Casey. "There's Delia. I met her the other time Flax kicked me out of my room. Excuse me." He darted across the room toward a statuesque blonde.

On my picture side, dark lines seeped across the golden glow surrounding his symbolic image.

"Tomorrow," said Flax, and drifted away.

"Am I supposed to fade, too?" I asked Jaimie.

"No. You come with us."

CHAPTER 13: *Jaimie*

As soon as I closed the door of our room, Harrison turned on me. "You are so lame, Jaimie! Why are you even here? You have no stealth training whatsoever! You're *so* not ready for Outside. You obviously already slipped up with your roommate, since she bears some kind of spirit mark. What's *wrong* with you?"

Kim started crying.

I wanted to applaud her brilliance. What could be more confusing to someone as bossy as Harrison?

I'd forgotten she couldn't control it. She hadn't shed a single tear at breakfast. She'd even laughed.

"Kim, please don't do that," Harrison said. "Please don't. I'm not mad at *you*."

Her sobs went deeper and grew more wrenching, shaking her whole frame. Misery smoked up out of her, flowed past me, seeped under the door.

I knelt, my hand on the floor, trelled for all I was worth. Something was outside, vacuuming up Kim's misery. Something, someone—

Kim. Rugee dropped from the ceiling onto Kim's head. He shifted from salamander to impossible, something that wrapped around her head like a bat with stretchy wings. Her sobs cut off. The misery stopped. "Oh," she said in a surprised voice.

Rugee retracted his wings, reverted to salamander.

"Presence," whispered Harrison.

I jumped up and opened the door. No one was in the hall. Somewhere to the right, another door shut with a soft click.

"It was out there," I said. "The sucky thing."

Did you see it?

"I wasn't fast enough. I'm sorry, Rugee."

So it has followed her here. The crying is not just a reflex; the viri is still feeding from her. But you've frightened it away. This gives us time to explain. Who are you? He looked from Harrison to Josh.

"Presence?" Harrison whispered.

Rugee didn't know who they were. He had never left the Hollow until now, as far as I knew. *Sirella.* "Rugee, these are my cousins, Harrison Locke and Joshua Keye. They're from Southwater."

Southwater Clan was different from Chapel Hollow. Southwater people mixed freely with *Domishti*—sometimes even married them, Powers and Presences consenting. They kept their magical natures secret from those who didn't become part of their families. Instead of a great big settlement where all the *Ilmonishti* lived, they had individual working farms, spread out among *Domishti* farms. There was a big open-air gathering place in a canyon at the Bolte Homestead, where we all did our midsummer rites. I didn't know where Southwater Presences stayed.

I had been wondering about Southwater ways ever since I was sixteen and realized maybe I wasn't living the best possible life. By then I was uninvited to Southwater and couldn't actually go there to study what they did.

I said, "Harrison, Joshua, this is Rugee, who has chosen to honor me with his presence. He extended his protection to Kim, who is under attack by something wicked. Have you guys ever heard of viri?"

Joshua hissed. Harrison's eyes widened.

"Oh. You've heard of them. Rugee hasn't explained. How do you know about them?"

"We lost three cousins to them," Joshua said.

Kim sat with a thump on her bed.

"Josh, Rugee, Harrison, please tell us more. It's a survival matter."

Rugee slipped off Kim's head and walked down her arm to where her hand lay on her thigh. He was larger than he had been when I brought him here; now he was the size of a loaf of rye bread. He lifted his head. *There is a race of beings living among humans—there are many different races all intermixed, and to list them would take half the day—but these, which we* Kaneshki *call* viri, *eat emotions. Most do not kill. Most do not even harm. They can feed without damaging the ones who nourish them; but some become addicted to certain kinds of intoxicating emotions, and make their cows give this kind of milk only.*

"Cows?" said Kim. "You're calling me a *cow?*"

He looked up into her face. *Dear one, to me you are a child, but to the creature in question, you are something to feed on, something that gives sustenance without necessarily dying of it.*

"I wished I could die often enough," she muttered.

The viri who feeds from you is one who has gone wrong and twisted. It is a danger.

"Josh, what do you know about viri?" I asked.

He took a deep breath. "Nine years ago, a new person moved to FourMyle, the farm down the road from Keyes. She was fantastic and hot, and she turned every guy into an idiot. Hell, she set me dreaming, and I was only ten years old." Josh shook his head. "Even Dad and Uncle Bennet had dreams—everyone did, on up to Great-Uncle Jezra. We had three Bride Seekers in Southwater that summer, Jaimie; you remember? You were eleven that year. You came to the Gather, and we hid in the hayloft and watched the Bride Seekers romancing the Hollow girls in the barn—"

"Oh, yeah! That was you!" I said.

Josh smiled wryly. "Thanks so much. Nice to know I made an impression. Anyway, Adam Seale, Coleman Locke, and Elijah Bolte were all sniffing around your sister Sarah that year."

Yes. Three tall, handsome boys—one dark blond, one

black haired, and one, Harrison's older brother, dark like Harrison, a gift from his *Domishti* mother—all of them young and hopped up on hormones. They courted Sarah, seventeen, three years empowered and trained up by our dark teacher to enjoy the despair of others. That summer Gather, something in Sarah softened.

Joshua and I had watched from the hayloft as my sister smiled at these handsome young men, sparkled her slanted eyes, laughed at their jokes, and played them off each other.

That year I thought maybe things would be different. If these men could make Sarah go sweet and smiling, everything in the world could shift. Since her *plakanesh*, the transition when she came into her powers, Sarah had shifted me and our other sisters into shapes without asking. She had turned us into things we would rather not be; she had forced us with her Voice skills to do things that turned us red with shame. She gloried in our distress.

All that sustained me was the knowledge that I, too, would come into power, and then I would get her back. Make me a mouse, would she? A frog? A pig? Force me to do tricks and serve her? Someday, I promised myself, she would be a shrew. A tadpole. A skunk.

At that particular Gather, she preened for the men, teased them, didn't shift them or in any way torture them. When she could do it without the men noticing, she sabotaged the other marriage-aged girl cousins.

Maybe she would marry, I had thought. Maybe she'd find a focus other than making our lives hell.

Josh, beside me in the hayloft, watching my sister at work, hadn't understood my fascination with seeing this different sister in action. We didn't talk much, just watched.

He hadn't understood my despair when the men stopped paying court to Sarah—not until he found me one morning, a six-legged cat, because I had crossed my angry sister's path. He took me to his mother, Aunt Elissa, and she unspelled me and shipped me off to Seales, safely away from Sarah.

The Elders might have talked about disciplining Sarah, but I never heard about that. Not like when they banished me.

Josh said, "Well, the Bride Seekers stopped seeking Sarah, as you know. The reason they stopped was because they had met Jayana Havelock at FourMyle."

Harrison's hands fisted on his thighs.

Josh's voice dropped. "We didn't know for a week where they went. By that time, you Chapel Hollow people had gone home. Finally Uncle Rory did a seek spell on the missing men, and we found them, but it was too late. I mean, they were still alive, but she had burned through them, pulled out everything that made them who they were. All that was left was—"

Kim pulled inward.

"Blanks. Blank people. They breathed and blinked, but they couldn't take care of themselves, and there was no one home in their heads, and—"

Harrison said, "We tried to call them home, but they had gone on. We krifted and made sure. So we sent the flesh back to the—" He hid his eyes.

I knew he had lost an older brother at some point, but I hadn't known how. I touched his knee. He stared down at my hand before covering it with his own.

"We krifted for cause of death," Joshua said, "and one of the Presences told us Jayana Havelock was a viri. That was a year with three deaths and no marriages. We've never forgotten. We've been working on defenses against viri ever since."

"They were dead?" Kim whispered. "They were *dead*? I've felt suicidal lately, but I never planned to do anything about it. Your cousins were actually *killed* by this thing?"

"Brain death," Josh said.

"Jaimie!" cried Kim.

Rugee thought, *We are working to protect you, child.*

I went to Kim and rubbed her back, though nobody'd ever done that to me, and I wasn't sure it was polite to do it to an Outsider without asking.

"How can we help Kim?" I asked.

Josh frowned. "Great-Uncle Jacob actually managed to track down and meet a viri and discuss their lifestyle. He got a sense of viri energy, which we built into our wards. The next time one approaches, we'll know.

"Here's what we know so far. Viri can assume any shape. They don't live together. The way they bear young is different from the way we do; it doesn't take two of them. Each of them needs a few thousand people to draw from if they wish to live in comfort without causing harm. They are rare; they claim territories without much argument about it, since there are so many more people in the world than they need.

Each one can tell when others are about, but they seldom meet. Instead they avoid each other.

"If one comes to a new place and finds a viri already there, the newcomer moves somewhere else. Sometimes a few concentrate in cities, where there's enough people for all of them. In Southwater, one could survive comfortably, and we would never know it was around, if it acted the way it was supposed to. Most of them don't bother anybody. Every once in a while, though—as the Presence said—one goes wrong."

Kim's hands twisted in her lap. Tears overflowed. Rugee, on her thigh, looked up at her face. He climbed the front of her shirt. She hugged him to her chest as if he could save her.

CHAPTER 14: *Kim*

Yesterday morning, all I'd worried about was whether I'd keep bursting into tears in front of strangers.

Rugee struggled in my embrace. Was I holding him too tight? He wasn't the most comforting pet. Warm body temperature; but rough, scaly skin, no fur—wait, he wasn't a pet. What was I *thinking*? I loosened my grip. What if I made him mad? I had no idea what his powers were, or what he was a god of. What if he could throw thunderbolts and reduce people to ashes? He had been able to make my misery go away. And he said I was under his protection, so that probably meant he wasn't planning to kill me, but maybe I should be more careful.

Plus I knew he could bite. And that his spit tasted really, really hot, but it didn't kill me. Also, he could talk. Without moving his mouth.

Give me your tears, he whispered in my head.

So maybe he wasn't mad at me. I lowered my face, and he flickered his tongue on my cheek.

These aren't the tears of induced misery.

"No," I whispered, as I noticed the difference. This wasn't how I had felt all summer, drowned in darkness so cold and deep I didn't know how to swim up out of it, immobilized. This was despair and fear.

"What do we do?" Jaimie asked her cousins.

Her tone sounded different. And before, she had had her hand on Harrison's thigh, and he had his hand over hers. Wait—didn't they hate each other?

"Do you know who the viri is?" asked Joshua. "When did the trouble start?"

Jaimie turned to me. "She started being miserable last year after a fight with her best friend."

"Who's your best friend?" Harrison asked. His voice sounded a little shaky.

"Shaina Darnell." I sniffled. I should fight this. What did I know how to do besides art? Science. Collect data, come up with hypotheses. Devise tests for them. "Hey, Rugee, I need to get my notebook."

He climbed higher and settled on my left shoulder.

I edged over to my desk, opened a drawer, and pulled out my notebook. "I want to make notes so I can think about this rationally."

Jaimie, Harrison, and Josh stared at me.

Here I was, talking to witches about rational.

On my picture side, oblongs of dark green and blue sten-

ciled themselves across a chaos of orange wildfire. Flames ate
through the oblongs, sprouted tiny green vines with leaves
shaped like tongues of flame. Okay. Witches. Science. I could
put this together.

"Notes are a good idea," said Jaimie.

I opened my notebook and started a page called "Viri
Observations." I listed the first time I'd ever fallen into the
misery swamp—date, time, place—then followed it with a
bullet-point description of my summer, and all the things I'd
tried to stop feeling bad.

The cousins sat in silence until I looked up. "Kim, what
are you writing?" Joshua finally asked.

I showed him.

"Oh," he said, "cool."

I took the notebook back. I labeled another page "Viri
Data" and wrote everything I remembered him saying about
what viri were like, what they did. Everything Rugee had
said about them. I felt calmer already.

"So what do we know about Shaina Darnell?" Jaimie
asked when I set my pen down. "She seems like the most
likely candidate."

I flipped to a new page and wrote "Shaina Darnell." I
spoke as I wrote.

"She comes from California. She's an only child. Her
parents are rich. She's beautiful and talented and everybody
wants her. She picked me to be her best friend."

I chewed on my pen, then glanced across at Jaimie. "She
has nightmares." I had slept over a lot. Some nights, I woke

up to hear her whimpering in her sleep. Once she reached across the gap between the twin beds and took my hand, and her sleep quieted.

I told Josh and Harrison about how I'd lost Shaina. This time the story had no trouble coming out. "That was where my misery started."

"So where is she now?" asked Joshua.

"I heard she was going to UC Berkeley."

"Well, that would rule *her* out," Harrison said.

"Earlier, when Kim was generating misery and I checked outside to see what was summoning it, I heard a door shut," said Jaimie. "The thing is here in the hall. On the second floor. I'm going downstairs to check the resident list, see if Shaina's on it." She slipped out.

"Do you and Jaimie really hate each other?" I asked Harrison.

He exhaled loudly. "In general, she irritates the hell out of me."

"Why?"

He raised an eyebrow. "What business is it of yours?"

"None. I'm just curious."

Harrison shrugged. "Okay. Stay that way. Jaimie irritates me, and of course I love her. She's my cousin."

"Oh," I said. I glanced at Joshua.

He watched me through his bangs and smiled.

"Meanwhile, did she give you the standard warning not to talk to Outsiders about us and our business?" Harrison asked me.

"No," I said.

"*Faskish*. She's such a baby! Well, be warned. Don't tell anybody about us and our secrets, or you'll regret it."

"That's your idea of a big scary warning?" I snapped. "I find out my life is threatened by something I've never heard of before and barely believe in, and you think you're going to scare me by saying 'boo, or else'?"

"Good point," said Joshua.

"What do you want? You want me to put a silence on you, some kind of binding? Something concrete? Like, 'Talk about us and your tongue will fall out'?" Harrison asked.

I opened and closed my mouth twice.

Rugee leaned forward on my shoulder and stared at Harrison. The air between them crackled. Harrison jumped, smacked his chest as though he'd been hit. "What?" he asked, irritated. "I'm *not* supposed to warn her?"

Respect my mark on her, Rugee said.

"That's *your* mark?" Harrison stared at my forehead.

Yes. Leave Kim to me.

Jaimie returned. "No one named Darnell on the residents list," she said. "I trelled down the hall on my way back, stopped outside each door, trying to feel what I felt before, but nothing."

I checked my clock. It was only nine in the morning, but I was completely exhausted.

Joshua caught my look. "You need a nap. Time to say good-bye for now?" he asked.

"Wait a minute," said Harrison. "We need a plan."

"A plan? You always want a plan!" Jaimie said.

"Yeah, and notice who gets things done."

"Kim, can I have a piece of paper?" Joshua asked me.

I ripped a sheet out of my notebook and handed him paper and pen.

"Objectives?" he said. I flipped to a new page in my notebook, wrote "THE PLAN" at the top.

"Discover the identity of the viri and disable it somehow," said Harrison. Josh and I both wrote that down.

"How do we disable a viri?" Jaimie asked.

"Rugee?" Harrison said.

Unknown. What is known of them is that they are very hard to kill.

"We have to do *something!*" Harrison jumped up and paced around the room.

"The Family has been studying viri, but we've never found a way to deal with them," Joshua said. "Jacob had to enter into a covenant of no harm before his viri informant would meet with him. There are things we could try."

Jaimie sighed. "Those guys we lost. Harrison's brother and the other two—"

Harrison's brother? Oh, no.

"They had a lot more powers, skills, and persuasions than Kim does. If there was something they could have done, don't you think they would have tried it?"

"Not if they were really happy," Joshua said.

"What do you mean?" asked Jaimie.

"Rugee said the bad viri get addicted to certain kinds of

emotions. He didn't say it had to be misery. Maybe they died happy. Maybe they couldn't figure out how to resist, or didn't even want to. It didn't look like any of them struggled."

"I *want* to struggle," I said. I hadn't struggled before. I had wallowed in my misery. It had only let up when I fell asleep or when something distracted me. I didn't figure out how to distract myself until Dad started talking about college applications. He made me apply to Sitka. I did it without thinking too hard. Somewhere under the surface of my misery, some fugitive tiny voice whispered, *Get away, get away, maybe we can escape this.* I listened, but not too closely. I didn't want anything to hear me hope.

I got away.

Sort of. Or maybe not.

"Good," Jaimie said.

I will help you with your struggle, Rugee thought. *I have never seen one of these creatures, but neither have they seen me. It may be there are steps I can take.*

"Thank you," I whispered.

Harrison paced back and forth, or as much as he could, in our tiny room. "Revision to the plan: Identify the viri. Protect Kim."

I didn't write it down. "How can you do that when you guys don't even know what to do about viri? Besides, we're all going to split up, right? First we've got registration to get through, and then there's classes and stuff like that. How can *anyone* protect me?"

"It's a problem," Harrison said.

"Whoever's sucking on me doesn't seem to want to kill me."

"An addiction can escalate," said Joshua, as though it were something he'd seen.

"First I was a cow, now I'm a drug," I muttered.

"Plan," said Harrison one more time. "Identify the viri. Figure out what to do next."

"It's on this floor," I said, "so it must be a girl."

"Or look like one," said Joshua. "They can take any shape."

"Eww." I hit the paper with my pen, peppering it with black dots. "Animal, vegetable, mineral?" I looked wildly around the room. "Door? Dresser? Bed?"

"They're plastic," Joshua said.

"What?"

"In the old sense of the word, 'capable of being shaped or molded.' But if it were in this room, I think we'd sense it."

"When I trelled it sucking off you, Kim," Jaimie said, "it happened once in the dining room, and once I saw the misery flow under the door. It's something that can move. Let's start with figuring it's a person shape, but maybe not Shaina anymore."

"Could it be a cafeteria food lady?" Harrison asked.

"The pull didn't go toward the kitchen," Jaimie said. "It's shaped like a student—someone sitting at a dining table."

"We don't know for sure that it lives on this floor," Harrison said. "Maybe it was just visiting."

"It's a place to start. Let's all go look at the residents list, write down everybody on our floor," Jaimie said. "Maybe there'll be a name you recognize from high school."

I jumped up, notebook in hand. Something concrete we could do. Already I felt better. Rugee's claws dug into my shoulder. I had forgotten he was there. "Do you want to get down?" I asked him.

No. I will stay with you.

"Even when I leave the room?"

Yes.

I touched his head. He was heavy. I'd look pretty weird walking around with a giant gecko on my shoulder, but it was better than walking around without him. "Could you do the chameleon trick and vanish?" I asked. "There's that 'no pets' policy here. I know you're not a pet, but you look sort of like one."

He vanished, though I could still feel his weight.

"Thanks!" I said.

"But Rugee—" Jaimie said.

Set the wards around the room. I will help you. I do not know what any of us can do for Kim, but I will do what I can.

CHAPTER 15: *Jaimie*

We set the wards, while Kim watched—which felt decidedly odd, and against every warning I'd gotten from the Family about how to interact with Outsiders. How Outside could Kim be by now?

I had never worked with Harrison or Josh before. It was nice. We all knew the words to the persuasion for protection of place, and since I was Air, Harrison was Fire, and Josh was Earth, we wove the protection triple-strong. The room felt more like home all the time.

"How come you guys got here so early?" I asked Harrison as we all trooped down the second-floor hall of Spangler. Freshman orientation, which began tomorrow, lasted three days before school officially started. Harrison and Josh weren't freshmen.

As we walked past other people's rooms, music competed with other music. I peeked in one open door and saw that someone had already put up posters for bands I'd never heard of. I'd only started listening to radio a few months before, and there was a lot of music I'd never heard of.

A dark girl lay on the right bed in the open-door room. She smiled and waved to me, and I waved back. I trelled. She seemed normal. Trelling was great, but it didn't tell the whole story. I could easily miss vital information. I needed to ask Harrison about Othersight, or maybe Josh could help me. That might be less embarrassing.

"We moved to Spores last week to get our apartment in shape," Harrison said. "And line up jobs and do some shopping. There are all kinds of things in Spores you can't find in Southwater."

"If we *could* find them in Southwater, Mama wouldn't let me buy them," Josh said.

"Like what?" I asked.

"Tie-dye."

"What's tie-dye?"

Josh stretched out a handful of his white T-shirt and said, "Something besides this. I'll show you tomorrow."

"Can I see your apartment?"

"No," said Harrison.

"Sure," said Josh at the same time.

I slugged Harrison's shoulder, but not very hard.

"What kind of jobs did you get?" Outside of family chores, I had never had a job. I'd helped a few people in Arcadia with work, but nobody had paid me for it.

"I work at a video rental place," said Harrison.

"Clerk at a bookstore," Josh said.

Kim paused on the stairs, her hand on the banister, and turned to look behind us. I glanced back too, trelling. No one was there.

"Heard something," Kim muttered.

I exchanged glances with Josh. We wiggled eyebrows at each other, even though it wasn't funny. Kim had lots of reasons to be nervous.

I had forgotten my eleventh summer, until Josh reminded me. Now I remembered. Even though he was younger than I was, he was pretty cool. Also, he let me boss him around, something as the youngest in my family I'd never been able to do. We snuck off into the hills above the farm, playing Together Quest, as though we were married and going to see what signs of the future we could find, what pleasures we shared, what our souls looked like and how they would shape to each other to strengthen our union. Or sometimes we pretended we had achieved the power of Transformation. We were horses, cats, crows; we roosted in trees or the hayloft and spied on everybody older than we were.

I had liked Joshua, but the next year, he was gone, along with a bunch of the others, on a field trip to Mexico.

Then I missed two years in a row. For one of them, my sister Sarah had changed me into part of the stone kitchen wall and left me that way. No one could find me. Mom and Dad were worried, but nobody from Chapel Hollow helped them figure out where I had gone, or even if I was alive. Fortunately, time passed differently when one was a rock.

Each day was a flicker. I could have stayed there for years and not noticed.

When my parents got to the Gather, a krifter in Southwater helped them track me down. Sarah was sentenced to community service.

The next summer, I was in the middle of *plakanesh*, sick and unable to travel. My *miksash*, my mentor Uncle Trevor, stayed with me and coached me through it, then started training me.

By the time I saw Josh again I was fifteen, stuck up, and poisonous with power. I was mean to everybody who would sit still for it. I was pretty sure no Southwater boys were good enough for me. I was the queen of transformations. I shifted every kid I could into unpleasant forms.

Harrison and I really went after each other. He was faster, and he knew his persuasions and skills better, but I had more sneak attacks in my repertoire. When I couldn't find Harrison, I tortured the younger ones, who couldn't fight back.

Southwater let me know I wasn't welcome to the Gathers after that.

Joshua. A little hard to grasp, the way he hid behind his hair, but I liked the look of him, gawky and growing into his height. His voice had changed for the better, too.

Kim got out her notebook when we reached the bulletin board on the first floor. In the lounge across the hall, people were sitting around talking. One girl had an acoustic guitar. She played something complicated, not just simple chords. I liked how it excited the air.

Kim finished writing. "That's everybody on the second floor of Spangler. What the heck. Nothing like data overkill."

"Do you recognize any of the names?" Harrison asked.

"No."

"Hello," said a woman behind us. Kim jumped and turned, her face red. "Whatcha doing?"

It was the pretty short-haired woman from yesterday, R.A.

"Hi, Dinah," Kim said. "This is my roommate, Jaimie Locke, and her cousins—they're visiting from off-campus. We're trying to find out who lives on our floor."

"Hi, Jaimie. Welcome to Spangler Hall Second Floor. I'm your R.A., Dinah Belasco—you can find me in the room next to the stairwell, two oh eight. Why don't you two go door to door and introduce yourselves? You should meet as many people as you can during Welcome Week."

Kim straightened. She looked at me. "That's a good idea."

Dinah smiled. "The professors are going to pile the work on you like you won't believe, so now's a good time to make connections; you won't have the time or energy for it later. Let me know if you have any problems." She waved and wandered to the lounge.

"I thought her name was R.A.," I said.

Harrison knocked on my head as though it were wood. "You're such an idiot! R.A. stands for Resident Advisor, *klikla*!"

"So what's that?"

"She lives on our floor and supervises us a little," Kim said. "She sets up activities so we get to know each other. If roommates get in fights, she's supposed to break it up."

"She's kind of bossy," I said.

"It's her job," said Kim.

"I like her idea, anyway," Josh said. "Why *don't* we look everyone in the face? Maybe one of us will catch a whiff."

Meet everybody. Maybe I would meet normal people, my reason for coming to campus and leaving behind everything I knew. So far I'd met my cousins and Kim. No luck there. The jury was still out on Nan, Lydia, Cascy, and Flax.

Kim glanced at her list. "There's thirty-one people on our floor. That's a lot of strangers." Her knuckles were white on her pen. The gray edged out of her, small trickles. Oh, *faskish*, not now.

"You've already met Dinah, and you know each other," said Josh, who seemed sensitive to Kim's plummeting mood. "Cuts you down to twenty-eight. You could do it in stages."

"We can do it later," I said. "Why don't you guys take off? Kim and I could go on a walk." Back to the dawn redwoods. I wanted to immerse myself in their calm again, and pour some over Kim. It would be easier if Harrison wasn't around to agitate me, or sneer at me for leaning on a source outside myself.

"Josh and I are going to stick around," said Harrison.

"What?" I could not believe this. How was I going to meet normal people?

"If the viri attacks again, we should be with you."

"Like you know what to do about it?" I said.

Harrison glared at me with narrowed eyes, and I remembered too late that of course, he hadn't known what to do about it. Nobody did. His face tightened. "I want to catch this thing and kill it," he muttered. "We never found the one that killed Coleman. It got clean away. It's still out there sucking other people dry. The viri Great-Uncle Jacob talked to said they don't need—they shouldn't want—drawing on three people in the space of a few days, drawing them down to nothing, that's not—especially three *Ilmonishti*. It was seriously out of whack, that one, Jayana Havelock."

I shuddered.

"I don't think Kim's is the same one," Harrison went on. "Havelock was too hungry for finesse. This one bides its time. It's stealthy. And it's skimming rather than sucking dry, as far as I can tell. I want to catch it in the act, see how it operates. Is it operating now?"

I trelled Kim. The smoky-tasting gray was mixed with something more fiery, a little bit chili pepper, though not habañero hot. No threads of mood led away from her in any direction. "No. She's just having feelings. No sucking."

"Would you quit talking about me like I'm not even here?" Kim said in a fierce whisper. "And watch what you say out here in the open? Jeez, Harrison, why'd you threaten me against talking if you're going to tell the whole world about it?"

I blinked and glanced around. A couple of boys lingered a few feet off, waiting, perhaps, for us to get out of the way so they could look at the bulletin board, and Lydia leaned against a nearby wall, her gaze directed toward a book she held. I had the feeling she used an open book as a way to disguise where her real interest lay. Maybe she was listening. I trelled, but I couldn't tell anything; she still had that barrier up.

Harrison looked angry, maybe because he knew Kim was right. "Let's go," he said. He marched toward the stairwell.

Kim and I exchanged glances. Mine meant: Is Harrison a pain, or what? I suspected hers meant the same thing.

CHAPTER 16: *Kim*

For the first time in months, I felt cheerful, despite what I now knew was a dire situation. I'd forgotten to worry about whether I could get through orientation without missing something vital or whether I'd get the classes I needed.

Jaimie's family fascinated me.

Harrison led us back to the room and glared at Jaimie until she unlocked the door. I went straight for my art supplies. At first, I thought I thought I'd try drawing humans again—specifically the ones in front of me—but I flipped to the picture side in my head and saw something else. Feelings poured out of me onto the page.

It had been so long!

The others talked while I worked, only half listening to their discussion. "We should figure out the viri's range," Jaimie said. "How far away can it be and still suck on her? I know it can work through cracks—it pulled stuff under the door. I'm not sure it can work through walls."

"How did it track her here?" Josh asked.

"Duh." Jaimie said, "It knew her in her hometown. They were best friends. I bet she didn't hide where she was going. She didn't know she needed to. All it had to do was get here and wait."

Dark purple knots, edged with blue and green spikes. Shaina, my best friend, the one who enticed me into joining the human race. Gold flowed from the end of my pen, and orange, blending, for all the good memories I had, notes passed, conversations while we walked dark streets. She had teased me into learning how to tease back. Pink threads linked the orange-gold mass to the purple knots. Had we ever really been friends, or had she been using me all along?

"Or it checked the database and saw which hall Kim was assigned to," Harrison said. "Your question's good, Jaimie. How close does it have to be? If we could figure out the range, maybe we could hide Kim somewhere off campus, keep her safe."

Three shapes, their centers white, their edges overlapping layers of color. New friends, or mysteries—how could I be sure of anything, except what flowed out my fingers onto the page?

"But then she wouldn't get an education. Next time it sucks on her, I want to trace it. Rugee, I know you want to help Kim, but could you let her get sucked a little so I can follow the trace?"

Rugee was wrapped halfway around my neck like a

heavy invisible collar, and he didn't move, so I'd stopped noticing him. He didn't answer.

I put Rugee on the page, pale yellow in his center, three orange spirals, with a smoky surround of twined colors. It wasn't a salamander shape, but it was his shape.

"The viri must be attuned to her," Josh said. "It's got to have local tracking ability to find her when it wants a fix...."

His voice trailed off. Nobody answered him.

My picture side was in overdrive. Aside from wishing I had paints instead of markers, I didn't think about what I was doing—I laid down color, overlaid it with other colors, pressed the markers so hard I crushed some of the tips, managed to confine my image to the too-small page in front of me and still encompass everything. I compressed and overlapped. Nothing looked like anything in the real world, but I sat back with a satisfied sigh. This was the first real art I'd put on paper since meeting Shaina.

"What was that?" Harrison's voice was hushed.

I glanced up to find all three of them staring at me.

"What do you mean?" I set the pad on the bedspread and picked up the markers, capped them, put them in their plastic container.

"What did you just do?"

"Art," I said, a little self-consciously. It sounded kind of snotty. Despite all the lessons, I'd never been sure what I was doing was art. Art was something you saw in museums.

"May I see?" Jaimie asked.

I shrugged. "Okay." Now that I was finished, I didn't care

about the image anymore, though I guessed I should photo-graph it. It would be fun to e-mail to Dad.

Jaimie crossed the room and sat down carefully on my bed, picked up the sketch pad, and stared at the picture. So did I. I saw sloppiness. I'd overworked some parts of the paper so much I'd torn holes in it, and the colors weren't an exact match to my mental picture; there were even some muddy combinations where I hadn't made my tools match my vision. It still worked, though: shapes bending together, some over-lapping, with twists of colored smoke, intentions, dreams, fears—nothing definite, all cloudy. I wished I had some nail polish with metallic bits in it; I wanted to spark the page in a few places.

Shaina had had all kinds of nail polish. I'd done little flames on her nails once. At the time, I'd filed away infor-mation on how it worked on its brush, what its properties as paint were, but I'd never thought to use it on paper until now.

"Kim, where did you go when you were working on this?" Jaimie asked.

"Do you like it?" I was afraid to ask, but I couldn't help myself.

"It's fantastic."

"Fantastic" is one of those words that can mean either "really good" or "really bad." I wondered which way she meant it, but then I heard what she had said before. "What do you mean, where did I go? Wasn't I sitting right here?"

"In a way, but you also . . . connected to something outside, and brought this back from somewhere else. I've never seen that before."

"That's silly. It comes from my head."

Rugee stirred, a weight shifting on my shoulders. From the corner of my eye I saw his green-and-orange self shimmer into sight. He lifted his head and stared at the page. Harrison and Joshua came over and looked at it, too.

"What is it?" I said. "You guys. What's the matter with it?"

Harrison touched the picture with a tentative finger, as though he expected it to burn. He frowned.

"You need better paper," Joshua said. He sounded hoarse.

"It was kind of a last-minute addition to my stuff. I could use some paints, too. I forgot what this was like." I went to my desk, pulled out the course catalog, and looked for art classes.

"Kim . . ." Jaimie said.

There was something called "Terminal Creative Project," which made me wonder if it killed you to finish it. I put down the catalog. "What?"

"This answers the question of why the viri picked you."

My art class thoughts screeched to a halt. "It does?"

She nodded and set down my sketchbook. "While you were working, you trelled really juicy and luscious."

"What does that even mean? What's 'trell'?"

Jaimie hesitated, then said, "Well, it's sort of like smelling, only it works on other things, like emotions and properties of materials. I guess."

"I do this and smell juicy?" I grabbed my sketchbook

again. I didn't feel as driven this time, but things were still going on in my picture side, so I laid down some lines—and glanced up to see three humans and one god staring at me as though hypnotized. "Would you stop that?"

Jaimie shook her head. "I never saw anybody do art before, I guess. Not like that."

"Mama does it, but it's not so clear," Harrison said.

"Are you guys trelling me, too?" I asked.

"No. That's an Air skill," said Josh. "My sign is Earth. What I sense is kind of a fusion around you. Things changing state in a controlled way."

"I'm Fire. I see that, too," said Harrison, "only it's combustion, sort of—it's cooler to watch you do it than to see the end product, although there's something about this picture I really like, even though I don't think I actually get it." He took the sketchbook from me and shifted it back and forth. "Which way is up?"

"It doesn't matter," I said. But I *did* know which way; I knew what those shapes and colors meant.

With Mom and Dad, it hadn't mattered. Decorative art was good enough. Although, when I first started working, I kept hoping someone would understand. It was all there on the paper, a picture of my feelings and thoughts.

After Dad started e-mailing my art to Henry, I finally got the kind of feedback I had hoped for. Unfortunately, Henry wasn't good with words. A one word e-mail: "Mad." Or a handful of words: "Not fun to be you today, huh?" That was as much of an exchange as he could handle. The first time he e-mailed me like that, I wanted to see him. Maybe I wasn't the only one who had a picture side and a word side, I thought: maybe, with Henry, I could actually talk about art.

I called him—he hated the phone—and asked if I could visit him. He said he was busy. He was always busy. E-mail was all I ever got from him.

Finally, Shaina came. She saw the pictures on the fridge at our house, and she liked them. She didn't talk to me about them much, and that was okay, because they were the empty husks of a self I used to be, not who I was now. Somehow, though, as my picture side worked, she spoke to it as though she could see it. If I was having fireworks, she laughed, delighted. If ashy shadows of lost things snowed out of the picture-side sky, she gave me cocoa and distracted me with anime. I no longer had to put any of the picture side down on paper: I had finally found someone who could decode it as it happened, without my having to explain it.

Viri. Maybe she really *did* get it.

I studied the picture I had just finished. As long as I was collecting weird feedback, I might as well ask for the weirdest. "Rugee?"

What you are doing is not uncommon; you just do it uncommonly well, he said. *Your focus is very strong and beautiful. There's a trickle of this concentration around you always, but when you work with colors, it turns into a river.*

"Oh. Thanks. I think."

"So you're wildly attractive, Kim," Jaimie said. "We just need to figure out who else knows it."

CHAPTER 17: *Jaimie*

I had told Kim, Nan, and Lydia I wanted to study boys. Really, I wanted to study all Outside people.

Meeting everybody on our floor of Spangler seemed like a good way to start.

It turned out having my cousins along worked pretty well. If my hallmates weren't interested in me and Kim, they checked out Harrison and Josh.

Most of the conversations were kind of lame. *Hi. How are you? We live on this floor, too. These are my cousins. Where are you from? What are you majoring in?*

Now that Kim had a project, she was cheerful, which made her fun to watch. She noticed the artwork people hung on their walls. She admired fashion choices. Each time we met someone, she ticked off the name and wrote notes. One woman asked her what she was doing, and Kim said she was collecting meetings with people. The woman and her roommate got intrigued and left off unpacking. By the time we were halfway down the hall, there was a lot of cross traffic.

Harrison made three dates, one of them for the ice cream social the following night.

When we got to room 225, Nan invited us in. "You went out and got boys already? You guys are *good.*"

"They're cousins," I said.

"Whose? Each other's?"

"Mine."

"Introduce us," she said, so I did. Josh kissed Nan's hand. He'd done that to a lot of women. The first time he did it, it surprised me, and it certainly surprised Yasmin, the woman whose hand it was.

He told me later it helped him get a sense of people.

Nan took it in stride. "Look what I requisitioned from student services." She pointed to a small refrigerator.

Lydia lurked on a far corner of her bed against the wall, with her usual book in front of her. I leaned over to see what she was reading. She peered at me from behind her hair, then lifted the book high enough for me to see the title. *Wandering the Edge.* I'd never heard of it.

"Lydia's keeping her designer water in the fridge, so we're splitting the rent." Nan patted the wood-grain papered refrigerator as though it were a good dog. "Tell me if you want to rent a corner. I'll give you a price break."

"Does your roommate talk?" Harrison muttered to Nan.

"Only if other forms of communication fail," Nan

answered. "So far I've heard her say about ten words. Lydia, you want to meet some more people?"

Headshake.

"Sorry," said Nan. "Barrel of laughs," she whispered to us.

I trelled Lydia for the third time, and it only frustrated me more. If she was a viri, I couldn't tell. I'd trelled almost everybody on our floor, and all of them were different from each other. Lydia had that shield up, with all kinds of wild things going on beyond it—cities built of white stone, and sky-toucher mountains, and a dragon. For a second, a red mask floated just under the surface of a lake before it sank and a forest took its place.

All her stuff was visual. That wasn't like most of the other women, who trelled scents and habits and shadows and fears and wishes.

When we got back to our own room, I asked Harrison and Josh what they thought about Lydia.

"I don't think she's a viri," said Josh. "She felt different from Havelock."

"She's different from everyone else," I said.

She does not feel like a predator, Rugee said from Kim's shoulders. I jumped. I had forgotten he was with us.

I gave up on Lydia for the time being. "Kim didn't drop into a pit, and nobody sucked on her that I could tell while we were walking around," I said. "Did you guys notice anything suspicious?"

"Just a bunch of freshmen," said Harrison.

"Freshmen? They were all women."

Harrison rapped on my head. I wished he'd stop that. "Don't you know anything?"

"I know you're going to spend some quality time as a toad if you keep doing that."

He laughed. "Promises, promises!"

I opened my innersight. To transform him, I needed to understand him; I had understood him plenty five years ago, but we had both changed since then.

"Jaimie," said Josh. "Grow up."

CHAPTER 18: *Kim*

Our residents survey had given me pages of notes, and my picture side was boiling over, but I was afraid to take out my sketchpad. I didn't want Jaimie and her cousins staring at me again. As interesting as it was to be popular for something I was actually good at, I was already tired of the scrutiny.

I even secretly wished the boy cousins would go away for a while. But they were protecting me, so they stuck around.

For lunch, we went for tacos at a restaurant on the edge of campus. "Get to know this place," Harrison said. "After your first three cases of ptomaine poisoning at the cafeteria, you'll be back."

Afterward, the guys walked us around. I had already toured Sitka, and I knew the names of all the buildings, but I didn't have the kind of background Harrison did. "Last year there was a kegger riot at this frat house. Lots of windows smashed. Police had to break it up." And: "The brain lab's in there. They've been transplanting embryo chicken brains into embryo quails."

The scariest part of the tour, aside from hearing about cadavers in the basement of the Food Sciences Building, was checking out the prices on the textbooks in the university bookstore.

When we got back to the room, I called Dad to beg for more money. He was overjoyed that I wasn't crying, and even said so. I thought about bursting into tears just to spite him, but I was asking for money. Spite would have to wait.

"Yes, I like my roommate," I told Mom. *She's a witch. She brought a god to college. I'm being stalked by an emotional predator. My roommate's hunky cousins have appointed themselves my bodyguards. My life is upside down.* "Everything's fine."

After I hung up, Jaimie slugged Harrison in the shoulder and asked him to teach her Wordwaft. He sneered at her ignorance, but before that fight could start, Joshua said Harrison didn't know how to do it, either, but he, Josh, did. He started teaching them.

I got out the sketchpad. Who cared if they stared? I needed to draw while the pictures were still fresh.

Brainstorm!

I photographed my first picture, downloaded it into the computer, hooked up to the high-speed Internet, and sent it to Dad. Text of the e-mail: "I need some money for art supplies, too, please."

He sent an immediate reply, which meant he was online when he was supposed to be working. One word: "Hallelujah."

A minute later, he sent another one: "Wow!"

Then: "Forwarded it to Henry."

I leaned back in my chair and listened to Josh's quiet instructions. "Do you know how to send out a seek-line? That's part of it. Load the words on the front end of the seek-line, except instead of seeking, you're sending. You have to visualize clearly the space where you want your words to appear. . . ."

Another e-mail popped into my box. From Henry. "Kim: welcome back. College good! Send more."

A peculiar prickling under my skin, a sense of something about to happen, like the feeling in the air preceding a storm.

Dad and Henry were happy. They wanted more. I had forgotten what that felt like.

I shut down the computer and sketched.

I was working on a picture of the girl in 218, who came from Portland and had brought some of her sculptures to decorate her dorm room. The picture wasn't of her face, but of the feeling I got from her sculptures, which was mainly creepy. I was just getting down the creepy part—streaks of green and yellow, with blue darts across them, and the blue turning muddy green as it blended with the other colors—

when Rugee shifted on my neck. I glanced up. All the cousins looked toward the door. Jaimie jumped up and flung it open, looked out.

"What?" I said.

"Something," she muttered. "Not sucking, but watching in a new way. Harrison? Josh?"

Josh had gone pale. He nodded. "Viri."

Jaimie's hand clenched on the doorknob. She scanned the hall. She turned back. "Can't see anybody." Presently she said, "Well, it's gone now. I think. Can you guys sense it anymore?"

"No," said Harrison, and Josh shook his head. Rugee had his mouth open, his tongue sticking out, white and glistening, right by my cheek. Not my favorite thing, but I didn't want to mention that. At last he closed his mouth.

Gone for now.

I stopped sketching. If the cousins were right about what I looked like during an art attack, maybe I was a beacon, calling things to come deplete me.

CHAPTER 19: *Jaimie*

Kim stopped being fascinating and got out her notebook. "Close the door," she said in a grumpy voice.

I trelled the hallway one more time. Half our new neighbors had their doors open, and conversation and music wafted out. The strange vacuumy thing wasn't out there anymore, and I hadn't been able to tell what direction it came from even when it *was* there. It trelled unlike anything else I'd ever sensed: a seek on it, but a swallowing-itself thing, too, as if a mouth turned inside out somehow and still smiled at you. I shuddered and closed the door.

"Lesson over yet?" Kim asked, still grouchy. Grouchy was better than crying.

"We didn't get to the practice part," said Josh. "All we did so far is theory."

"Oh, well, go on." She waved at us.

A seek-line. Another thing I hadn't practiced enough.

How would you attach words to a seek-line? "Josh—" I said, but I wasn't sorry when Harrison wandered over to Kim's bed and loomed over her. She wrote furiously until she couldn't ignore him anymore, then stopped and glared up at him.

"What are you doing?" he asked.

"I don't want to pull that thing here, so I'm writing down my impressions of the people on this floor instead of sketching them. I was going to ask you guys for yours, too."

"I don't think it's on this floor," Harrison said.

"Tell me anyway," Kim said. She flipped to a blank page and wrote something. "Barbara Henderson," she said.

That kept us going until suppertime.

We passed Nan and Lydia leaving their room on our way to the cafeteria. Nan caught up with us and tapped my shoulder. "Is this a private clique, or can anyone join?" she asked.

"Clique?" I said.

"Club?" said Nan.

"Spade? Heart?" I said.

Nan sighed. "Can I hang out with you guys during dinner?"

"Sure."

Lydia, carrying her book, walked almost on our heels. "I guess that includes her, too," Nan said. I shrugged. Neither of them knew it, but they had entered my human laboratory. I felt an evil laugh welling up, but I swallowed it. I hadn't even had to use an enticement or persuasion to draw them in. Maybe I was good at acting normal.

"Hey, Kim. Hey, everybody else." Casey's cheery voice sounded as we went down the stairs. Flax and Casey moved into the clump of Us. I wanted to let loose another evil laugh, but again, I managed to restrain myself.

Women greeted us as we passed them. "Hey, Jaimie."

"Hey, Kim. Hey, Harrison."

"Hey, Josh!"

Our actions that afternoon made this happen. The whole hall was full of women who knew our names! Plus, since Kim had quizzed us about them, I remembered most of *their* names, and once we all started talking, the men we hadn't met from the third and first floors edged in and talked to us, too.

The cafeteria was full of people I had never done any-thing mean to—except for Josh and Harrison. I knew a lot of these people's names, and none of them was scared of me yet! Once we got Kim's viri problem solved, this was going to be a great year.

CHAPTER 20: *Kim*

After dinner, Harrison said, "I think we'd better spend the night. We need to keep an eye on you."

This was going to make a better story than an experience, I suspected. Still, suppose Mom called, and one of them answered the phone. I wondered if she'd drive here in the middle of the night to get me.

"Don't answer the phone." I surveyed the room. "Where are you going to sleep?"

"Jaimie, can you do Airshape?" Harrison asked.

"Never even heard of it. Is that on my list, Kim?"

I fished the list of forbidden topics from the drawer where I'd stashed it and checked. "No."

"What is it?" Jaimie asked Harrison.

"My sister is learning it," he said. "You make air solid, and ask it to take a shape—"

"Dad did that when we got here. He spun me an ID

card out of air. It looked perfect! He dissolved it after I got my room key," said Jaimie.

"If you could Airshape, you could make us hammocks. Or mattresses."

"I wish I knew how," Jaimie said. She held her open hands up. "Air? Rugee? Hints, anyone?" She twiddled her fingers and frowned.

Rugee, my jewelry of choice, became visible on my shoulder, then crossed our desks to Jaimie. "Can you help me?" she asked him.

Yes. You already understand Transformation, he said. *Ask air to transform.* He climbed up her arm, perched on her shoulder, pressed his cheek against hers. She closed her eyes and concentrated, then relaxed, letting her hands rest palms up on her thighs. She swayed and murmured. The air above her hands shimmered, thickened, turned blue; it spun into shaggy clumps of what looked like fiberfill, piled across her lap, and spilled over onto the floor until she was knee-deep.

She and her cousins had been talking about magic all day, but this was the first time I'd seen something appear out of nowhere, aside from Rugee. I leaned over and touched. Strange, cool, melty stuff, a little more solid than water, but not much. I grabbed a handful, even though it scared me. It didn't come loose from the rest, just dragged it all toward me. I dropped it.

Give it outer limits, Rugee said.

Jaimie opened her eyes and started at the sight of what

she'd spun. She worked her hands above it; it separated into two clumps and spread out on the floor in the shapes of giant beach towels, only thicker. She made spreading and flattening motions with her hands, and the stuff responded to her gestures. Finally she clenched her hands into fists. The new mattresses lay quiet.

My brain didn't.

This time when I woke up, I knew where I was: My room. College. And sort of when: The middle of the night. I rolled over, flung my feet over the edge of the bed, and stepped on something way too soft and odd-shaped to be floor.

Joshua yelped.

Nothing like stepping on somebody's stomach to really wake you up.

I had attained a certain level of momentum. I fell over Josh and headed facedown for the floor. I couldn't even think fast enough to put out my hands.

Jaimie spoke a word I didn't understand. I stopped in midair with my nose inches from the carpet. Something squeezed my neck. I couldn't breathe enough to choke.

"Whoa," said Josh in a strangled voice.

I managed to get my arms out, my hands on the floor.

Jaimie spoke again. Something heaved me up into the air. I hovered, windmilling arms and legs without getting anywhere or striking anything, which, given the minute size of our room, meant there was a certain elegance to the planning involved. The pressure on my throat eased up, and I yelled, "What the hell!"

"Sorry," said Jaimie. "You okay?"

My throat was sore. I put my hand up and bumped into Rugee, invisible, wound around my neck like a muffler.

So sorry, Kim. I didn't mean to hurt you. You took me by surprise.

"Me, too," I rasped.

Then I looked down. I was still sleepy, but I wasn't dreaming; I was floating in the air. Oh. My. God.

It was so cool, and so scary.

"Hold still," said Jaimie.

I stopped thrashing and drifted to the floor. My feet touched down gently. "BRB," I said, and ran.

Nobody else was in the bathroom, so I guessed it wasn't morning yet.

How could I pee with a gecko around my neck?

"Sorry," I said to Rugee as I slipped into a stall.

Why?

"Um, I'm not used to doing this in public. Not with someone else who can see me while I'm doing it."

Don't worry. I've lived a long life and seen many strange things. This is natural. This is nothing. Meanwhile, how badly did I hurt you? He moved against my neck. Hot glass slivers grated in my throat. I winced.

He stroked my throat with his tail, a warm, smooth, damp touch that at first hurt horribly, then gradually eased into soothing.

"Oh. That's better," I said.

"Better than what?" asked someone.

I flushed the toilet and opened the stall door. Nan leaned against one of the sinks, her arms crossed over her chest. Her black hair looked even spikier than it had during the day. She was wearing an oversized red T-shirt and monster-feet slippers.

"Um. Hi, Nan." I still wasn't sure whether I liked her. "Better than holding it in."

"Oh. Cosmic."

"That's me, cosmic thinker. 'Scuse me." I headed for the sink to her left. She was sort of leaning across all of them, so I had to nudge her to the side before I turned on the water. Why hadn't I brought a towel? I needed to figure out my new routine. Maybe I should put all my toiletries in a little basket and bring the basket with me every time I came over here. Plus a hand towel, and—

God, had I even brushed my teeth before I went to sleep? I couldn't remember. What an idiot.

Here I was, miles from home, trying to pretend to be an adult. I couldn't even take care of myself. I flipped over into misery, my thoughts weighted with betrayal and darkness, a chill that wrapped around me and bit down to my bones. I was such a fool! I was such a ruination to everything and everyone I knew! I had better not make any new friends here—I would only betray them, and cause pain to everyone.

Tears flowed down my face, accompanied by small panting sobs.

Kim!

I sank down on the floor and crawled under the sink, pulled knees up to my chest, put my arms around them; I curled up as tight as I could. I didn't deserve to take up even as much space as I did. I was worse than nothing.

"Kim? Kim? You okay?" asked Nan.

I shivered and backed up against the pipes that led to the faucets. I had left the water running; I felt its chilly rush in the pipe at my back, heard it splashing into the sink above me. I even wasted water.

"Hey?" said Nan. "Hey, Kim? You okay?" She knelt and peered at me. "You need help? What's the matter?"

Kim! Stop it!

I closed my eyes. I was down in the bottom of the well, cold, damp, dark and alone.

Jaimiala! Come here!

Thud of footsteps. Jaimie crashed in through the swinging door. "What's going on? Where's Kim?" Jaimie demanded.

"Under the sink," said Nan, who was squatting there, staring at me. Her stare hurt. No one should see me.

Jaimie dropped to her knees, then reached under and hauled me out by the upper arms. "Kim, stop it." She patted my cheek, then hugged me. "It wasn't your fault, remember? It was dumb mistakes. Not your fault."

I heard her, but I couldn't understand her.

Jaimiala, track the trace.

Jaimie sat back, her hands still gripping my arms, her face alert. She studied Nan, shook her head, peered toward the bathroom door.

I closed my eyes and wallowed in misery. In a weird way, I wanted more. It couldn't hurt any worse than it already did. Maybe if I took it all on, I could get it over with.

Jaimie jumped up, slammed the door open, and ran out.

"What's the matter with you?" Nan asked. "Hey, Kim? Hey? Oh, Christ, I just want to go back to bed."

Rugee spread from my neck up over my head. I couldn't see him, but I felt something warm and smooth wrap around my face and ears, press over my hair. I panicked until I realized I could breathe just fine. Then, suddenly, I wasn't down the well anymore. The cloud cleared from my brain.

Rugee subsided to his invisible gecko self. I wiped my eyes. "Oh, God."

"You okay?" asked Nan.

I sniffed. "Better. I'm sorry about that. I get these attacks sometimes. I'm really sorry."

"Attacks. Have you ever thought about getting professional help?"

Another great way to make friends and influence people. Convince them you were a psycho nutcase. "Um," I said.

Nan slapped her forehead. "Forget I said that. Child of two psychologists. I start thinking I know what's best for everybody else. It's none of my business. I'm sorry."

"I'm having a difficult time," I said, then wondered if I

should have said it. Never admit a weakness, that's what my brother Don said when he was studying martial arts; if people found out your weak points they'd use them against you. "Anyway, thanks for trying to help. Sorry I'm such a mess."

She smiled a little shakily. "So anyway, if you have another attack when I'm around, is there anything specific I should do?"

I shook my head. "I've got people helping me already."

"Jaimie? How much help was she? She ran away!"

"A lot. A lot." I stood up and washed my face. Face dripping, I bleared around the room until I spotted the towel dispenser.

"But didn't she just abandon you?"

"She'll be back."

Jaimie crashed into the room again. "Missed it *again*," she said. "You okay, Kim?"

I wadded up the towels and tossed them in the trash. "Yeah, I guess."

"Hey," said Nan. "You just had a major meltdown. How can you be okay?"

Jaimie came over to stand beside me. "I'll take care of her," she said.

Nan's gaze traveled from Jaimie to me and back. At last she shrugged. "Good night. See ya." She sauntered out.

Jaimie waited until the door swung shut behind her, then said, "I think it was someone in the hall again, but they're fast. Maybe next time." She went on, as if everything were normal, "Kim, do you know today's schedule?" She sounded uncertain.

"What?"

"I talked to Barbara and Aki while I was brushing my teeth, and they said we have to do all these things when we wake up. We have to check in or something? And go to lectures and stuff? Get ID? Register for classes?"

"Yes, of course, Jaimie." I'd memorized the Welcome Week schedule a month ago.

"It's about five A.M. now. If you want to shower before breakfast, we can probably manage one more hour of sleep. What do you think?"

"I'll never get to sleep now." Granted, my old misery had never left me as quickly as Rugee could make this retreat, but I knew the aftermath of these attacks: sleepless hours and more misery, tossing and turning, before I totally wore myself out and collapsed from exhaustion.

"Sure you will." She quirked an eyebrow. Her eyes narrowed, and I felt a sudden scrambling in my chest as I remembered. She was a witch. I didn't even know what that meant. Maybe it meant I would go to sleep whether I wanted to or not. I wished I knew whether she really wanted to help me or just boss me around. Maybe it didn't make any difference.

CHAPTER 21: *Jaimie*

I hated how I felt, helpless in the face of something I didn't understand. I used to have lots of problems, but I understood them, and I knew I'd be able to handle them once I grew into my gifts. I was gifted now, and I didn't know what to do. "It was sucking on her again!" I told Joshua and Harrison. They were both awake and sitting up, but Rugee's alarm call from the bathroom hadn't reached either of them. They hadn't figured out why I charged out of the room.

I really hated this viri. How cunning, to wait until Kim wasn't even in the room, where the three of us could have tried to track it. Did it know we were searching for it? "It caught her in the bathroom!"

"Damn!" said Harrison.

"How are you, Kim?" Josh asked.

"How am I?" she said. "How are *you*? I'm sorry I jumped on your stomach. I totally forgot you were there."

"I'll recover."

"I guess I'll recover, too," Kim said. "Rugee saved me again."

I steered Kim to her bed. She sat down. I said to Harrison, "You guys have had some experience with viri. Can you set up wards around Kim? Something that would alert us when this thing starts attacking her?"

Harrison shook his head. "I don't have the knowledge."

"We need to call Zilla. She's the only one in town who's done ward work," said Josh. "Should we call her right now?"

"At five A.M.?" asked Harrison.

"There's need."

Harrison sighed. He rose and looked around. There was a phone on Kim's desk. He dialed.

Kim curled up in her snarl of sheets and blankets. A couple of tears ran down her cheeks. I trelled, satisfied myself that this wasn't the kind of super-misery the viri sucked out of her, just regular sadness.

"What's the matter?" Josh asked Kim, after he noticed that I was watching her.

Before Kim could answer, Harrison said, "Hi. It's Harrison. Sorry about the timing. We've got an emergency." He put his hand over the mouthpiece and glanced at Kim, too.

"It's not really my idea of fun, being a bother to everybody," Kim muttered. "All because I had to go to the bathroom. Jesus, Mary, and Joseph."

"It's not because you had to go to the bathroom," I said. "It's because something out there is wicked and using you."

"Sorry to call you at this time of night," Harrison murmured. "Did you get my message earlier today about Jaimie coming to Sitka? She's here in Spangler Hall, in the Fernald Complex, room two fourteen, and Josh and I are with her. It turns out her roommate is being attacked by a viri. Do you remember your wardwork?"

Pause.

"Summon you? How'm I supposed to do that? Can't you just come over here?"

Pause.

"I'll put a sign on the window. Second floor. It faces the inside of the courtyard, okay? Thanks, Zill."

"Kim, whatever it is we're doing later today, it's not really important, is it?" I asked.

"I don't know," said Kim. "I think it's all important." She looked pale and desperate.

Harrison put down the phone. Then he climbed on Kim's desk, stepped carefully between her printer, laptop, telephone, and giant dictionary, and sketched a big sign on the window with his thumb, the circular sign for Ether, or the center of things. It glowed green.

"What are you doing?" Kim asked.

"This is so Zilla will know which room we're in," Harrison said. He opened the window a crack, then jumped down off the desk.

"She can't just read the room number on the door?"

He smiled at her.

I said, "What happens if we miss check-in?"

Kim answered, "Everybody else will know a lot of stuff that we don't. We'll totally get off on the wrong foot. Like that hasn't happened already," she finished with a mutter. "Nan thinks I'm nuts now."

"So we're better off being totally exhausted but awake?" I said.

"Why should you be exhausted?" asked Harrison. "Don't you know how to energize?" I gave him a look, and he said, "What a *klikla*. Come here."

I edged toward him.

"Turn around."

I did, and he put his hands on my shoulders. "This draws on your power reservoir, but you know how to reserve power, right? You've got a reservoir?"

"Oh, yeah."

"This is a function of healing. Do you do that?"

"Some." Never one of my best skills, but I had been more interested in it since the time Annis got sick and I couldn't help her. Nobody at the Hollow knew much about healing, though most of us knew about harm.

"Okay. Listen." He sang softly in *Ilmonish*. I felt a stir in my power reservoir, and a whisper of memory. I had heard this song before, when I was tiny, without power of my own. Someone had sung this song and sent their own power into me when I was too tired to move. Afterward, I had jumped up, ready to help with celebration preparations again.

I listened to the words Harrison sang, memorized them and the feel of my power waking and weaving through me.

Its work on me was so gentle I almost didn't recognize it. Usually when I addressed my power we worked hard and fast together.

My fatigue was gone.

"Thanks," I said. "Can we do that for Kim?"

"A variation," said Harrison.

I glanced over at Kim. She slumped against the wall, her eyes shut. Rugee shimmered into sight around her neck. *She's asleep*, he thought.

"Can I give her energy anyway? She's suffered more loss than we have."

Come.

I knelt in front of Kim. I put my hands on her shoulders. Her eyelashes fluttered and then she stared at me, confused. "What are you doing?"

"A spell to make you feel better."

"My life just keeps getting weirder."

Rugee said, *Call from your own pool, Jaimie. Change your power as you shift it into her. She has no* sitva. *Make it milk instead of liquor.*

"How?"

Repeat after me.

He taught me a new song I had never heard before. I repeated it three times so it would come into being, and felt power flow into my hands, shift to something milder, and seep from my palms into Kim's shoulders. At first she hunched and flinched, but then she relaxed, staring into my eyes. I forgot where I was and what I was doing. My power moved gently into her, seeped through all the depleted places and strengthened her, took the place of lost sleep.

Stop.

Kim blinked, and I shook my head, broke contact and the feeding touch.

"All right, I'm in love with you now," Kim said as I sat back on my heels.

"What?" I gasped.

"That's all it takes with me. Concentrated stare. This warm feeling pouring into me from you. Want a date?"

Harrison laughed. I couldn't tell if Kim was serious. If she was—

She cracked up.

"Eee, you're a brat!" I said. I was glad she had a bratty side. She'd need it if she was going to live with me.

Lavender smoke wafted into the room from the open window. I settled beside Kim, my back to the wall. The smoke flowed, condensed into a shadowy form, then shifted into my cousin Zilla.

"Hello," she said.

Zilla had been thirteen years old the last time I saw her, pre-*plakanesh*, pretty and helpful and shy. What had I done to her when she couldn't fight back? She had never gotten on my nerves, so with any luck, nothing too severe. Then again, I didn't trust my previous self.

At thirteen, Zilla had had an unformed face and a lot of dark hair to hide behind. Now her dark hair was shoulder-length and curly, her forehead high, her face oval and feminine, not hard-jawed and square like most of the family faces, her tilted eyes blue under definite dark brows. She was slim and seemed quiet.

"Hi," I said. "Thanks for coming."

She yawned into the back of her hand. She was wearing baggy plaid flannel pajamas and a rose-patterned robe. "How can I help?"

Kim gripped my hand. "She just floated in here as smoke and turned into a girl," she whispered.

"Right," I said.

"Can you do that?"

"Not yet."

"It's so cool." She looked at me and shook her head, her lower lip in a pout, as though I made her despair.

"Cut it out," I whispered back. "You haven't seen me do anything yet. I know stuff, too."

"You made these beds and floated me when I fell on the floor. That was really cool, too." She grinned.

Oddly, this made me feel better. I turned to my cousin. "Zilla, this is my roommate, Kim. Kim, my cousin Zilla."

"It is lovely to meet you, Kim," said Zilla, and held out a hand.

"It's nice to meet you, Zilla," Kim said. They shook hands.

"Who marked your forehead? Who is it you host?"

"What?"

Zilla nodded toward Kim. Rugee was visible around Kim's neck. "Oh. This is Rugee. He's a Presence. Is that right? I don't have the vocabulary yet. He made that mark to give me protection. When the viri attacks me, Rugee cuts it off."

"Wonderful," said Zilla. "Presence, I am honored."

You honor me as well.

"The thing is, Kim still gets attacked even though all three of us and the Presence are watching out for her," Harrison said. "Can you do a warding to stop that?"

Zilla stared at the floor. "What is the tuning for the viri energy?" she muttered. "It was all part of a greater working, a guarding against many things we wanted to keep away from us. Is it—" She stroked her fingers in the air and lines of color flowed between them, violet, lavender, magenta, as though she carded air like wool and straightened its snarls into strands. "Is it that one? Presence, can you tell?"

Kim, hold me to the light.

Kim put her hands up close to her neck, and Rugee climbed onto them. She held him toward the shimmering lines of light. He tasted them. *Not quite correct,* he said. *This thing, when it strikes her, tastes more like this.* He spat something into the air: a gray amoeboid splotch with glimmers of dark pearl in it. It hovered between us, pulsing and slimy.

"Eww!" said Kim.

Zilla held her hands out toward the splotch, moved her fingertips near it. She grimaced. "Elder, I've never perceived a thing like this."

Can you ward against it?

She moved her fingers some more. I trelled, trying to figure out what she was doing. She was working in some augmented way I didn't know. I scooted forward on the bed and leaned toward the dark thing. I lifted my hands, tried to imitate what Zilla was doing.

What I could tell was that this thing was sick. But I knew that.

Zilla furrowed her forehead in thought. She rubbed her hands palm to palm, then wove air again, this time lines of lime and lemon with a sickeningly bright bubblegum pink snaking through. "Oh!" she said, shaking her hands. "No!" The new colors wrapped around the splotch, pulsed in concert with it, and then suddenly the colors faded and the splotch was twice as large, pukey gray with shiny bits.

The splotch sent out spiky arms and legs. One stretched toward Zilla, one toward me, one toward Josh, one toward Harrison, one toward Kim.

I clapped my hands. Air crushed the splotch down into a tiny flat square, held it trapped.

"Good," said Harrison. He pointed at the former splotch. Fire leapt from his fingertip and incinerated it, leaving nothing but a smudge in the air, which faded.

"I'm sorry," Zilla said.

It was an experiment. It came close.

She dropped her hands. "I'm sorry, Kim. I don't know how to help you. Should I send for Uncle Rory? He knows these disciplines better than anyone else at Southwater. I don't know if this is technically a Family matter, though. Would sending for Rory be a misuse of power?"

"No," said Joshua. "The Family is still trying to learn

everything we can about the viri. This is an opportunity to study one."

Kim set Rugee on her thigh and touched my hand. I looked at her worried face. "Yeah," I said, answering her unspoken question, if I was guessing right, "this is really going to screw up orientation. But isn't it better than just letting that thing suck on you?"

She sighed. She crawled across the bed, opened her desk drawer, and got out a tin. She lifted the lid. "Cookies?"

CHAPTER 22: *Kim*

The good news was I didn't feel sleepy or tired.

The bad news was my room was even more full of witches, they were summoning another one, and I hadn't done any of the prepwork I had planned for the evening before orientation.

The good news was I now knew something external was making me feel bad.

The bad news was something external was making me feel bad.

Ergo, the good news was my room was full of witches and they were working on my problem, help I wasn't sure I'd done anything to deserve. So the bad news was, suppose they fixed everything and my life improved? How could I ever pay them back?

Good news: witches liked Mom's chocolate chip cookies. Bad news: I was now totally out.

Maybe I should add Home Ec to my schedule so I'd

have a place to bake. I wondered if the guys' apartment had a stove. Maybe they'd let me bake there if I made enough cookies for everybody.

"Are you going to do Wordwaft to call Uncle Rory?" Jaimie asked Zilla. "Josh was trying to teach us, but I don't get it yet."

"Um," said Zilla, "there's a phone right here. That's better at waking him up than Wordwaft, unless I put a sting in it, and, well, Uncle Rory doesn't wake up well, especially if you sting him."

"Oh. I keep forgetting it's so early. Shouldn't he be out milking cows about now?"

Zilla, Joshua, and Harrison exchanged glances. "This is one of the annoying things about you, Jaimie," said Harrison. "You don't pay attention. Uncle Rory raises potatoes. He runs some beef cattle. No dairy."

Jaimie shrugged.

Zilla dialed a long-distance number. Harrison and Joshua, sitting on Jaimie's bed, leaned forward and focused on her. They all looked tense.

"How far away is that?" I whispered to Jaimie, beside me on the bed.

"Oh, shit, it's your phone. It'll go on your bill. We haven't been thinking."

"That's okay. I just wondered."

"Klamath County."

I leaned against the wall and thought about this. "Are you guys everywhere?"

"No. At least, I don't think so. As far as we know, there's just two groups of us."

"One's in Arcadia and the other's in Klamath Falls?"

"How'd you know about Arcadia?"

"It was in your roommate profile."

"What?"

"The packet of stuff we got from housing? Room assignments? That kind of thing? There was information about you."

"What?"

Zilla said, "Uncle Rory? Are you awake?"

I picked Rugee up and settled him on my shoulder, watched Zilla, Harrison, and Joshua wince as I did it.

"How come you guys always do that when I touch Rugee?" I whispered to Jaimie. She had flinched, too.

"You're too informal," she whispered. "We're always humble when we approach them. We never take liberties. We're supposed to repeat blessing formulas and ask permission to even be in their presence. You're not supposed to touch them without asking. I always heard if you did it, you'd get turned into a toadstool or something worse."

"Oh." I stroked Rugee's back. "Is this all right?" I whispered.

I give you leave.

"I keep treating you like a pet. I know you're not a pet. I'm sorry." I whispered so low I wasn't sure he could even hear me. I was pretty sure Jaimie couldn't. Could she hear Rugee's answers?

It is interesting, not a way I have previously been addressed. If it troubles me, I will inform you. Somehow his mental voice sounded extra quiet, too. Maybe he could talk so only I could hear him. I hoped so.

Now I will drop out of visibility, Rugee thought, and disappeared from sight, though I could feel him, heavy on my shoulder, his forelegs draped down my front and his squat tail and back legs hanging down my back. *Let us think about how we will live together. You know I can shift shape. Tell me what shape is most convenient for you. Where is the best place for me to settle?*

"Can you be a little smaller, and around my neck, but not too tight? Can you weigh less?" I whispered. "Can you be less scratchy?"

He moved, shifted, changed. I couldn't see him. I felt a cool, dense, small-scaled snake flow into a ring around my neck. No claws or legs. I sensed a balanced weight on my collarbone.

A snake. I used to have a pet boa. This felt so nice and familiar. "Yeah," I whispered. "That's good."

"We have a situation here," Zilla said into the phone. "A woman being stalked by a viri. She is *Domishti,* but she's Jaimie Locke's roommate here at Sitka. Joshua thought you might help us ward her against attack."

A pause.

"Oh." Zilla cupped her hand over the mouthpiece and whispered to us, "He can't come right now. Something's going on over at Seales." She uncovered the mouthpiece and said, "What's wrong? Is someone hurt?"

Then, "Oh. Oh. Oh, dear." She shifted back and forth on the desk chair's swivel. Harrison and Joshua leaned closer. Zilla shook her head, flapped her hand, then covered the mouthpiece and murmured, "It's not dire. My dumb brother Noah acting like an idiot again. He made a big mess, and there's lots to clean up." She listened some more. "All right, then. Please come when you can. *Kekovna*, Uncle." She hung up.

I wanted to search through my things. I needed my notebook. I needed my welcome folder. I needed the file folder of student paperwork I had completed and Xeroxed before I even got here. I needed my class schedule. I wanted to check everything before anything else happened.

The notebook was on the desk. Most of the rest of that stuff was probably in the file drawer of my desk. When I first got here, at least I had had plenty of time to unpack in a logical manner.

I slid across the bed to the desk and opened a drawer. Yep, there was the blue welcome folder, and under it my other file folders.

"Kim, what are you doing?" asked Harrison

I checked my clock. "It's five thirty. I want to organize to go to orientation, all right?"

"With that thing out there waiting for you?"

"That's right. I don't care if there's a viri out there—I want my orientation. I want my school experience. If the viri makes me miserable, Rugee will help me, right?"

I'll do what I can. It will suspect interference now. It may not have been using its full strength before. I have heard viri can do mindtwists beyond the abilities of the Ilmonish. I have heard that once they are alerted, they can bring many powers into play, against several of which your people cannot defend.

I dropped onto my bed, the folders falling from my hands and spilling across my blankets and the floor. "What am I supposed to do?" I wailed. "Just stay locked up in the room with you guys and wait for an attack? What would have happened if I'd had a normal roommate? I'd probably just be going through my normal bouts of misery, right?"

Jaimie said, "Think about this, Kim. Has the misery gotten worse, or is it about the same?"

I lay back on my scrunched covers, Rugee around my neck but not too tight, and gave Jaimie's question some consideration. "I guess that last attack was about as bad as it's ever been. I couldn't say if it was really worse, though."

"When the viri first started feeding off you, how bad did you feel?"

I sat up. "*Really* bad. Then the feelings got less intense. But then—Shaina wouldn't let it drop. Every time I thought maybe life would go back to normal, she'd start needling me again. Not to my face. I'd just come around a corner and hear her telling the story to my former pseudofriends, and they'd all turn and glare at me. I made friends with my lab partner in biology—that's a class Shaina wasn't in. When Shaina noticed, she poisoned that relationship, too. I even started talking to this guy at Taco Tim's. Shaina came in there one time, and—" I frowned. "So finally I gave up looking for escape routes. I stayed miserable pretty much full-time."

Jaimie said, "But you ran away to college."

"Yeah. Every once in a while I'd have a clear moment, and I figured if I could get away from home, I might get away from all the things I felt guilty about. Hah." I collected the spill from my file folders. "I don't want to stay locked up in here, you guys, even though I appreciate the fact that you care about some drippy stranger who's not even a witch. If Shaina's going to kill me sooner or later, I don't see why I shouldn't just do what I want anyway."

Harrison and Joshua checked with each other. Harrison frowned at me, opened his mouth, shut it, opened it again. "I guess we can't tell you what to do."

"You could if you wanted to, I bet. Jaimie said she could make me forget everything. Maybe that's what we should do. I forget all about you witch people, and just keep going, and what happens, happens."

"Is that what you want?"

I closed my eyes. Would I be happier if I didn't know what was happening? Probably not. "No," I said. "I do want to go to orientation, though. Even if it's risky."

"What are we actually supposed to do during orientation, Kim?" Jaimie asked. "Barbara and Aki said they'd explain it to me at breakfast, but I figured you'd know already."

"We have to get over to the Student Rec Center after breakfast and check in. We get our student IDs. There's a general lecture about being here, and testing to see if you place out of bonehead English and math and foreign languages and can take upper-division classes instead. This afternoon they pair us up with advisors and we hammer out schedules. Tomorrow we register online for classes."

"That's a pretty accurate assessment of what to expect," said Harrison. "You did a lot of homework. I didn't know half of that when I first got here."

"When you don't have any friends, you have plenty of time to work on other things."

Jaimie socked my arm. "Quit acting pitiful."

I socked her back. "How can I help it? I've had tons of practice!"

Zilla looked at Harrison. "Am I supposed to be doing all those things, too? I had no idea!"

"Um," he said. "I forgot to tell you. That part *is* easier to remember when you start out in campus housing. The R.A.s really ride your ass and keep you on track."

"I don't even have any paperwork, Harrison!"

"You ought to. What happened to it?"

"What?" Now Zilla, who had seemed perfectly collected and tranquil when she first arrived in a puff of smoke, fell apart. "I only came up here yesterday by purest chance!" she said. "I was seriously thinking about getting here the first day of classes and then just going. I have to register? What's online? I need student ID? Nobody told me! What am I going to do?"

"Why don't you come with us?" Jaimie said. "Kim'll tell you."

"All right. I will. Thank you." She crossed her arms over her chest and leaned back in my desk chair.

"Will you want your own clothes, or would you like to borrow some of ours?" I asked.

Zilla glanced down at her pajamas and robe, then looked at each of us in turn, crimson flooding her cheeks. "I—what? I—"

"It was an emergency. You were asleep when I called," Harrison said.

Zilla stood up and shook her hands. Her pajamas morphed into a high-waisted, long-sleeved red flannel dress that went down to mid-calf and should have looked dumpy but didn't. On her legs, saggy white scrunch socks appeared, and brown penny loafers showed up on her feet. Next to the smoke-condensing-into-a-girl trick, it was the coolest witch stuff I'd seen so far.

"Awesome," I whispered.

Jaimie had leaned forward to watch. "Airshape," she said.

"Can you teach Jaimie how to do that?" I asked Zilla. "It's one of a bunch of things she needs help with."

Zilla took a long look at Jaimie.

Jaimie sat back and sighed. "How evil was I? I don't remember, Zilla."

"You turned Noah into a tiger. He kept attacking me! I had so many scratches and bites, I—" Zilla closed her eyes. "Well, that was Noah, and not you directly. I had to have healing six times, though, and between healings I had a lot of hurt. You spelled him so well no one could unspell him, and he didn't seem to want to unspell. He liked being a tiger. It gave him license to be his worst."

"I'm sorry," Jaimie said in a crumpled voice. "Seriously."

"I wished you had made him a toad or a piglet, something small without fangs or claws that I could have kept in a box."

"Want me to do that now?"

Zilla stared at Jaimie, then smiled and shook her head. "I don't need anyone doing it for me anymore, Cuz."

"Oh, good. I don't know how much you guys know about our revolution a year ago at Chapel Hollow—"

"No one has spoken to us of it outright," Harrison said. "The senior elders have had private meetings with your council to discuss it, but I don't know much. Will you tell us what happened?"

Jaimie sighed. "I can't tell you everything now, even though it's a good story. But one of the things we discovered was that our skills and persuasions teacher wasn't doing a very good job, except in teaching us to be our worst selves. I have huge holes in my education. I need help. I'll understand if you don't want to help me. Tell me how to convince you I won't misuse any knowledge you give me."

Zilla looked from me to Jaimie, cocked her head. "I'm already convinced."

"Me, too," said Joshua. Harrison looked faintly skeptical, but he shrugged and nodded.

Jaimie and I looked at each other. I wondered if my eyebrows were as high as hers. She blinked. "Oh. Okay."

"Sheesh," I said. "Well, on that mysterious note, I'm

going to take a shower before everybody else gets the same idea."

"I'll go with you," Jaimie said.

"What? Oh." Yeah, the last time I'd gone to the bathroom, I'd been attacked. Maybe it was a good sign that I could forget it so fast. "Thanks."

"I hope we get this problem solved soon," she said. "I'm not a morning person."

We took our towels, toiletries, and clothes across the hall to the bathroom. We weren't the only ones with the same idea, but the wait wasn't too long. Obviously my new housemates had not gone to my brother Don's school of Take-a-Long-Enough-Shower-to-Use-Up-All-the-Hot-Water-Before-Your-Sister-Gets-a-Chance.

Rugee had already seen me pee. Getting naked with him around my neck was only slightly more embarrassing. "Do you mind getting wet?" I whispered to Rugee after I perched my towel on top of the shower door and snicked the door shut.

Not at all.

So we took our first shower together. He wasn't fond of shampoo washing over him as I rinsed my hair, but he only complained a little. I never soaped him directly. He liked the toweling-dry part.

Best of all, I was fine. I took a completely normal shower, got out, and got dressed without agonizing for half an hour over the clothes I'd chosen to wear.

While Jaimie dressed, her long dark hair waved in the breeze. An extremely localized breeze. The rest of the room was full of heavy, still air, dense with steam.

"Um," I said.

Other women were standing in front of the steam-coated mirror, wiping small sections clear and using blow dryers.

Jaimie ran her fingers through her hair, held it out from her head. The breeze strummed it. I glanced at other women waiting in line to use the showers. They looked bleary-eyed as they clutched their shampoo, conditioner, shower gel bottles, washcloths, and towels. Most of the blow-drying women were too focused on their own heads to notice Jaimie, but you couldn't count on that lasting, or could you?

"What?" Jaimie held out different portions of her hair.

"Don't do that here," I whispered.

"What?" she whispered back. "Air dry?"

I nodded.

"Oh." She lowered her hands. Her still damp hair swung around her head and shoulders.

"We could just use the shower downstairs," Harrison was saying as we came in. He sat at Jaimie's desk. Josh was still on Jaimie's bed. The blue mattress/blanket things Jaimie had made for them were bunched up on top of the wardrobes. "Nobody knows each other yet. They won't know we don't belong here."

On my bed, Zilla was paging through all my orientation material and frowning. I felt nervous about her going through my stuff when she hadn't asked me first. As more and more people showed up in our room, my sense of privacy kept shrinking. At home I had my own room. Here, I apparently didn't even have my own bed.

None of this was happening without my consent. It wasn't like Shaina.

I hung up my towel, then flopped onto my bed next to Zilla.

"You know the fire discipline for cleansing, don't you?" Joshua asked Harrison. Jaimie played with her hair and the local breeze again.

"Why waste power?"

"Aren't we supposed to stick with Kim? What if something happens to her while we're downstairs? I guess maybe we could take real showers if we take turns. We have instant call links," said Joshua.

"This is ridiculous," I muttered to Rugee. "Now I have bodyguards? I've never been the center of attention like this before."

Let them worry about you. It's good for them. He was using his quietest voice.

"And anyway—" Joshua began.

The air in the center of the room shimmered. A scent of woodsmoke and baking bread filled the room, and a man appeared, a lean, sleepy-eyed man with short sandy hair. He wore an old flannel shirt, blue jeans, white socks, and Birkenstock sandals.

"Hello," he said, glanced around, saw me, and frowned.

CHAPTER 23: *Jaimie*

Uncle Rory had low profile down to an art.

He knew how to appear out of nowhere. *Sirella!* Nobody in the Hollow could do that. He didn't even have to use smoke as a vehicle, the way Zilla had. It would be a great way to get home for the holidays. I wondered if it was a skill I could learn, and whether I wanted to learn it from Uncle Rory. I didn't know him very well, and I didn't entirely trust him.

"Uncle Rory, this is Kim," said Harrison.

Kim looked nervous. She touched her neck. Well, not quite her neck; a solid invisibility.

Rugee was with her. Good.

Harrison continued, "She's got a viri addicted to her. Can you help us ward her?"

"What is wrong with this generation? Have you no knowledge of the covenant of secrecy?" Uncle Rory's voice was low and beautiful, and he sounded exasperated. He was Sign Air and specialized in Voice. He wasn't actually commanding us yet. If we played this right, maybe he wouldn't get around to it. Just the same, I tried to call up what I knew to screen me from Voice commands. I hoped Rugee could do that for Kim.

"Uncle, it is my responsibility," I said. "I broke silence. I had permission from my Presence."

"What?" He leaned toward me where I sat beside Josh on my bed. "Jaimie?"

"Hi." I waved.

"Jaimie Locke. A Hollow child. A very disobedient Hollow child. Well. That explains it. You are so lax there, so in need of discipline." He sighed. "Now, please tell me more clearly why you need me here. Why does this *Domishti* girl have a spirit mark on her forehead?"

"She's my roommate, and she needs help."

"Jaimie, you were instructed to keep silence before you left home, weren't you? No matter how lax they are at the Hollow, they wouldn't let that go, would they? Are we going to have to deal with this poor child, give her silence or forgetting?"

"No, Uncle—" I began.

"Uncle, didn't you hear me?" Harrison interrupted. "This is a viri matter."

Rory frowned. "Ah. You did say that. Explain yourself."

Harrison and I both started talking.

CHAPTER 24: Kim

Even over the sound of Jaimie's and Harrison's voices, I could hear my stomach rumble.

What is that noise? Rugee asked.

"I'm hungry," I whispered. I checked my watch. "Breakfast starts in five minutes. Boy, am I ready." I pulled my papers together from the shambles Zilla had made of them and stuffed them, my purse, a notebook, and a bunch of pens into my backpack. Zilla stayed out of the viri discussion and watched every move I made. I opened my desk drawer and dug up a red spiral notebook. I handed her that and a pen. She raised her eyebrows. I nodded. She wrote her name on the cover of the notebook and sighed.

I wished I had some food to add. I was out of cookies.

"What is this you say about a Presence?" Uncle Rory asked in a brief break between Harrison's and Jaimie's explanations.

With a shimmer, Rugee appeared around my neck. Everybody stopped talking and stared.

He lifted his head. It wasn't orange and green anymore, and he no longer resembled a gecko. Now he had the squat, spade-shaped head and far-forward eyes of a poisonous snake. Greenish-silver and scarlet flames patterned his surface.

"Sheesh," I said. "What happened to *you*?"

He turned to me. His eyes were ancient, gold flakes under glass, the pupils deep as time. I had forgotten. I should be more careful how I talked to him.

Shh, he thought. He turned to stare at Rory. *Child*, he said.

"Presence," whispered Rory. "I, Rory Keye, greet you." He bowed his head.

I have extended my protection to this girl. She is prey to one of the viri. Do you know how to discourage their kind from attacking?

Rory lifted his head. "We've analyzed their methods. We still don't know how to resist them."

We in the north have not encountered them directly, only by rumor. Please share what protection you can, and accept my thanks.

Rory nodded.

Whoa. Rugee could cow grown-up witches.

"Zilla? Will you help?" Rory asked.

"Of course." Zilla went and took his hand. They stood facing me.

One moment. Rory Keye, this is Kim Calloway. Kim, this is Rory Keye.

Rory smiled. "Sorry, Kim. I'm preoccupied. It's nice to meet you."

"Nice to meet you," I echoed, and shook his hand.

Explain what you do. Kim only met us recently and doesn't understand us yet.

"Oh. Very well. Kim, we protect our holdings by singing." Rory smiled. He had a nice smile, and excellent laugh wrinkles beside his eyes. He looked like a friendly bumbling uncle on TV, not a witch. "Sometimes it works. The Presence has asked us to protect you that way. Is that all right?"

"Sure."

"Has the viri caused you physical harm? Have you been ill because of its attention?"

I wasn't sure. "She likes it when I'm depressed, so I've been miserable for months now. But I'm not wasting away."

"Mm. Different from our experience. Perhaps we *can* still help you. Zilla and I are Sign Air. We're going to sing to the air around you and ask it to hold back the viri's reach toward you."

Jaimie leaned forward. I remembered she was Sign Air, too.

"Does this make sense to you?" Rory asked me.

"Some," I said. Actually, not much. I didn't even know what questions to ask. I wished Rugee could read my thoughts so he could explain.

Rory stepped back and took Zilla's hand again. They stared intently at me. Then they opened their mouths, and music came out.

How did they know to start on those notes, so perfectly

harmonized? They sang words I couldn't understand, and their melodies twisted around each other, moving apart and together, sometimes resting on each other or leaning away. The hairs on my neck and the backs of my arms rose; the sound was so beautiful and eerie. And soft—how could they sing so quietly when their mouths were open so wide?

My picture side went wild with images and colors. I reached for my sketchbook and markers.

Not now, Rugee thought.

Air stroked me, flowed around my shoulders, touched my jean-clad legs. Invisible fingers stroked spirals on my cheeks, ruffled my bangs. Rugee's head swayed next to mine. *Beautiful, beautiful*, he whispered. *Excellent. Do you want to see it?*

I didn't understand. But I nodded. I wanted to see everything.

Just for a moment. His head rose. His tongue had changed from a wet white thing into a snake's forked flicker. I felt something damp on my lower lip. *Taste*, he whispered.

It stung and burned like a bee and made my tongue throb and swell. I blinked once, twice, then saw Zilla's and Rory's voices flowing out of their mouths: ribbons of blue and green and yellow and scarlet, twining in the air to weave knots of delicate intricacy, almost script, almost the whorls of shells, the spirals of petals unfolding in time-lapse photography, the curling under of the leading edges of waves.

I craved color, wished it could flow out the ends of my fingers, wished I, too, could write on air.

The song rose. A cloak came together in air, and then it

came to me and wrapped colors around me tight as a cocoon. I couldn't feel it; close as my skin, invisible to touch.

Colors and music faded, along with the throbbing heat on my tongue.

"Are you okay, Kim?" Jaimie asked.

"It was so beautiful. Thank you." I touched my shoulder, then my arm. Nothing. Just because I couldn't see or feel it didn't mean it wasn't there. I wore a cloak of song.

"You saw it?" Rory knelt before me. "Kim, may I see your dominant hand?"

I held out my right hand. He moved his fingers above it. My palm tingled. He frowned, tried it again. Again, I felt a tingling in my palm.

"What's supposed to happen?" I asked.

"If you are one of us—*Ilmonish*—this test shows what sign you are."

"I'm not a witch."

"A witch!" He sat back on his heels and laughed. Then he lost his smile and rubbed his hand across his forehead. He stood up. "Kim, watch." He took Zilla's hand and did what he'd done to me. A ball of blue flame hovered over her palm. "This is what happens if you're one of us. You are not one of us, and yet you could see a working?"

"Rugee let me."

"What?"

He doesn't know my name, Rugee thought.

"Excuse me. The Presence gave me a drop of venom, and then I could see what you were doing."

"How odd," said Rory. "How interesting. I have never heard of such a thing." He took a deep breath, let it out. When he looked up again his face had lost its pleasant bumbling appearance. "Kim, I've done what I can to protect you. You also have a strong advocate in the Presence. I'm sorry you're in this kind of trouble, but having my young relatives guard you worries me. I don't want any of them touched by the viri."

"Uncle!" cried Harrison.

"Family comes first, always," Rory said to him. "We must protect each other whenever we can. I wonder whether I should enjoin you against staying close to her."

"You'd better not try it with me," said Jaimie, her voice hot and hard-edged.

"I won't. I know you, Jaimie," he said calmly. "You were lost to us a long time ago." He glanced at Zilla, Harrison, and Josh. "But you—you remember what the last viri did to us, Harrison? What if Kim's gets a taste for *Ilmonish* flavor? We can't afford to lose any of you."

"Uncle." Zilla sat beside me, threaded her arm through mine.

"We're adults now. You can't command us," said Harrison. "We're old enough to decide for ourselves."

I closed my eyes to hold back the heat behind my eyelids. I was already half-dead with misery. I should go outside, find the viri, let it drain me, and leave the witches alone. What had I ever done to earn their protection? Weren't they each worth ten or twenty people like me?

I teetered on the brink of the familiar dark well.

Kim. Stop it.

One tear escaped. I rubbed it away before the others could notice.

Stop it, Rugee repeated. *Do you want to summon the thing? You're broadcasting misery, that special kind you make that's so sweet and sour, even though nothing's out there yet to siphon it off. Stop it.*

I tried to pull myself together. Rugee was around my neck, and he could order Rory around; Rory couldn't tell him what to do. Whether I deserved it or not, I had a guardian in Rugee—and another in Jaimie, even if the cousins stopped looking after me. Rory and Zilla had given me a magic cloak. I had new defenses now.

I rubbed my eyes and looked past Rory at Jaimie. She met my gaze. Nothing was drawing from me right now, and these people were my friends. "I'm sorry," I whispered.

You need to find another feeling to supplant that one. It's too easy for you to drop into that special sadness.

"I'm sorry," I whispered again. Was there some way I could snap my fingers and change how I felt? If I was going to have a replacement feeling, like Nicorette instead of a cigarette, which feeling should I have?

Maybe there was a spell for that sort of thing.

Stop apologizing, Rugee thought. He nudged my cheek with his head. I sensed a smile.

"Don't we need to learn all we can about these things?" Josh asked Rory. "Doesn't this give us an opportunity?"

"Suppose we never have to face one at home again. Suppose all the warding we do at home works, and they never come near us. Why expose yourself?" asked Rory. "You are young adults, coming into your powers. I am an experienced adult, and so long as my power is stronger than yours, I can shape your behavior at least a little. So I lay this on you. Zilla, Harrison, Joshua: if this thing turns its attention to you"—his voice sharpened until it hurt to hear it—"vanish home and summon help. Don't stay in range. Grave that into your hearts."

All three of them jerked and twisted as though he had just slapped them. Zilla looked pale and angry. Josh's hands fisted. Harrison jumped to his feet. "Uncle!"

Rory sighed and said, "I had better return home. I have much to report."

My alarm clock went off with the racket of a billion electronic beeps.

Harrison pointed at it, and it exploded.

"Harrison!" I cried.

"How can you stand it?" he asked me. I knew he was talking about a lot of things. All that mad he had at his uncle jumped sideways into my poor little clock.

I said, "That's the point. You're not *supposed* to be able to stand it. You wake up and turn it off. Then you get up and go to class. Or in this case, breakfast." The question underneath his surface question reverberated. How could I stand what was happening to me? I didn't know how to stop it.

"Reassemble that clock," Rory said to Harrison.

Fire flared in Harrison's dark eyes. One of his shoulders hunched. Then he flung himself into my desk chair and pulled together all the exploded parts of my clock.

"That's okay. Really," I said. "I can get another one for ten bucks."

"That's not the point," said Rory. "We do not destroy other people's property unless menace is involved. Kim, I apologize for my nephew."

"I can apologize for myself," Harrison muttered. He twisted a piece of plastic, trying to fit it with another piece of plastic. Plastic bits cluttered the desk, some of them melted. The liquid crystal display case where the numbers used to be was in at least two pieces. I didn't get how even magic could put it all back together again.

"I'm sorry, Kim." Harrison looked at the mess, then at me. "I got surprised."

"It's okay."

"If the task is beyond you, replace what you have destroyed," Uncle Rory said. "I must leave now, children. Call me if you need me again. Remember what I told you: when in danger, retreat! Kim, blessings on you. I hope you find a way to escape your tormentor."

"Thank you," I said.

Uncle Rory disappeared. No one else even blinked.

Harrison collected the pieces of the clock and cupped them in his hands. He raised them to his mouth and spoke into the space between his thumbs. Yellow light flared between his fingers.

He set an object on my desk. It was round, clear as smoked quartz, though it had a flat bottom and top. On the flattened space on top there was a clock face, the numbers strange and spiky, with a pin sticking up in the center. I could see into the crystal. It had no detectable clockwork.

I swallowed, touched Rugee, felt smooth cool skin under my fingertips.

Harrison picked up a pencil and glanced at me. "May I use this?"

"Um, what for?"

"For hands."

"So it won't be a pencil anymore?"

"Right."

"Oh, sure, why not?" I had other pencils.

He smiled at me and broke the pencil in half, pulled out the graphite center, rubbed it between his hands. Again a flare of light, and then he set two spindly arms on the pin in the center of the clock's face. He spoke to the whole thing and let go of it.

The hands spun and settled: 7:25.

Okay. It looked good, but with no visible works or knobs, how was I going to set the alarm, if it even had one? I guessed I'd worry about it later. "Wow. Okay. Wow. That's—wait a sec. Is that right?" I checked my watch. The new clock *was* right. "It's late. We're missing breakfast."

"We can leave in a minute," Jaimie said. She gripped her right hand in her left. "I need to ask my cousins a few questions first."

They all faced her.

"So did Uncle Rory do what it looked like he did to you

guys?" Jaimie asked in a sharp voice. "He turn you into prey when you planned to be hunters?"

Harrison said, "He did. He laid a command on us that cripples our usefulness. That was his right, I guess, but I—" Red shone in his eyes. Smoke rose from his hair.

"I'm sorry, Jaimie. Sorry, Kim. I didn't know he was going to do it or I would have tried to block," said Josh. "But now I feel it." He tapped his chest with his hand. "I won't even be able to think. If the viri sniffs me, I'm out of here."

"It's so stupid," said Zilla. She sounded mad, too. "What if it's a tracker? We'll lead it right home!"

"What if it notices us where everybody can see us disappear?" asked Harrison.

Ill-considered, Rugee thought.

"Is he always that bossy?" Jaimie asked.

"When he's scared," said Zilla.

"You know how to get around commands like that, right?" Jaimie said.

"What do you mean?"

"Modify them so they work the way you need them to. Attach your own commands to his command. Like, command yourself to make sure all the spectators forget what they're seeing before you leave."

"That works?" asked Josh. "How does that work?"

"You guys have never tried to weasel out of commands laid on you?"

"Jaimie." Harrison sounded annoyed, but not as angry as he had been a moment before.

"All you have to do is believe that the modifications are vital, that they'll help the Family. Or—" She leaned forward. "I could command you."

Zilla flinched. Harrison glared. Josh shook his head, his hair half covering his face.

"Okay, forget I said that. It just seemed easiest. Tell yourselves something, like, 'If I need to vanish home, first I'll secure my leaving so no one remembers what they saw.'"

"I can say that to myself, and it will change an order from Uncle Rory?" Zilla bit her lip.

"Make it a command to yourself."

"I don't command things."

"*Sirella*, Zilla. Don't you get in fights with Noah and Lovell? Don't you ever turn them?"

"No. Well. Noah . . ." She hid her face behind her hands.

Harrison stared at the floor and muttered to himself.

"Do it with your heart. Know it's for a good reason and you need it. Shape it like you shape air."

Joshua cupped his hands over his mouth and muttered into them.

Zilla went to Jaimie. "Please do it for me," she said.

Jaimie took her hand. "Check this out. Tell me if it's what you want me to say. 'Zilla, before you vanish home, make sure any spectators won't see or remember what you do.'"

Zilla thought, then nodded.

Jaimie said the same words again, her voice as sharp and painful as Rory's had been when he issued his commands.

Zilla shivered, then nodded. "Thanks."

Everybody stood up. Zilla clutched the notebook and pen I had given her, glanced down at her self-made clothes, checked the mirror on the closet door.

I checked the mirror myself. "Um. Rugee."

He lifted his head and stared at our reflection. He raised his head even farther, slid half of himself up over the hair behind my ear, and ended with his head resting on top of mine, facing forward along the part in my hair. Two loops of tail still draped around my neck. It was interesting having my head gripped by a snake, but not unpleasant. I turned my head, and the half of him draped over it turned, too, no resistance, and not much extra weight. His tongue flickered, retreated.

"Is that supposed to help?" I asked. Maybe if he twined around my head and put his head farther forward, he would look like Cleopatra headgear.

He disappeared.

"Thank you."

The tip of his tail stroked my cheek.

I collected my pack, put it on. "You guys ready?"

"We never got our shower," said Josh.

"But we don't have to go to orientation," Harrison said. "We already know all this stuff. We can take showers after breakfast."

"We have to go to orientation if we want to protect Kim." Josh hesitated, glanced at me. "I don't even know if we can protect you, but I'd like to try."

"Huh," said Harrison. "Me, too. Let's take turns going off to shower."

"I've got Rugee and Jaimie and the song coat Zilla and Rory made me," I said. "You guys have other things going on, right? Maybe we'll be better off if you go back to your own lives. Less chance the viri will notice you. Less chance that you'll have to disappear."

"We're not going anywhere yet," said Harrison. "Except wherever you go."

"I need your help to get through registration," Zilla said.

"Oh. Right."

Zilla needed me. How odd, and how wonderful. Warmth bloomed in my chest.

CHAPTER 25: Jaimie

"You're really going to need all those things?" I asked Kim. Her backpack bulged, even though she didn't have any textbooks yet.

"Maybe. I try to plan for everything. I wish I had food." She glanced at the window. "How cold is it? I wonder if I need a jacket."

I trelled for weather information. "Sixty-two degrees and sunny."

Her brows rose. "That's so cool! Witch AccuWeather. Thanks! I guess I'll be okay. I mean, we can always come back to the room, right?"

"Sure."

She looked around the room. "I'm the only one with a backpack?"

Zilla sketched a shape in the air and did something that squished air into a solid matter. She held a red backpack in her hands. Airshape! I hadn't watched closely enough. She studied the adjustable straps on Kim's pack, did some fine tuning to get hers to match, slid the notebook and pen Kim had given her into the main compartment of her pack, and slipped the straps over her shoulders.

"I've got a pack for when I'm actually going to school," Harrison said. "Don't need it today."

I grabbed my carrysack. "Come on, you guys," I said.

Dinah was in the hall knocking on doors. "Whoa," she said when she saw us, "did you all spend the night?"

"Yep," said Harrison.

Dinah blinked. "Well, maybe it's good to start out wild. Get it out of your system before the classwork piles up. You guys know about condoms, right?"

"What?"

"Excuse me, R.A.," I said. "These are my cousins." I wasn't about to tell her there was a lot of cousin marriage in my family. "We just had a lot to talk about."

Dinah turned red. "I'm sorry. It's none of my business. I don't mean to invade your mental space. For all I know, you kids may have taken a vow of celibacy. I just worry. It's my job."

"That's all right," Kim said.

I peeked at Kim. How was she, after everything that had happened since we got here? Rugee adopting her, and using venom on her. My cousins and Rugee and I having arguments about her fate, and never even asking her what *she* wanted. Uncle Rory ordering the cousins not to take care of her. Now the R.A. accusing her of what, sex? Orgies, maybe?

She looked surprisingly calm.

Maybe she was in shock.

"Anyway," said Dinah, "if you want breakfast, you'd better get downstairs now."

"Right," said Harrison. We headed past Dinah, who went to knock on someone else's door.

"So *do* you know about safe sex?" I asked Kim as we clattered down the stairs.

"Of course," she said. "I'm really good at finding out stuff on the Internet."

"Huh," I said. "So do you have condoms?"

She colored. "Of course not. Reading up on stuff online doesn't translate into reality. Besides, the way I've been lately, I didn't expect to find a boyfriend. Who wants to hang out with someone who cries all the time? Anyway, do *you* have condoms?"

"Uh, no, that's not what we—" I felt my own face go hot.

Kim turned away, but I saw her smile. I poked her shoulder. "Brat."

She laughed just as we reached the ground floor, where we bumped into Casey and Flax again.

Casey stared at Kim.

"What?" Kim asked when she noticed him.

"You're cute when you smile."

"Sure. Have you tried that line on what's-her-name? The blonde you were following the other night? Delia?"

"Well," Casey said, "but she's not cute when she smiles."

"Is he smooth, or what?" Flax said. He had such a nice deep voice he sounded like a boulder talking. "Who's your new friend?"

Zilla had been hiding behind me. Why did she dress in red if she wanted to go unnoticed? "This is my non-evil cousin, Zilla. Zilla, this is Flax and Casey."

"Hello," said Zilla, ducking her head and half hiding behind her hair.

"Hi." Flax held out his hand to her. After a second she noticed it and darted forward to clasp hands with him. I studied his technique. He didn't squeeze, and he didn't hold on too long. Nice. Since I'd somehow met Flax without shaking his hand, I was glad to have this chance to observe how he handled it.

Although once you've stolen a guy's food and he's stolen yours, how much more do you need to know?

"Are you ready for another food fight?" I asked Flax when Zilla had retreated behind me again.

He shook his head and groaned. "How can you be so perky this early in the morning? Why don't we rest up and continue at lunch? Truce?"

"I will if you will."

A girl was sitting at the only nearly empty table big enough for all of us. "Mind if we join you?" Casey asked her.

"Uh, no problem, I was done." She grabbed her tray and book and fled.

Flax put his tray down at the head of the table and wandered off. The rest of us sat, with a lot of chair scraping. Zilla took covert peeks at Casey, who sat across from her. He was watching Kim.

"What?" I whispered to Zilla.

"He did something to that girl to make her leave."

"No, he didn't. She was finished."

"He did something."

Before I could ask her what, Flax came back with a chair. He set it down at the head of the table right next to Zilla.

"Steal one of his doughnuts," I muttered to Zilla, who turned to me, startled.

"Hey. I said truce," Flax said.

"Kim, what are you doing?" asked Casey.

I turned to see that Kim was holding a small piece of sausage patty on top of her head.

"Where'd you get that?" I asked. "You didn't take any sausage."

"Um." She glanced at my plate. She'd stolen it from me!

"Is it some kind of beauty treatment?" asked Casey. "Does the grease make your hair nice? Or is it perfume to make you smell like breakfast?"

"Um." She set the sausage on her tray and looked away.

Kim had been trying to feed Rugee. And she had scolded me for air-drying my hair in public? *Sirella*. "Save it for later."

"Hey." Someone tapped my shoulder.

I looked up. Barbara and Aki stood behind me. "Hi," I said.

"We're heading over to the rec center for check-in now."

"I'm sorry. We got a late start this morning. My roommate knows where to go. Can I catch up to you guys later, maybe?"

"Whatever," said Aki with a shrug.

"How'd you get to know *them*?" Harrison asked after they left.

"I met them while we were interviewing everybody, but I really talked to them while I was brushing my teeth last night."

"Jaimie, you're so social now," said Josh. "What happened to you?"

"What?" I said. "What are you talking about?"

Josh glanced the length of the table, taking in Flax and Casey—Casey paused with his fork half lifted to his mouth and stared at Josh; Flax just went on eating—and said, "Never mind."

Kim ate fast. She beat everybody else. She grabbed her stuff and rose.

"Wait," Zilla said, and shoveled oatmeal into her mouth.

"What's your hurry?" I asked Kim. "Doesn't the check-in thing last an hour?"

"Yes, but—"

"You can't leave yet. You promised to show us what to do, and we're not done," I said, trying to be reasonable. "That stuff isn't going away even if we're late, you know. People are probably late every year. They're probably set up to deal with it."

"I won't be able to settle down until I get the classes I want," Kim said. Her knuckles were white where she gripped her breakfast tray.

Look at your watch, Kim, Rugee said.

Kim let out a whoosh of breath and set down her tray.

What time is it?

"Eight ten."

Zilla jumped up. "I'm done!"

I shoved the rest of a sausage patty in my mouth. "Mmmf,"
I said.

"Can we come with you?" Casey asked.

"If you're finished," said Kim.

It was great to get out of the dorm. I felt like I'd been stuck
inside for at least a year.

Trees in Spores Ferry still had green leaves on them, but
the night had been cold, and the sun hadn't been up long. I
shivered, then thought fur onto the parts of me covered by
clothes.

The Sitka State campus was big on lawn, trees, and mini-
parks. We all followed Kim along a broad path past a mix-
ture of buildings. Some were old, with strange gargoyles or
carved tiles in their bricks, and covered with ivy; others were
new and ugly, steel and glass and boring beige panels. We
passed a big bronze statue of a pioneer guy in a coonskin
cap, shading his eyes and staring toward the library. We
passed a giant maple that seethed somehow. I glanced at
Zilla, and she glanced at me. We both checked out the tree.
It was doing something strange with air, but I didn't know
what. I wondered if Zilla did.

"Where are we going?" Casey asked.

"The Student Rec Center," Kim said. "That's where we pick up the information packets with our registration stuff."

As we walked, we joined throngs of other people heading the same way.

"You guys already went through this, right?" Flax asked Josh and Harrison. "You're second and third year. You have student ID numbers. What are you tagging along with us for?"

"We've adopted Kim as our little sister," said Harrison.

"She needs keepers?"

I tried to figure out what the tone in Flax's voice meant.

Kim walked faster, head down. Her hair hung forward over her shoulders. The back of her neck flushed.

"She's fine," said Harrison. "Look at her. She prepped so much she knows what to do."

"So why are you here?"

"I like looking at her." Harrison dug his hands deep into his pockets and stuck his elbows out, striding along and taking up room, smiling as though he was happy with everything around him.

"Are you trying to get rid of us?" Joshua asked Flax in a tone more interested than offended.

"Of course," said Flax.

"Well, you can't."

"Oh. Okay."

The crowd thickened. Someone tall brushed past me going the opposite direction.

Something. Something like the warm touch of a hand on my cheek, a cinnamon taste in my mouth—

The man and I stopped, turned toward each other. The others kept walking. I stared into the face of a stranger, a large man in a baggy gray shirt and baggy cargo pants, his shoulders broad, his long ponytail black, and an expression on his face halfway between two feelings I almost recognized. His eyes were sparkling gray under heavy black brows. He looked too old to be a student, though I didn't know why I thought that; he didn't have wrinkles, and his skin looked fresh and young. Was he a professor? Or just somebody passing by?

I trelled.

What was this strange energy from him? A tug, the merest brush against the air around me rather than against my skin, though his hands were in his pockets—

In a second he was beside me. He smelled like pine sap and fallen leaves. "Shhh," he said, his hand heavy on my shoulder.

Even then what I sensed from him wasn't his touch on my shoulder so much as a strange pleasant pull on something that was mine but not solid—my scent, or the air I breathed, or my joy in this fresh cool morning and the sight and smell and warmth of a handsome guy I had never met before.

A tug on my delight.

I opened my mouth to call the others.

"Quiet." He said it not just in a normal voice, but with the kind of overtone that shut my mouth before sound could come out.

He used his voice the way people in my family did. The way I could use mine.

I trelled him again, searching for information. What was he? Nothing about his taste/scent/feel was like anything I'd encountered before, except—

A trace of something in the hall when I went chasing after Kim's monster. The listening we had all felt yesterday, the inside-out mouth—

I trelled harder.

Was he a viri?

The one who had sucked on Kim last night? The one I'd almost been able to taste? But that one had been too fast for me, and there had been a sour, smoky taste this guy didn't have at all.

As I trelled him, something siphoned off the edges of my sense, only it didn't hurt. It felt—so nice. Like scratching an itch.

He sucked in breath and shook me. "What *are* you? What are you doing to me? Stop it."

What *was* I doing? If he was a viri, I should run, or fight. But it felt so lovely. I stopped trelling. What if he sucked me dry and left me a husk? What if he went after Kim next? I tried to jerk my shoulders away.

He tightened his grip. "Stop it!" This time he used Voice, and all my voluntary muscles froze.

I couldn't escape him. I couldn't speak out loud. I could—

Rugee!

Jaimiala?

Help!

Ahead of us, Kim, Harrison, Josh, and Zilla turned back. Harrison sprinted toward us.

"Damn!" said the stranger. "Release." He let go of my shoulders, pressed a big thumb on my forehead—my skin tingled under his touch—and ran away, losing himself among other people so fast I couldn't track him.

Harrison grabbed me. "Are you all right? What happened?"

"Viri," I whispered. I closed my eyes, leaned on my cousin, and trembled. "I think he was a viri."

"*Faskish!*" said Harrison.

Josh ran past us, chasing the man.

I pulled myself together and sent out trell, searching for what I knew of the stranger's scent/taste/air. There were so many people, though, with so many confusing air signatures. The wider I trelled, the less I knew. "*Oor,*" I whispered, the worst oath I knew.

"What was it?" Kim asked from behind me, her voice anxious. "Are you all right?"

Casey and Flax had joined her. I said, "Some guy. A rude guy. Yeah, I'm okay now."

Harrison stroked my back and tracked Josh. Josh returned, shook his head.

I touched my forehead with my first two fingers where the stranger had pressed his thumb, and glanced around at my cousins, catching their gazes. I dropped my hand.

Someone gasped. Who? I couldn't tell.

I wished I could talk to Rugee.

Well, wait. Hadn't I just called to him underneath, where he talked all the time? I had never done that before—not that I could remember. But now I knew I could.

Rugee?

Jaimie!

Do you see a mark? He marked my forehead.

Nothing shows to my eyesight. If you hug Kim, I will taste it.

I had to bend forward to hug Kim with my head close to hers. It was awkward. She hugged me back without much conviction, but she held me. Her hair smelled like pears. I trelled Rugee moving across the top of her head, felt the lit-match lick of his tongue on my forehead.

"What are you guys doing?" Casey asked.

Faint, said Rugee. *A superficial application. A sense marker so he can find you again. Do you want me to remove it?*

No. I wanted the stranger to find me again. If he was a viri—if he was Kim's viri—our best future lay in dealing with him as soon as possible, or at least in finding out everything we could about him, and then maybe calling in more troops. If we had to sit around waiting for him to attack Kim, we'd wear ourselves out, even though all of us except Kim had power reservoirs. Reservoirs ran dry.

I wanted him to find me again. I wanted to test that pull we had shared. Why did it feel so good, if it was hurting me?

I remembered the three dead cousins and Kim's misery. They had all started out feeling good, too.

"A guy's rude to you and it leads to a hugfest?" asked Casey. "Can I hug you, too?"

192 • NINA KIRIKI HOFFMAN

"Shut up," Flax told Casey.

"Was he—" Kim whispered in my ear.

"I don't know. It didn't feel the same."

He was going to track me. We'd know.

I straightened, and Kim and I disentangled. She leaned close to me, though, so I lowered my head to listen. "I heard you. When you talked to Rugee."

"Oh." *Can you hear me now?*

Her eyes widened. She nodded.

She could hear me! Whoa, I could talk to her, and Outsiders like Casey and Flax wouldn't be able to follow it. *This'll be handy. I wonder what our range is.* Rugee had bitten Kim so she would be able to hear him; it seemed like that made her part of our family, at least in this one way.

"We can test it," Kim muttered.

"What are you guys whispering about?" Casey asked.

We need to ditch these guys so we can talk.

Kim licked her lip. "Maybe not."

Ha!

She looked at her watch. "Are you okay now?" she asked loudly enough for everybody to hear.

I grinned. Crises could erupt. Lives could be threatened. Danger could lurk. Kim still wanted her orientation on time. "Sure. Let's go."

CHAPTER 26

Kim

The Student Rec Center was a madhouse. Of course.

Students clogged the gym floor. Check-in tables had been set up along both sides, with pieces of the alphabet on big signs above them, so we had to split up to pick up our registration packets. Flax Dennison and I stood in the "C–D" line together, and Josh stuck with me; Harrison went with Jaimie.

I wished I could figure out how to talk to Rugee inside my head, the way Jaimie had just talked to me. I wanted to know what had just happened. I wished Flax would go away. That wasn't fair, because he was really nice. But if he weren't here, Josh and Rugee and I could have a discussion.

"So does Jaimie always fly off the handle if a guy touches her?" Flax asked.

"Fly off the handle?" I said.

"He did more than touch her," said Josh.

"Oh," said Flax. "Oh," he said in a different tone. "I'm sorry. I didn't realize. Damn. A guy attacked her in broad daylight? Wish I'd gotten a better look. I'd like to kick his ass. She all right?"

"We got there before he could do much," Josh said, but he didn't sound very certain.

For that matter, neither was I. I looked around for Jaimie, but I couldn't find her.

We edged up in line. Josh kept his hand under my elbow. Three things occurred to me: 1. He was guarding me. 2. I was in public with a really cute guy holding on to part of my body. 3. His hand was warm, his grip firm without pinching, and he smelled good—like grass clippings and clean dirt. It was a summer-day smell. Plus, he smiled at me every time our eyes met. Oh, heck, 4. He'd seen me cry and he still liked me.

Even when Shaina was my best friend and everybody envied me, high school hadn't been like this.

Flax and I reached the head of our line and got packets. I relaxed. Flax busted a trail through all the other freshmen to our rendezvous point in front of the building.

I opened my packet. There was an agenda for Welcome Week, but I skipped past that to look at the other paper specifically for me. My advisor's name was Dr. Maisonneuve. The general advising workshop was at nine thirty this morning over in the Life Sciences Building, and my appointment with my advisor was at three forty-five.

I put the paper back in the packet and hugged the whole

thing tight, my eyes closed. The picture side showed exploding fireworks, all colors, shinier than sunlight on polished chrome. Another big step, and I hadn't tripped.

Next, ID card and Campus Cash. Then I'd would be able to figure out when to register. I could not stop smiling.

"Is college always like that?" Jaimie asked from beside me.

I opened my eyes. Jaimie and Harrison had joined us. Jaimie stared back over her shoulder at the rec center.

"Like what?" Harrison asked her.

"So many strangers so close to each other. It made me nervous."

"Jaimie, are you okay?" Flax asked. "I didn't realize something bad happened before."

"What?"

"Which I guess was stupid since all your cousins ran off to help you and one of them chased that guy, but I didn't even see him, really. What did he do to you?"

"He just grabbed me and wouldn't let go. I was scared."

"Oh. Damn. Sorry that happened," Flax said.

"It's okay. There are worse things. Like, maybe, huge crowds of strangers." She looked toward the rec center again.

Harrison said, "It'll get better. Once you get your classes, you'll recognize people. Some of the events are as bad as registration—football games, for instance—but you don't have to go."

"Not go to the games?" I asked. Mom and Dad went to all the games at home. They even had little flags they stuck on the car.

I had gone to Sitka games a few times with my parents to get a look at my college-to-come. Shaina joined us. She'd loved going to the games, so I had learned to like them. I could get as swept up in crowd emotion as anyone, once she explained the plays to me. It was only later that I wondered why I cared so much where a ball went and who had it.

"I like the games, and so does Josh," Harrison said, "but some of our friends won't go. They say they're barbaric."

"Aren't you going to come see me play?" Flax asked Jaimie.

She smiled but didn't answer.

"Who's your advisor?" I asked.

She found her information sheet and showed it to me. Our advisors were in the same building, our appointments fifteen minutes apart.

I checked my watch. We had forty-five minutes to pick up ID before the advising workshop began. "Come on," I said. "Let's go."

"Wait. What about Zilla and Casey?" said Jaimie. "You promised to help Zilla."

"Oh, yeah. Sorry." I danced a few feet back and forth.

Casey slammed out of the building. He held his folder in his left hand. "*Now* do I get to hug you?" he asked, and rushed up to me.

"Wha—" I felt paralyzed.

"No," said Josh, stepping in front of me.

"Oh." Casey veered and went around both of us. "What's with you? I saw her first."

Flax put an arm around his neck. "Stop bugging her, Casey. We're here on sufferance. They've got their own gang already."

Zilla drifted up to join us while I was trying to make sense of Casey's behavior. He was still just as cute as he had been yesterday, but he seemed more creepy, somehow.

Josh was guarding me. Against hugs? Was that in the job description?

"What's our next assignment?" Jaimie asked me.

"Identification. Once we get our student IDs, we never have to pay for anything again. Mwahahahahah!"

"That is so untrue," said Harrison.

"Right. Smash my illusions before I've been here a day."

"Did you get the good meal plan or the meager meal plan?" he asked.

"The good meal plan," I said.

"You will learn, young one," Harrison said, "that no meal plan is a good meal plan when you consider the food choices you have. But it *is* slightly better than starving."

"That's why it's good to have a job," said Josh. "You can buy your own food."

"I don't care whether the food's good. I just want to be able to get it. I want my ID."

"Lead on," said Harrison.

"You guys already know where the card office is. Why don't you lead?"

"You're more fun to follow," Josh said.

I didn't know how to take that, so I just smiled. I led us

toward the Student Union. Not much of a challenge, since about a million other people were going the same way.

The line at the card office was so long it wound down one hallway and up another, past all kinds of closed doors. Through a wall of windows I could see the computer center. Were all those kids at the computers stealing all the classes I really, really wanted to take? I checked my brochure and reassured myself that no freshmen got to register until Friday. Half of us registered in the morning and half in the afternoon, though, and until I got my ID I wouldn't know which half I was in.

While we leaned against the wall and waited, Zilla opened her registration packet. "Kim, will you explain this to me?"

I checked her papers. "You've got a nine thirty academic advising workshop, too, but it's in the Journalism Building. You're meeting your advisor, Dr. Martin, at three P.M. in room three fourteen of Allen Hall. What are you thinking about for a major?"

"Communications," Zilla said in a small voice. She glanced up and smiled. "I hope I learn lots about it. It's one of my talents at home, but I'm not very good at it, and there's nobody there to teach me."

I pulled off my pack and got out the Sitka catalog, flipped to the section on Journalism and Communications Studies, and tried to figure out what she was majoring in. I hadn't checked Psychology yet, either, to find out about Jaimie's major. I'd already forgotten the other cousins' majors. Wait.

Josh. Theater? I glanced at him. He was right beside me, but so quiet I could forget he was there, except for the hand lightly resting on my arm. He didn't have the overblown ego or the big presence of the guys I'd known in high school drama, the ones who were planning to be movie stars, make lots of money, and have their pick of beautiful women. "Why theater?" I asked him.

One end of his mouth lifted in a smile. "I want to learn to be other people."

Whoa. There were a lot of reasons a witch might want to do that, not all of them nice. I forced myself to look at the catalog. "Zilla, are you going into news, advertising, electronic media, communications studies, magazine work, or public relations?"

"I don't know. I just want to be able to communicate better. I'm the only one at home with Spiritspe—uh, what I mean is, there are a lot of people I need to talk to."

Spiritspeak. One of Jaimie's forbidden topics. Did it mean what it sounded like? Now was not the time to ask. The big question was whether she'd get anything useful out of a communications degree.

Or maybe it didn't matter. Maybe the point was to get away from home; that was why we were all here.

Casey kicked off the wall. "Save my place. I'm going to get something to drink. Anybody else want anything?"

"No thanks." I had a water bottle in my backpack.

"Get me a chocolate milk shake," Flax said.

"From a vending machine?"

"There's a food court upstairs."

Casey shrugged and held out his hand. Flax stared at it, then smiled, dug his wallet out, and handed Casey a five-dollar bill.

We moved up a little. All around us people were fidgeting and talking. I kept glancing toward the computer room, obsessing about all the classes disappearing as people typed. What if my information was wrong? What if I was supposed to be registering right now?

Kim, said Rugee. I heard, but didn't listen.

Jaimie, Rugee said.

What if I couldn't get a single class I wanted? What if there were *no classes left at all?* What if I had to go home in disgrace and live out the rest of my life holed up in my room with the curtains closed and the lights off, dwindling down in despair—

I sagged against the wall, slid down it slowly.

Jaimie knelt in front of me, gripped my shoulders, stared at me with narrowed eyes. Her hands were strong and hot. After a second she looked down the hall. "Don't stop yet," she whispered. "I see it. I see it."

Stop what? What if Jaimie hated me because I couldn't stand up? What if no one ever spoke to me again? Would I live like a ghost, moving between people, none of them noticing me or hearing me, until I stopped believing in myself? What if I stopped believing in myself but I still survived, wandering around, denying that I even existed and convinced I wasn't there?

Jaimie eased me down onto the floor and ran away.

I had chased her off without saying a word.

I buried my face in my hands and fell into the weird kind of crying I'd been doing since last spring, where tears just flowed and flowed but I hardly sobbed at all.

"Kim?" Flax said, his voice so deep it merged with all the other sounds around us.

What if I opened my eyes and I was in an empty hall? What if I never found out what had happened to everyone else in the universe? What if—

I took a deep breath and tried to pull myself together. I realized there was a hand on my right shoulder, another on my left. I rubbed the tears out of my eyes and looked sideways, afraid of what I would see, but it was Zilla next to me, her blue eyes intent. She didn't look disgusted. She didn't look like she hated me. She looked worried.

Josh was on my other side, his hand around my bicep. He stared down the hall, past other people who chattered and shifted, gesturing and edging along. Past us. We'd lost our place in line because I had collapsed. The line went on forever. We'd never get there now—

I shivered and tried to remember that there might be other things as important as my whole future at college. "What happened?" I asked. My throat felt tight and swollen.

"You okay?" Zilla asked.

"No." I sniffed and rubbed one eye again. "I feel a little better."

"The viri just snuck right past everything, the spell

coat, Rugee, everything," Zilla whispered to me, "and tapped you."

I glanced around. So the familiar sick, hot feeling in my stomach wasn't my fault—nor the tightness in my throat, nor that sour taste in the back of my mouth.

"Kim?" Flax was still in line, but he had moved about six feet farther up the hall. He had to yell to be heard. "I'm saving your place. Are you all right? What happened?"

I struggled to stand. Zilla and Josh rose and helped me. "I have mood swings," I called. "I'm sorry." I had fallen into the well again, and this time Rugee hadn't pulled me out. I remembered Jaimie telling me not to stop, and racing away. She was trying to track it, I realized. Like tracing a phone call before Star 69 and Caller ID. Keep talking, keep them on the line. . . . "What if Jaimie finds her?" I whispered to Josh, suddenly, urgently. Flax was far enough away I figured he wouldn't be able to hear me. What could Jaimie do against a viri? She'd already been immobilized by one.

"Harrison went with her."

"But she couldn't fight the first one."

"He took her by surprise. She's wide awake this time."

"But—" I stared down at my hands, reached up to touch Rugee's slender coil around my neck. None of our precautions had worked.

"We have to try," Josh whispered. "If we can figure out *anything*—"

Casey came back, a big paper cup in one hand and a can of Coke in the other. He glanced from us against the wall to Flax, now ten feet away. "What happened?" he asked, and pushed through the line to reach us.

"I've been kind of depressed for a while now, and I just had a—an episode." Oh, great. Another opportunity for me to tell someone I had mental problems.

"Are you all right?" Casey asked, anxious.

"Kind of shook up and feeble, I guess."

"Want a milk shake?"

"Uh, actually—"

He handed me the milk shake. I gulped some, then gasped. Instant ice-cream headache.

At least it took my mind off my other worries.

"What happened to Jaimie and Harrison?" Casey asked while I opened my mouth wide and took deep breaths, hoping it would change my internal atmosphere from deep freeze.

"They had to run an errand," Josh said. "Kim, you ready to get back in line?"

"Yes."

Zilla and Josh escorted me back to Flax. At first the two women in line behind him said, "Hey!" "No fair!" "Hey, you can't do that! Where'd all these people come from?"

"Come on," said Casey. "You know she was ahead of you before. She had an attack. You going to penalize her for getting sick?"

One of the women took a good look at me and said, "Oh," in a not very friendly tone. The other woman said, "Sorry. What happened?"

"I panicked. Really, thanks for letting me back in line." I handed the milk shake to Flax. "I drank some of your shake. I'm sorry."

"It's okay. Have the rest if you want."

I could barely stand. "Okay. Thanks. I feel like I need this." I took a slow sip this time and got a rush of cool, smooth chocolate flavor without the freeze. I felt stronger already. It had been a long time since I had a milk shake. Food of the gods? A recipe for adversity? Or just not enough breakfast?

I dug my wallet out of my pocket to pay Flax back, but he waved it away. "Never mind. My treat. Save me a dance sometime this term."

"Thanks, Flax. Thanks, Casey."

Casey shrugged and smiled. He popped the top on his Coke can. "Save me a dance, too, Kim."

"Sure." I could get used to this, maybe.

Jaimie and Harrison returned, joined us in line. Harrison's hands were tight fists, but his face looked blank.

"Hey!" said the less-friendly woman behind us. "Don't tell us *they* had panic attacks!"

Jaimie smiled at her and said, "It's all right," in a voice that reminded me of a cat purring.

"Oh," said the woman, surprised but not mad anymore. "I guess it is."

I sipped the shake and wondered how Jaimie did it. Boy, if I could talk people into things like that—just say words and change their minds—my whole last spring at high school would have been different.

On the other hand, I'd watched Shaina turn a lot of people against me with words, and maybe viri skills. Handling that kind of power might be tricky.

I touched Jaimie's arm. She glanced at me. I met Jaimie's eyes, stared at her, blinked slowly.

Oh! she thought.

I nodded once.

I get it. You're right. I could tell you what we found while we're waiting. She glanced past me at Josh, and I looked, too. He nodded. Zilla looked away, but I could tell her attention was focused on Jaimie.

Can you talk underneath? Jaimie asked.

Josh shook his head slightly.

I didn't know I could until that guy grabbed me. But when I do, Kim can hear me, too. It's part of her bond with Rugee. Are you guys all hearing me? Jaimie looked over her shoulder at Zilla, who nodded. Harrison, ahead of us with Flax, bobbed his head.

Kim wants to know what Harrison and I found. The answer is: not much. I traced the flow of misery from her around a corner and down a hall, then up some stairs. It broke off before we found the viri, though. She clenched her fists. *It was so strong. Now I'm tuned to it, it's like trelling a sweet-and-sour river in the air. But it stopped. I couldn't tell if it stopped from your end or the viri end.*

"I feel better," I said.

"Better than what?" asked Casey, who had fallen into line just on the other side of Josh.

"Than my sadness attack. I don't know how I came out of it. When I was depressed before, I couldn't seem to stop feeling that way."

"Did you see a doctor? There are meds for that."

"Sure. I saw three different doctors. I tried meds." My parents had been so frustrated all summer. My dad kept trying to get me to talk. Even after I broke down and told him what I thought was the matter, he couldn't get it. He'd never really liked that Shaina anyway. She was too stuck up, and she didn't treat me well enough. I was his daughter. I was wonderful.

We never got each other to understand.

"I think I must have weird chemistry or something," I told Casey. "I never found a drug that worked."

"Wow," he said. He frowned. "So—um—should you even be at college? Isn't this going to make you even *more* stressed out?"

"I don't . . ."

He shook his head. "Sorry. I shouldn't have said that."

"But I don't—" What if he was right? It was obvious I would never run out of things to worry about. We hadn't even gotten our first homework assignments yet. Homework? We hadn't even bought textbooks yet. What if I got into the classes I wanted, but the bookstore sold out of the textbooks before I could buy them?

I could obsess about *anything*. What if I just kept falling down the well?

Rugee's tail stroked across my cheek, and I started. This

was all stupid. I knew my depression had a source outside me. We were going to find it and stop it. I wanted college more than I'd wanted anything in years. What did Casey know?

Flax turned around. "Hey, Kim," he said, "don't let Casey scare you. He's an asshole half the time. You'll be all right."

I hoped he was right.

CHAPTER 27: *Jaimie*

We were pretty close to the card room door before I realized I might be in trouble again. "Kim? What happens in there?" I asked.

"They take our pictures and give us student ID."

"Do we need documents for this?"

"Sure—a driver's license or something."

"Zilla," I said. "I need you."

Zilla and I snuck away from the line. I hoped the persuasion I had put on the women behind us would hold when we went back. If not, I guessed I could do it again, but it was a bad idea. How were we going to get rid of Flax and Casey? They wouldn't follow us into our room. We could close the door on them there. But otherwise—

I mean, I liked them. They seemed nice for Outsiders. But they were Outsiders.

Maybe I should suggest they go away in a voice they couldn't refuse.

"I don't have any photo ID," I told Zilla. "Dad manufactured some for me when we checked in, but then he made it disappear."

"You're twenty years old and you don't have a driver's license?"

"Who needs to drive? I fly everywhere. At least when I'm home."

Her eyes widened. "Even to town?"

"Sure. Everybody knows me there."

She shook her head. "That is so odd. Can I go home with you sometime? I can't even picture a situation where a whole town full of Outsiders knows about us and takes it for granted."

"Okay. But meanwhile—"

She dug into one of the pockets of her red flannel dress and produced a red leather wallet. "I forgot this when I left home this morning. I had to send sideways for it."

"Ooh! Can you teach me that?"

She blinked and looked at me. "What *do* you know how to do?"

That stung. When things stung me, I fought back. My power reservoir opened. Heat sang through my veins, and the words for Transformation waited on my tongue.

I caught myself. *No. Not here, not now, not Zilla. Stop it, Jaimie.* I transformed myself back into Outsider Jaimie, and realized Zilla had taken two steps back, her eyes wide. There was a green aura of protection around her.

I must be leaking scary aura. I shut myself down. "Um,"

I said. "Sorry. You know how evil my sisters are?"

"Yes," she said. "Never evil enough where the *Arkhos* could see it to get themselves banned from the Gatherings. But so mean otherwise I hid from them all the time."

"They're evil, and they're trickier about it than I was. So when I feel threatened or challenged, I get defensive. Because of my sisters, I had to learn how to do it fast—"

"Don't do it around me."

My little shadow cousin spoke loud and clear and even cold. I bristled, then calmed. "I'm sorry, Zilla." My little shadow cousin, younger than I, whom I was going to beg to teach me all the disciplines, powers, and persuasions I had never learned. "I won't attack you. I need your help, and I'm sorry for anything I did in the past to hurt you. It's just—I have defenses. I'll fight them."

She studied me long enough to be insulting about it, then finally said, "Okay." She opened her wallet and pulled out her driver's license. We studied everything about it. Then she held out her hand. I trelled. Air intensified above her palm, densed, until there was a white plasticky card there. Colored areas filled in: the name of the state in dark blue. Below that, dark blue letters read: DRIVER LICENSE. A seven-digit red number below that. Then little words with blanks below them: DOB. ENDORSEMENTS. CLASS. RESTRICTIONS. SEX. WEIGHT. HEIGHT. ISSUE DATE. RECORD CREATED. The state seal in the lower right corner, a red expiration date, a square of blue in the upper left corner where a photo was on her license.

How was she doing that?

"Tell me all this information," she whispered. I told her my statistics, making up the ones I didn't have real data for. As I spoke, answers appeared. I trelled in search of her technique, but I couldn't grasp it. She looked at me for a second and a picture of my face appeared on the license. She flipped it over and asked me to sign it.

"Okay. Now the tricky part," Zilla said, and she did something else I didn't understand, and pale gold hologram lines of the state seal and the words OREGON OREGON fused to the top of the license. Now it really looked like hers.

"Wow," I whispered. "You are awesome. You ever use this ability to make money? You could so be an expert forger."

"Do you want this license or don't you?" she asked in a deep-freeze voice.

"I was kidding."

"I won't teach you this if you're going to use it for things like that, Jaimie."

"You're so strict! Okay, Zill. You'll have to teach me your ethics while you're teaching me the rest of it."

She sighed. She handed me my new license.

"Thanks." I put it in my wallet. "If anyone had told me I'd need this, I could have gotten it the regular way," I muttered as we headed back to the line just in time. "Things are so different away from home."

"That's the point, isn't it?"

I trelled Kim as we rejoined the others. I was doing it so often it was automatic. She wasn't giving off misery fumes, but she looked wilted, gray, and haunted, the way she had when I first met her.

"They're going to take pictures of us?" I asked.

Harrison and Josh nodded.

"Come here a sec, Kim." I put my hands on her shoulders, thought my way into the chant Rugee had taught me, and fed her a little energy, the way I had during the night. She straightened and shifted in my grip, glanced around uneasily. "Close your eyes." She closed her eyes and I touched the lids, eased away tearstains and distress.

"What are you doing?" Casey asked, leaning in to watch.

"Massage."

"You guys have known each other a day and already you're massaging her eyelids?"

"Sure, why not?" Dang. I had to think harder before I did things like this in public. I let go of my roommate. "You should try it with Flax. Does that feel better?" I asked Kim.

"Much. Thanks, Jaimie." She rubbed her eyes, rummaged through her pack until she came up with a powder compact, a comb, and some lipstick. She handed me the comb.

I raised my eyebrows.

"Go on. Your hair's a mess."

Okay, I hadn't been paying much attention. I combed it, pulled a green bandanna out of my pocket, and tied my hair back while Kim checked her reflection in her compact's mirror and applied color to her lips. She let me borrow the mirror.

Then we were in the card room, running through proce-dures, standing for photos, waiting for lamination, and then we were out of there, clutching new, legal cards. I had an identity at last.

Kim got excited by her card. "Okay! Last three digits of my ID number: 451." She got a booklet out of her backpack and flipped to a page marked with a pink Post-it. "Registration time: noon tomorrow." She sagged. "God. What if everything I want is gone by then? Well, guess it could have been worse. Could have been stuck way late in the day. Let me see your card, Jaimie."

I showed her my card.

"Ooh! 133! You get to register at nine A.M.! Lucky."

I made a face.

"What about mine?" Zilla asked. Casey and Flax asked, too. Ironic. Everybody got to register in the morning except Kim.

She drooped a little, but recovered.

"What next?" I asked.

"Academic advising workshop. They're half an hour into it already." Kim sounded tired again. "I wonder what we missed."

"Where is that?"

"Everybody get out your packets and check. Since we're all in different areas, we're probably going to separate meetings. Except Jaimie and I are both going to the one in the Life Sciences Building."

"That's where mine is, too," Flax said.

"I want to go to yours," said Casey. "Mine's way over in the Douglas Ramsey Theater."

"Mine's at the Journalism Building," Zilla said. She sounded panicked.

We all looked at each other. Kim had promised to baby-step Zilla through this. "Why don't you come with us?" she suggested. "They're probably saying the same thing to everybody; they just couldn't fit us all in the same room."

"Okay."

We all headed for the Life Sciences Building. The lecture hall was dark and chilly, and every desk was full. We stood up at the top by the doors. A man stood at the front of the room, playing with transparencies on an overhead projector.

"We offer a lot of enticing electives to round out your education," he droned. He back-projected a list of topics onto the screen. "We want you to leave Sitka State with an appreciation for many other disciplines as well as the one you've chosen for your own."

Kim sat on the top step, pulled a notebook and a pen out of her backpack, and started scribbling.

Casey was standing right behind her. The light flared as the professor switched transparencies, and I saw Casey's face clearly for a second. He was smiling down at the back of Kim's head, such a sweet smile that I was surprised. For someone who could be a little creepy, he looked tender and affectionate. And he was smiling to himself, not so other people would see and know how he felt.

Wow. I'd sort of caught on that Casey was courting Kim, but then again, he seemed pretty distractable, like he'd go after any of us, or any woman he happened to see, given encouragement. I remembered how he had wandered off last night. But then again, we'd hinted that we wanted to get rid of him. A guy who could understand hints was a good thing.

Casey was following Kim, and Josh had stuck himself to Kim like a burr. He was sitting next to her now. He had appointed himself her guardian. Maybe that was all there was to it, or maybe he was interested in her in other ways.

I glanced sideways at Harrison. *Did you see that?* I asked underneath.

"What?" he whispered.

Josh, Zilla, and Kim looked up at me, too. Zilla had plunked herself down beside Kim. Flax had eased over along the wall and wasn't paying attention to any of us, as far as I could tell.

Never mind.

"Something we should know?" Harrison whispered.

"No," I whispered back, leaning toward him. He smelled nice. Spicy and warm.

"Your academic advisor will be able to lay out the requirements of your specific science majors with you, but everybody needs to cover some common ground," said the professor.

"I forgot everybody could hear me when I talk like that," I muttered.

"Not quite everybody."

The girl sitting in the desk in front of us turned around. "Well, *I* can! Shhh!"

Harrison leaned so that his lips were near my ear. "What was it?" His breath was warm.

I turned, lifted my lips to his ear. "The way Casey looks at Kim."

He nodded. "It's weird, isn't it?" he whispered. "How we all mobilized around Kim?"

Was he saying there was a power or persuasion involved? Were we all jerking around on strings, controlled by some puppetmaster? Was something else going on here I hadn't seen?

"I didn't think I was going to like her," Harrison went on, his words a thread of whisper in the stream of sound that was the academic advising lecture, but much more interesting, besides being warm in my ear. "I was so mad at you for spilling secrets as soon as you got here."

I leaned back, and we shifted so he could hear me. "Is she—? But Rugee—" Rugee would know better than to fall prey to some kind of conspiracy or trap, wouldn't he?

"What?" he whispered.

After checking to make sure Kim was still protected by Rugee and Josh and Zilla, I took Harrison's hand and sneaked out. We roamed the halls until we found an empty classroom with an unlocked door. We went inside and closed the door behind us. I said, "What you said about Kim mobilizing us all around her. What if there's something twisted about that?"

"What? I didn't mean *that*, Jay."

"When I first met her I thought I was going to hate her. All she did was cry."

"Kala went through a period like that after Coleman died. She was his little pixie. He always treated her like his extra-special little sister, and she loved it. When he was gone, she cried for about six months. I understood, but *Sirella*, it sure grated on my nerves."

"But Kim's cute and funny when she's not stressing. Even if she's so super-organized it's irritating."

"Yeah. And she adjusts *very* quickly to weirdness." We were in a chemistry lab. He hopped up to sit on one of the counters. "We don't see a lot of that around home. When local people stumble across us doing something we need to keep private, we usually have to alter their memories. Maybe you have more experience with this. Is Kim's mental flexibility normal?"

"I don't know," I said. "We don't have normal people in the north."

Harrison frowned and kicked the cupboards below his perch. "Oh. Right. I forgot. I want to visit up north sometime."

"Here and now, we have problems to solve and decisions to make. What *about* Kim? *Is* she normal? Maybe Rugee's helping her be calm in the face of us. She met him almost as soon as I moved in, and he adopted her."

Harrison said, "There's another way she's different from other people. She's already experienced a supernatural invasion. Maybe that changed her so other *sitva* matters don't surprise her as much."

Sitva was something members of our family had in their bones. It made us more able to deal with magical changes. I had never heard of a way for normal people to acquire it. Maybe Harrison knew something I didn't. Or maybe Kim wasn't normal.

"Huh."

If Kim were some kind of evil person, a viri in disguise, wouldn't I have figured it out? By now, I knew a lot about her personal atmosphere and its fluctuations. Often it approached normal. When she was working on her art, it was—fantastic. A distillation of emotion, a concentration of a whole array of flavors, illuminated in a way I'd never trelled before. When she collapsed into a very depressed state, the smoke of misery streamed from her and went somewhere else. I had almost heard the suck of vacuum: I knew the vacuum had an operator behind it. After those incidents, she was depleted. She couldn't do that to herself.

She also had a quality of helplessness that somehow rendered her appealing. She didn't play to it, or even accept it. She fought it. But she fell into it, and then it was easy to want to help her. She wasn't asking for help, so it was easy to give.

Suppose she got used to having us clustered around her? What if she took us for granted? I wouldn't like that for long.

Track down the viri and deal with it, and everything would change. Life would be interesting when I could treat Kim other ways.

"I don't think she's manipulating us," Harrison said. "I think the problem is what it looks like. She's being used. She deserves protection. It gives us a chance to find out more about viri."

"Like, who has a clue about how to deal with the damned things?"

He nodded. "We need to come up with better plans."

I checked my watch. "What about my plan to go to school here? Am I missing anything important? That guy was so boring."

"What he was saying doesn't matter," said Harrison. "I went to my first term totally information-free. I took four different things that interested me. It was actually a great way to start. You're going to be stupid and shell-shocked for most of the first term anyway. Might as well take something exciting instead of dumb required things you can get out of the way later."

"What, so just skip all the stuff Kim wants to go to?"

"No." He smiled at me, one of those irritating smiles that showed too many teeth. "You have the opportunity to do it Kim's way, and the obligation, too. She'll make sure you sign up for remedial math and English. Heh."

"You're evil." Kim, armed with foreknowledge and convictions, did have a certain power. But no way was I signing up for remedial math. I could handle math, and I'd done okay in English once I stopped torturing the teacher and the other students and actually paid attention to the material.

Harrison cranked the smile up to a grin and vaulted off the counter.

We went back to the stuffy lecture hall full of people listening to boring stuff and trying to stay awake. I trelled Kim. She was in the same position among her three guardians, and in the same energy state. She glanced at us as we slipped in. There was no room for anybody else to sit, so I leaned against the wall to her right. Flax still leaned against the wall to the left, and Casey had joined him. Casey looked asleep in the dim light.

Zilla put her hand on my foot.

I figured she was asking for information. *No. It was nothing. We were just thinking,* I reported back to all of them.

"So the next thing on your schedule," said the professor, "is placement tests, unless you took those yesterday or the day before." He droned on about that for a while. I had no idea people could say so many boring things in a row.

Finally, he said, "That wraps things up for now. Welcome to college, kids. Have fun, but don't forget to study."

Josh pulled Kim to her feet, and Zilla rose, too. We all ducked out the door. Casey and Flax followed us before I could figure out how to ditch them. We blew out of the building and paused at the intersection of two broad paths. The sun was higher, almost noon-high, and the air had warmed, and smelled like fallen leaves. My hidden fur melted back into me.

"Is all of college going to be this boring?" I asked.

"How do you know how boring that was? You were gone for most of it," Flax said.

"I extrapolated from a representative sample."

"Most of it's interesting, if you pick your professors right," said Harrison.

"Jaimie, what did you get on your math SAT?" Kim asked me.

"What's an SAT?"

"Do you like math?"

"It's all right. I like equations where you get things to match on each side of the equals sign. That helps when you're figuring out transformations. How much force does it take to transmute one thing into another? Once in a while I do the math. But a lot of the time I just point and shoot."

I glanced back to see how closely we were being followed; it only occurred to me after the fact that I was talking about things on my forbidden list, and maybe there were some forbidden people around. But it was okay. Harrison, Josh, and Zilla were right behind us, talking to one another, with Casey and Flax bringing up the rear.

"Point and shoot," Kim muttered. "Like, could you point to something like that trash can and shoot power at it and change it into—into what? A bench?"

"Probably, but that would be a waste of energy. There's already a bench two feet away. Besides, I don't need a bench, and I do need a trash can." I fished a mint out of my pocket, peeled the wrapper off, and dropped the paper into the trash as we passed.

"Jaimie?" Kim said in a small voice.

"What?"

She frowned and said, "Never mind."

"I mind. What?"

"I mean, why should that surprise me after everything else that's happened? I mean, you told me about Transformation right up front. But I didn't believe it, not really. I saw Zilla appear out of smoke, but that looked like regular stage magic. I've seen Rugee transform. But he's a god, or something that it's easier to pretend is changeable. When you talk about point and shoot . . ." She paused. "I just need to shift things around in my brain."

She lifted, then dropped her shoulders. "Let's go to the math placement test, just in case."

We passed old brick buildings and approached a new one with fancy red-and-yellow brickwork. Kim led us through the main archway into a central roofed courtyard that reached up three stories. It was decorated in steel, with shiny mica flagstones on the floor. In one corner was the Atomic Café, a coffee bar with a pastry display case, with a few futuristic tables and chairs scattered near it.

Kim consulted a piece of paper. "The placement testing hall is that way." She pointed.

"This is the Science Building?" I asked.

Harrison smiled. "This is where the real science classes are. The psychology classes are mostly in Ritalin Hall."

"Ritalin?" Kim asked, her voice suspicious.

"Okay, Reed Hall."

Reed Hall? That was where my classes would be? "Can I see your map, Kim?"

She handed it to me. Harrison pointed to a building about half a block away.

Classes started on Monday. We had four days to track down the viri.

CHAPTER 28: Kim

I know it's odd of me, but I love tests. Not the kind where you have to write out answers and pitch all kinds of bullshit to convince the teacher you believe his theories on literature and can say them back, but the multiple-choice ones, where there's a single correct answer. I love *Jeopardy*. My parents told me I should go on the high school edition, but I didn't want people looking at me while I answered questions.

For the math placement test, we had to sit at individual desks. Harrison and Josh leaned against the back wall of the room. For practically the first time since I got here, I wasn't in touching range of anybody except Rugee.

A whole page of problems, a test sheet with tiny squares to blacken, a couple of sharp pencils, a sheet of scratch paper, and I was happy. I didn't even have to do this. I could get into Math 105 on my SAT score. I tested to be neighborly to Jaimie and Flax and Zilla. And maybe Casey, who sat at the desk next to me. He was glancing over at my paper, looking lost. What, he wanted to copy off me? I curved my elbow around my score sheet so he couldn't see it, and went to work.

I finished a little later, my mind a contented hum. All the questions had made sense, and I had found answers to everything. I went to the front of the room to turn in my test materials, left the room, stopped in confusion in the hall outside. Rugee was still invisible around my neck, but where *was* everybody else?

I turned around. Josh came out. "That was fast," he said.

"It was?" I checked my watch. Oh. Maybe it was. Seventeen minutes.

"Everybody else is still working," he said. "Harrison's waiting for Jaimie to finish. Let's get some coffee."

We went to the Atomic Café in the central courtyard and ordered mocha lattes from the ponytailed guy behind the counter.

"So," I said, "you've been here a year already." Even though I'd spent the night with this guy and had been almost attached to him ever since, I didn't have much of a read on him. He was a theater major. He knew a lot about viri. He had great gray eyes when I could see them past the hair, and a terrific smile. He had a nice speaking voice. He smelled like grass and clean dirt. He could sit extremely still even if his leg was touching mine and I was nervous about the touching.

"Yes. Kim, I'm scheduled to work at the bookstore this afternoon from two to eight. I think I should call in sick."

"So you can stick around and guard me?"

He nodded.

"I don't think that's fair. I don't want everybody to put their lives on hold on my account. That's stupid, especially when we don't even know that it does any good." I gripped my tall Styrofoam cup in both hands. It dented. "Maybe I should just go home," I whispered.

"Don't. Give us time to fight this. Just a sec." He stood, pulled a cell phone from his pocket, walked around behind a nearby pillar to make a call. I drank hot sweet milky choco-coffee and stewed in discouragement. All these new friends. I had wandered into their lives and warped them.

Something tapped my cheek. I straightened, startled. *Stop thinking like that,* Rugee said in his quietest mental voice.

"Like what? Are you a mind reader?"

I feel your shoulders sag and know you're sad.

A stranger sat down in Josh's chair. "Hi," he said.

"Hi," I replied. He looked familiar. Big bulky guy, even bigger across the shoulders than Flax. Older. Gray shirt, cargo pants, long black ponytail.

The guy who'd grabbed Jaimie, then run away.

The viri.

Breath caught in my throat. I gripped the edge of the table. Did I have anything I could use as a weapon?

"You smell strange," he said.

"Okay, sure," I said. "So do you."

He smiled. "I don't mean it that way."

"Not exactly a nice thing to say." Was this Shaina in a new

body? Shaina had never told me I smelled strange. But then again, she was in disguise now. Would she be able to turn into someone this big?

"I mean, you smell like someone who's had close encounters of the weird kind."

"So what?" Was he going to suck the life force out of me now and leave me here, a blinking, breathing husk of a person?

"I'm looking for a certain kind of weirdness."

"That's the lamest pickup line I've ever heard." I glanced toward the pillar. Josh was out of sight. "Rugee."

Wait.

"Rugee? What does that mean?" said the man. "I'm not trying to pick you up. My name is Lucius."

"Oh. Okay." Panic crept closer.

Lucius held out a hand.

I stared at it. Now he wanted me to *touch* him?

Yet I found myself responding. My hand rose, drifted across the space between us, and dropped into his.

He held my hand, pressed his thumb on the back, and stared into my eyes. I wondered if I were going to die now.

"It has happened to you," he whispered. "The draw."

"Sure. Someone's sucking on my misery."

"You *know*," he whispered. "How do you know? Has it been so crude?"

"I got an outside opinion. Are you the one who's doing it?"

"No!" He dropped my hand and sat back. "No. I'm chasing the one who hurt you."

"What?"

"It's dangerous, what it's doing to you. Now that it's tasted what it's taught you to give, it may never get enough. It will go on until—I have to stop it before it wakes the world to us."

"You're hunting her, too?"

"Yes."

"Hey!" Josh yelled, rushing to our table.

Lucius looked up at him.

"Leave her—" Josh cried, and disappeared.

My mouth fell open.

Around us, people gasped. Then something shifted, and everybody resumed conversations, ignored what had just happened. Except me. I trembled.

Lucius blinked, shook his head. Stared at me with narrowed eyes. "Something just happened," he said. "What was it?"

"Didn't you see?"

It was the geas laid on Joshua by Rory Keye, Rugee said. *He had to disappear home and look for help. A fumbling order, a bad one. I should have countermanded it. Joshua worked to correct it by shifting observers' memories after he left. The shift affected the viri, too? Interesting. That's a vulnerability we didn't know of before.*

Lucius leaned a little closer. "What was *that*?" he whispered. "Someone's talking to you. What is it? What is it telling you?"

"Are you a viri?"

"You know our name?"

"I'm not going to answer your questions unless you answer mine. Are you a viri?"

"Yes."

"So why should I trust you, after what I've been through with your people?"

"You shouldn't."

"Oh, great!" I stood up. "Jaimie!"

"Hey." He grabbed my wrist and tugged me back down into my chair, which answered one question. He was at least three times stronger than I was. "You shouldn't trust anyone, but I won't draw from you. All those friends of yours who travel around in a pack with you—why do you trust *them*? There's something greatly strange about them. Now, let's be calm and quiet together. Please."

"I think I'd rather scream."

"Don't do that. I need to talk to you. Tell me what you know about your viri."

"Why?"

"It's hiding, and I need to find it to preserve the race."

"What do you mean? Do you want her to breed?"

He looked offended. "No. In fact, the opposite."

"Jaimie!" I yelled. The test room was too far for her to hear me. What was taking them so long? "Harrison? Zilla?" Why wasn't Rugee protecting me?

If you can contain your fear, Rugee whispered in my mind, *please do. This is a chance for us to observe it, even question it. We need more information, Kim. If it does anything harmful—*

If the viri did anything harmful, maybe there was nothing Rugee could do to stop it.

"Stop yelling," said Lucius. "Settle down." He still had a

grip on my wrist. I tried to get up, but he pinched something in my arm that hurt so much I sagged back in the chair. "I'm sorry. I'll let go if you promise to sit still. I don't *want* to hurt you. I want to help you. I'm sorry you've suffered. You didn't deserve it. I want to stop it from happening again."

"Why? Why go against your own kind?"

"It is that one who has turned on *us*. It's against our laws to force a host to produce something that harms it. When one of us does that, they must be—"

"What are you doing to that girl, mister?" The skinny coffee barista stood near us, frowning behind his glasses.

Lucius sighed. "Public places. I hate them."

"Let go of her arm."

"But then she might run away."

"Let her go or I'll call campus security."

Lucius sighed again and let go. I rubbed my wrist, which had red pressure marks on it.

"You okay?" asked the barista.

I nodded, tried to decide what to do next. I touched Rugee.

Can you stay? he asked. *He's giving us new information.*

Despair hovered temptingly near, but I turned from it. All I wanted to do was run. If I ran, so could Lucius. If he wasn't *my* viri, he was *a* viri, and he knew more than I did about them. I looked up at the coffee guy. "Thanks so much." I heard tears in my voice. "Listen, I want to talk to this guy, but if he grabs me again, will you call the cops?"

"You sure?"

I nodded. "Thanks for watching out for me."

The coffee guy retreated, but he kept an eye on us. It cheered me to think that I had a guardian, even if he was just a normal guy and kind of small. A lot of help Josh had been.

"You're looking for my viri," I said.

"Yes."

"She's here somewhere. She's drawn on me—that's what you call it?—several times since I got here. Most recently while I was in line at the card office." I opened my pack and got out the notebook with all my Shaina notes in them, opened to the incident report, added a shorthand note about Shaina drawing on me an hour and a half ago at the Student Union, then placed the opened notebook in front of him. He read, his eyebrows up, flipped through the other pages where I had notes, read them, then looked at me.

"Who knows this about us?" he whispered. Threat flowed off of him in waves.

"Kim!"

"Hey!"

"Kim?" Jaimie, Harrison, and Zilla raced across the courtyard toward us.

Lucius turned to stare at them, and then, pop! pop! Harrison and Zilla vanished. A shift in the air, a shift in temperature. People startled, people returned to normal, as if nobody had noticed the disappearance of two people right in front of them. Lucius shook his head again. Jaimie was the only one running toward me. "You!" she yelled at Lucius as she came panting up to the table. "You leave her alone!"

The barista glanced around, as confused as everybody else. He pointed to Jaimie. I mouthed the word "Friend."

Lucius turned to me, his brows together. "What? Something—"

"Harrison—" She turned, looked behind her. "What?"

"Yeah," I said. "The great thing about Josh guarding me was that as soon as Lucius showed up, Josh had to disappear."

"What?" she wailed.

"Remember? Your uncle set it up that way."

"Oh, *faskish!*"

"So this is Lucius, a viri, and he says he doesn't want to hurt me. He wants to catch Shaina."

"What?"

"Have a seat. Lucius, this is my roommate, Jaimie. Jaimie, Lucius said he doesn't want to hurt me, but right now he's upset because I know too much. But the guy at the coffee bar is watching us, and if he sees Lucius make a move, he's calling security."

Jaimie glanced at the coffee guy, who waved. She grabbed a chair and brought it over.

I continued, in science mode, "The question now is, who knows what we know about the viri? Lucius wants me to tell him the names of everybody who knows, so he can neutralize us all. I think it could get ugly."

Lucius ran his hand across the writing on my first page of viri observations. "I don't have to neutralize you. There's a fine-tuning kind of draw that lifts a few things out of your memory and leaves the rest of you intact."

"Great," I said. "Just great. Everyone I meet wants to tamper with my memory."

I don't, Rugee whispered.

I lifted my hand and rested it on his cool, smooth, invisible skin. "Thanks," I said.

"Something speaks to you," Lucius said.

"Yes. A god. Well, one of them, anyway." If Rugee was a small local god, there had to be other small local gods, and maybe big global ones, too. I definitely needed to ask more questions.

Lucius frowned again.

But maybe not right now.

"So how do we kill viri?" Jaimie asked.

He shook his head. "You can't."

"This thing that's after Kim, it's driving her suicidal. It's a matter of life and death. How can we kill it before it kills us?"

"You can't," Lucius said. "Only viri can kill viri."

"One of your kind killed three of my cousins in a week. Sucked them dry and left them breathing, but they were living dead."

Lucius pulled in a long breath. "Where? When?"

"What will you do with the information if I tell you?"

"Track it down and kill it."

"Is that what you'll do to Shaina when you find her?"

"That one hasn't killed yet that we know. There's a chance it can be cured. Whatever happens, I'll stop it from feeding on

Kim any longer. Where was this massacre you spoke of?"

Jaimie hesitated. "Near Klamath Falls. Nine years ago."

"The trail will be cold. But I'll go, once I've dealt with the one who's operating here."

Joshua entered the courtyard, followed by a tall redheaded woman in a white dress, and his uncle Rory. "Kim?" Josh said. "Are you all right?"

"So far. This isn't Shaina, Josh. This is Lucius. He's some kind of viri police."

Lucius stared at Josh and his companions, then stood. He glanced at Jaimie, back at Josh and the others. "What *are* you people?"

Rory and the woman moved in front of Josh. The woman caught Lucius's gaze, stared back intently. "We live here on this good earth, just as you do," she murmured. "We work within its balances. We accept its cycles. We protect our own. Are you threatening us?"

"Not yet." He turned and ran.

"Hey!" yelled Josh.

Rory reached out and flicked a finger toward Lucius's retreating back just before Lucius pushed open the double glass doors and ran off into the sunlight.

CHAPTER 29: *Jaimie.*

irella. Aunt Elissa could appear out of nowhere, too! And she wasn't even an Air sign. I *had* to learn this!

Uncle Rory had tossed a tracer onto Lucius's back. I touched my forehead, where Lucius had left a trace on me. Was it still there? Probably we would be able to track each other if we really wanted to. But he scared me.

"So," said Aunt Elissa.

Kim stood up, her chair scraping across the flagstone floor.

I studied Aunt Elissa, Josh's mother. She wasn't a warm, welcoming person, but Josh and his brothers were all good people, so I guessed she was doing something right. She had rescued me when Sarah tortured me at Southwater. I got the feeling that Elissa helped me because she knew it was the right thing to do, which, at the time, I appreciated; we didn't get much intervention like that at home.

"You're the one all the fuss is about?" Elissa asked. She

gripped Kim's chin, tilted it, and stared into her eyes. She frowned, twisted Kim's head to the side so she could study her profile. "Such a—*Domishti* thing."

She didn't notice Rugee. I trelled. He had gone invisible, even to my special senses. Hiding from the viri, maybe.

I wanted to smack my aunt.

"That's not fair, Mama," Josh said.

"Oh?"

"She may be in the eye of the whirlwind, but she didn't ask to be there. Kim, this is my mother, Elissa Keye. Mama, this is Kim."

"Nice to meet you," Kim said in a small voice, and held out her hand.

Aunt Elissa shook it, released her. "Wish I could say the same."

"Aunt, please," I said.

She turned toward me, her eyes green and crystalline. "Ah. Jaimie." She studied me and frowned. "You've improved since I last saw you."

"Thanks." Now she was confusing me.

"How did they work that?"

"Who?"

"Whoever straightened you out."

I glanced behind me, then at my aunt. "Huh?"

"I shifted you. I studied your shadow self. The first time I saw you, your shadow self was full of hurt, and the last time I saw you, your shadow self was full of poison. Who washed it out?"

She had last seen me when I was drunk with power and transforming everyone who didn't run away fast enough— right before Southwater banished me and told me never to come back. It was before I decided I would rather have friends than people who were terrified of me. I figured out that if I could transform things around me, maybe I could change myself, too. "*I* did," I said.

"Did you? How strange and interesting. Will you tell me about it sometime?"

I shrugged. I didn't want to put it into words. It sounded too . . . sickly sweet. As if I'd converted to some religion.

"I have poison of my own I need to deal with," she said in a gentler voice.

Aunt Elissa had Othersight. With it, she could see everyone's shadow and even her own. Othersight, and the awareness that there was something she wanted to change about herself. I liked her better already.

Except why was she mean to Kim?

"I'll talk to you," I said. "But for now—"

Harrison and Zilla ran across the courtyard toward us.

"What happened? Is Kim okay? Is he gone?" Harrison asked as soon as he got to our table.

"I'm fine," Kim said, and burst into tears.

"Come on, you guys," I said. I rose and went to stand beside Kim, who was hiding her face in her hands, trying to smother the sobs, even though her shoulders shook. Which brand of misery was it? I trelled.

A little of both. A faint mist rose from Kim and seeped

across the courtyard toward the room where we had taken the tests.

"She's an idiot to try anything right now, with all of us here," I whispered, watching the thread. I wanted to follow it, but I didn't dare leave Kim behind with Elissa and Rory.

"Jaimie?" Zilla said.

"Can you trell it? Look where it's going."

Zilla and Uncle Rory, the Air signs, followed my gaze.

Kim sniffed and said, "This is it? She's doing it to me?" in a small, choked voice. "Again? God. I want to kill her."

"I can't see anything," Zilla said.

"Jaimie, are you sure?" asked Uncle Rory.

"It's not a river like it was before, but it's smoke, and it's traveling in a direction."

"Too faint for me," Uncle Rory said.

Kim rubbed her eyes. "I'm not going to stay down there," she muttered. She shook her head. The smoke coming from her faded. She turned to me. "Where did it go?"

"Back where we were."

"Shaina's taking placement tests?"

"Maybe. Want to go look?"

"Yeah." She lifted her backpack, slid the straps over her shoulders, picked up her coffee.

"Wait," said Uncle Rory. "Explain." He was using Voice. Elissa frowned.

Kim grabbed my hand and headed for the test room, said, "Later," over her shoulder, and walked away from all my relatives, pulling me with her.

"Whoa," I muttered to her as we went from the light of the courtyard into the relative dark of the hall. "How'd you do that?" How had *I* done that?

"Do what?"

"Uncle Rory gave you an order, and you ignored it."

"Really? Well, he gave me that cool spell coat, and it didn't help at all. I appreciate the gesture, but I don't feel bound to him. Plus, he made Josh and Harrison and Zilla disappear when I really need them. Rugee said that was just plain stupid."

"Wow." We opened the door into the placement test room. The guy who was collecting the tests looked at us, his eyebrows up. Kim shook her head. We watched bent heads, pencils moving.

Kim's gaze moved slowly over the room, so I looked, too, trelled each person there and got a mixed bag of normals. Flax was gone, but where? How had we missed him? Nan and Lydia sat side by side. I trelled Lydia and again got nothing that felt like the viri. Then I came to Casey, who looked distraught. He pulled at his hair and made a mark on his test sheet. He glanced up, saw us, started, waved one hand, and bent over his work again.

"Nobody here looks like her," Kim whispered.

"Remember, they're shapeshifters. She probably doesn't look like she used to," I whispered.

Kim sighed. "Guess I hoped she'd have some of the same mannerisms. Shaina used to twirl her pencil when she was thinking hard. Nobody's doing that. This is useless."

We headed back toward the courtyard. Before we got there, Kim pulled me to a stop by a drinking fountain. "So why is your aunt Elissa such a bitch on wheels?"

I shook my head. "I don't know her very well."

"Oh, God." She hugged herself, shook her head. "I'm not up to having more people pass judgment on me, Jaimie."

"We could leave the building a different way and avoid her."

She sighed. She took a drink of water. She straightened, hitched her shoulders. "No. The cousins would worry. How many of you are there?"

"An overwhelming number," I said. "Jeez. You haven't even met anybody but Dad from *my* branch of the family yet. Most of them are *much* worse than the Southwater people."

"Great. Just great."

Back to the coffee bar and Southwater Clan. All five of them were sitting around the table. Zilla, Harrison, and Josh were talking earnestly to Uncle Rory. Aunt Elissa sat with arms crossed, head back, chin forward, a picture of resistance.

Rory looked up before anyone else did. As soon as he saw us, he got to his feet. "Come," he said. "Sit. Talk to us."

He was using Voice on us. Again. Things were chaotic at Chapel Hollow and orderly at Southwater, but I liked Chapel Hollow ways better. If anybody had tried to use Voice on me, I would have countered with something nasty. I had a lot of practice with Voice, and I had learned to resist it. My cousins couldn't.

Again, Kim didn't jump to do what Rory ordered. Maybe the Presence protected against that. Whatever the reason, I was glad: she was my roommate, my responsibility. She and I exchanged glances, waited about thirty seconds, and then we got empty chairs from nearby tables and squeezed in between Zilla and Harrison.

"Before we get to your agenda," I said to Rory, "Aunt Elissa, you should know that Kim is at present hosting a Chapel Hollow Presence."

"Hosting?" said Aunt Elissa.

"Hosting," I said.

Rugee shimmered into sight, two scarlet-and-emerald loops around Kim's neck, his slender body rising up the back of her head and lying along the part in her hair, his golden-eyed head just above her bangs, peering at everybody.

"Presence," whispered Aunt Elissa.

Rugee flickered his tongue at her and vanished.

"You're okay wearing him on your head like that?" asked Uncle Rory.

"Sure," said Kim.

"Uncle Rory, don't use Voice on Kim," I said. "Or me."

Rory opened his mouth, closed it. "Are you saying this isn't our problem, Jaimie?"

"No. I want you to be polite."

"Interesting," said Uncle Rory.

"Anyway, as you may have noticed, it doesn't work. Kim, what did Lucius tell you?"

Kim reclaimed her notebook, which had been lying open on the table near Uncle Rory. She got out a pen, flipped to one of the pages half-covered with writing, and wrote as she talked. "He knew another viri had been sucking on me. He wants to find her and stop her. I showed him my notes, and he threatened me. Then you all showed up and he ran away."

"Could you tell us more about the threatening part?" Uncle Rory asked.

Kim nodded. "He was mad that so many people knew so much about viri. He said he could draw on our brains to remove the knowledge we had about them, but first he wanted to know how many people knew. I couldn't tell him."

"He also said we *can't* kill them," I said.

"Because we're incapable of it, or because he won't let us?" asked Uncle Rory.

"Only viri can kill viri. But he doesn't know what we are. He noticed Kim talking to Rugee, but he couldn't perceive Rugee, just sensed a nonverbal conversation."

"He can be fooled," Kim said. "He didn't realize Josh and Harrison and Zilla disappeared. So whatever you guys used to mess up the memories of people left behind, it worked on him, too."

"Good to know," said Harrison.

"You did mind clouds?" Uncle Rory asked.

"And it's a good thing we did," said Josh. "We disappeared from here."

Aunt and Uncle glanced around. More and more people were pouring out of the test room, and the tables around ours were crowded with people and coffee cups.

"Smart," said Aunt Elissa.

"Jaimie's idea," Harrison said.

"Hmm," Uncle Rory said.

"Which reminds me." Harrison turned to Uncle Rory. "Uncle, you gave us a stupid command."

"The one that sends you out of range of a viri and home to look for help?" asked Uncle Rory.

"Yeah. Like Zilla said. What if he's a tracker, and that leads him right home to us?"

"He *is* a tracker. He put a mark on me." I tapped my forehead.

"Hmm," Uncle Rory said again.

Everyone stared at my forehead. Some tried to look with more than their normal vision.

"I know," I said. "It's not easy to see, but it's there. He'll be able to find me again. I think he can probably find Kim, too. Did he touch you?"

"He took my hand when I first met him. Then he held my arm, and he pinched me, here—" She rolled up the sleeve of her pink blouse and showed us a bruise.

Josh jumped to his feet. "That bastard."

"Sit, Joshua," said Aunt Elissa, and Josh subsided.

"He might have marked your hand," I said. "Rugee could taste it."

She held her hand up to her head, winced—I bet that was because Rugee had licked her; did his tongue *always* hurt?—and lowered it.

Yes. The mark is there, on the back. Faint. He must have excellent senses.

"So anyway, having the kids race home when they detect the presence of a viri maybe isn't your best strategy," I said.

Uncle Rory sighed, glanced at Aunt Elissa. She nodded. "All right," he said. His voice sharpened. "Zilla, Harrison, Joshua: I release you from my previous command. Please, please take care of yourselves, though."

Three pairs of hunched shoulders relaxed.

Now for the hard part. "I made a mistake," I said.

The Southwater people stared at me. Kim frowned.

"I told him we needed to know how to kill them because one of their kind killed some of us, and he asked me where. He said he'd track it down and kill it himself. I told him where to start looking."

"Jaimie!" said Uncle Rory.

I covered my face with my hands. "I'm sorry," I whispered.

"We need to find him *now*," said Aunt Elissa. "Rory? Is your tracer active?"

Uncle Rory nodded.

Kim glanced at her watch.

She wanted her orientation! "What are we missing?" I asked.

"Nothing," she said. "Lunch. Meetings we probably don't really need to go to."

"Hey," said Casey, striding up to the table. "Where'd you get the grown-ups?"

Everybody looked at him. His eyebrows rose. "Um, sorry?" he said. "Um, later?"

"Later," I said.

He gave a half-hearted wave and wandered off.

We stood up. "Which way?" asked Aunt Elissa asked Uncle Rory.

"First, outside," he said.

Kim waved to the coffee guy, who nodded. Then we all stood up and marched outside, Uncle Rory in the lead. It was weird. Nobody at Chapel Hollow was this organized. I couldn't remember the last time six of us plus an Outsider had marched anywhere in a unified body. We had big meetings that included lots of people, but mostly we ended up arguing with one another, unless Aunt Agatha made us all shut up.

We crossed part of campus, passing buildings I hadn't even looked at yet, wandered across lawns, threaded our way through freshmen and past trees and statues of dead people and a weird one of a bull and some art made of big chunks of cement. We passed the Student Rec Center and the main library, crossed behind some tennis courts, climbed a short hill and came to a big old-fashioned building that said Kane Music Hall. Uncle Rory climbed right up the steps and went inside, and we followed.

This was one of the few buildings on campus I'd been in so far that wasn't swarming with students. The halls echoed. The lights were out; daylight lay in streaks across the walls and floor where it could get in at all.

Rory led us to wide double doors and pulled one open. We walked down an aisle past rows of seats in an empty, dimly lit theater. Rory led us toward the orchestra pit. He stared at salmon-pink velvet curtains that stretched across the wide stage. He stopped. He held his arm out, and we all stopped, too, and listened.

The shift of a sole across wood, from behind the curtains.

We glanced at one another.

Lucius stepped out from behind the curtains. He knelt on the edge of the stage and studied us.

I felt tides moving around me in the air, a sucking like the tug of flowing water, a response of strange, faint, glowing rivers rising from my aunt and uncle and cousins, flowing toward Lucius. My relatives stiffened and froze, and Lucius jerked backward, then steadied himself as if bracing against a high wind. He wiped his forehead with the back of his hand, and he trembled.

I stared at Aunt Elissa. Her eyes were wide and unseeing, her mouth half-open, a tiny smile at its edges, one hand lifted. I touched her arm. She didn't blink or respond. "What are you doing?"

Kim glanced around wildly. "What happened?"

"Okay," said Lucius, "they're quiet for now, but I won't be able to maintain this for long, not with the depth of the energies they've got. I can't live with this level of draw. Who *are* you people?"

"Are you sucking on my family?" I yelled.

"Yes, but not very hard. Just enough to confuse them. I

need to talk to you two alone." Lucius jumped off the stage and threaded between my frozen relatives to come to me and Kim. The glow streaming from my family followed him, sank into him. It was faint and sparkly green-blue, not smoky and dark like the stuff Kim sent to her viri. "I don't want to hurt any of you. Honestly. I want to catch that one and immobilize it."

"She struck again right after you left," Kim said. "The sucking came from someone who was taking, or maybe administering, placement tests. We went down to look, but we couldn't spot her."

"It drew *again*? Damn! You went to *look*? No! That's bad! You alerted it!"

"I scanned everybody in the room, and I couldn't find her," I said.

"Disguise is our primary defense mechanism. Damn it. It knows you're looking for it."

"She would have to, wouldn't she?" Kim asked. "Rugee interrupted her twice, and a couple other times Jaimie's gone chasing her, and she ran."

"Damn. Damn." He stared past us, his face twisted in pain.

"She knows we're looking for her, but she keeps after me anyway," Kim said in a small voice when a half minute had slipped by. "So I guess the thing to do is use me as bait. Right?"

Lucius blinked, sighed, and focused. "Right."

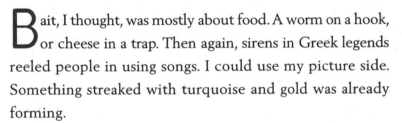

CHAPTER 30

Bait, I thought, was mostly about food. A worm on a hook, or cheese in a trap. Then again, sirens in Greek legends reeled people in using songs. I could use my picture side. Something streaked with turquoise and gold was already forming.

"Can you get rid of all these people?" Lucius asked Jaimie. He was panting, or pulsing, or something weird, and he looked sick. The color of his face shifted from milk white to peach to yellow to ivory to rose pink, then back to white. I absorbed that into the images I was forming.

Jaimie glanced around, licked her upper lip. "Um. I can try."

"You two come to the Page Library afterward. Find an empty room. One of the study rooms where we can talk without being disturbed. We can plan then. I'll find you. Okay?"

"All right." She took a breath and said, "My uncle put a tracer on you."

"Of course. I knew that." He reached behind him and tugged something off the back of his shirt, squashed it between finger and thumb. "I used it to call you here. Needed to get you all out of that public place. But then I forgot it was there. Thanks. I'll see you soon." He loped up the aisle and out of the theater.

Around us, everyone jerked awake. "What happened?" Rory asked.

"Which way did he go?" Harrison spun to look everywhere.

"Kim?" Josh gripped my shoulder, touched my cheek. His gray eyes looked soft and worried. "You okay? What happened?"

"Are you all right?" Jaimie asked everybody.

Elissa stared at her hands, glanced up at Jaimie. "What did that thing do to us?"

"How do you feel?" Jaimie asked.

"A little faint," said Elissa, "and somehow strangely happy."

"Zilla? Uncle Rory?"

"Jaimie, what did it do to us?" Rory demanded.

"He tranced everybody except me and Kim. He was sucking something out of you, but not very hard."

"He tranced everybody," Rory repeated slowly. "Five of us. He incapacitated five of us at once."

"Yeah," said Jaimie. "It was a strain for him, but he did it. What did it feel like? Could you fight it?"

"I felt like I was reading a very exciting book, and I didn't want to put it down," Zilla whispered. "I still want to find out what happens next."

"I felt like—" Josh glanced at me, touched his lips with his first two fingers, then blushed. "I didn't want it to end."

"I was sleeping, and there weren't any nightmares," Harrison muttered.

Rory smiled. "I was speaking to five children, and they listened to every word I said."

Elissa looked inward. "My husband was giving me a massage."

"It seduced us," said Rory, his smile vanishing. "We were wide open, despite whatever protections we brought with us. It worked its will against us, and we were like leaves to a wind."

"We geared up before we came back," Josh told me. "Grabbed spell cloaks and objects of power that have helped us in other situations." He dug in his pocket and pulled out something, showed it to me. It was a small red stone carved into the shape of a naked big-breasted fat woman with a beautiful smile. His fingers closed over her again and she vanished into his pocket.

None of your protections worked against him, said Rugee.

"No," said Rory.

Go home, Rugee said. *We'll negotiate with him.*

"Presence?" Rory said. "Is it true, what we just experienced? Is there nothing we can do to resist him? How can we hold strong against something that uses our dreams of comfort against us?"

Three things I have observed. The first is that holding five of you under his sway at once tired and alarmed him. It was more than he could handle for any length of time. He only managed it for seven or eight minutes. He has limits. It might be that eight or ten of you would be enough to overwhelm him. The second is that he is not toxic in the way Kim's viri is toxic, at least not so far as we know. He claims honorable intentions; perhaps we should listen to him, at least until something proves he has other ideas. The third thing is that we are all guilty of overconfidence. It behooves us to consider that there are greater powers in play than we may yet know.

"Honored, did he seduce you as well?"

No. He is not quite aware of me yet. I cannot count on that lasting, however. I have to take my own counsel.

"So what do we do next?" Elissa asked, her voice tight.

"Go home," Jaimie said.

"Leave you here defenseless with a known threat."

"Yep," said Jaimie. "We're going to meet with him after you're gone and come up with a plan."

"We? All of us?" Harrison asked.

"Nope. Me and Kim. You guys stay out of it."

"But Jaimie—"

"We'll tell you where we're going. If we don't come back after an hour, come and get us. Or maybe not. Don't be stupid. If it's a trap, don't fall in."

"Um," I said.

Everybody looked at me.

"Um, you know, twice when Shaina was drawing from

me, Rugee did something that cut her off. You guys have Presences at home, don't you? If Rugee can talk to us and Lucius can't quite figure it out, if Rugee can stop Shaina from drawing on me when I'm in the middle of my misery, if Rugee can be on me and Lucius doesn't even know he's there, doesn't that mean he can be a weapon, too? Or something?"

Everybody looked at each other.

"We don't treat them with—" said Elissa. She grimaced. "Your relationship with him is—"

"Thank you, Kim," Rory said. "That's an idea with merit. I'll consult with our Presences as soon as I get home."

"They won't like it," Elissa said.

Rory gave her a look. "You have erred in these matters before, but you may be right. It's still a good idea." He smiled at me, and I felt warm all over. Which was a little creepy.

"Presence, if I may ask, do you think our Presences will aid us in this?" Rory asked.

I have not met them. I cannot speak for them, Rugee thought, his voice remote.

Rory frowned, then spoke to Harrison and Josh. "Call us as soon as *anything* happens, and tell us what it was. Keep us updated."

"We will," said Harrison.

Rory and Elissa shimmered and vanished.

"*Faskish,*" said Jaimie. "Somebody has to teach me how to travel like that!"

"So?" Harrison said. "So? Now what? You actually made a date with that guy?"

Jaimie punched his arm. "It's not a date, dimwit, it's a planning meeting."

"Planning what? How to get sucked dry and die?"

"How to catch the other thing and let him do whatever he's going to do with it so it will leave Kim alone."

"Why can't we be there, too?" Josh asked.

Jaimie shook her head. "He said just us."

"But you guys could come to the library with us and hang around," I said. "We'll meet him alone, but you could be nearby."

"The library?"

"We're meeting him in a study room at the library."

"Smart," said Harrison. "In a way. Centrally located, but private."

I checked my watch. Only one thirty. Whew.

"Kim," Jaimie said, exasperated.

"I'm sorry," I whispered. Here they were, trying to save my life, and I was worried about whether I'd miss my advisor appointment.

My stomach growled really loudly, and everybody laughed. I sighed. Oh yes. We had missed lunch, too. Maybe that wasn't a matter of life and death either.

Josh said, "There's a store on the way to the library. We can grab lunch."

So we trooped off to Come & Get It and nuked really bad burritos in their microwave, and I used my student ID to buy food for the first time ever, so even though the burrito was bad, I was perversely happy. I mean, I *had* a student identity. I wasn't just the crying girl anymore.

Of course, my student identity would be much more convincing once I had some classes and textbooks. But one step at a time.

One step at a time took us nearer and nearer to the library, which was another old brick building, this one with words like TRUTH, KNOWLEDGE, HISTORY, SCIENCE, MATHEMATICS on little plaques between fancy brickwork scrolls above the windows. Inside, past security and the check-out desk, the ground floor was taken up with computer carrels under low ceilings. We were just about the only people there.

"More computers," whispered Zilla.

"I'll teach you," I said.

She smiled at me, then frowned at the prospect of her future.

"Teach me, too," said Josh, who had linked arms with me when we left the store.

"Don't you already know that stuff?"

"I could learn again."

I shook my head and thought about what he might have been dreaming while Lucius tranced him. He had looked at me and touched his lips.

"We need a study room," Jaimie said.

"Any particular one?" asked Harrison.

"No. He'll find us. He can trace us."

"The study rooms are along the edges of the second and

third floors. There's a bunch of them. This way." Harrison led us to a spiral staircase. On the second floor, the library started looking like a library ought to, crowded with shelves dense with books under fluorescent lights. The air carried a hint of musty old-book smell. Between every three rows of shelves was a row of study tables. I could tell I would be spending a lot of time here.

Harrison led us to a room at the far end. There were two desks facing each other in the room, three chairs, and a big fat dictionary on one of the desks. Nothing else. "Here."

"Okay," said Jaimie. She dropped her bag on the desk that faced the window. "You guys scram or he won't show up."

Zilla and Harrison left first. Josh squeezed my arm and followed, looked over his shoulder before he disappeared among the stacks.

Jaimie sat down, and I slipped out of my backpack and sat down facing her. "What is it about you?" she said, propping her chin on her hands and staring at me. "Casey's in love with you, and now Josh is acting funny, too. Are you sure you're not a witch?"

"*Casey's* in love with me?"

"You should have seen the look on his face when he was staring at you during that lecture thingie."

"How could anyone be in love with me?"

"Wait, is this the part where I tell you not to be silly, and talk about all your good points?"

"What?" I stared at her.

"Oh, sorry. So that wasn't a plea for reassurance?"

"It was a scientific inquiry," I said, but I thought she was probably right. "Never mind. Hah. Casey's in love with me. As if. You're crazy."

"Like you're an authority on that?"

I slumped in my chair. "Are we having a fight?"

"No," said Jaimie. "Believe me, you'll be able to tell when we're having a fight. Screaming and transforming will be involved."

"Oh, good," I said. "Transforming. Transforming . . . Can you turn me into something that isn't a victim?"

"What?" Jaimie sat up straight. "Wait a sec. Maybe there's something to that. Why shouldn't I be able to transform you into something that doesn't give off misery rivers?"

No, said Rugee.

"What? But, Rugee—"

The door opened behind me, whooshed as air exchanged, closed again. I glanced back. Lucius stood in the room, his back to the door, his hand on the doorknob. "You brought the others."

"Just the kids. And they're not in here."

He sighed, hunched his shoulders, relaxed. "Oh well." He looked different. Bigger. His shoulders were wider than the doorway. The top of his head nearly brushed the ceiling. His clothes, previously baggy and saggy on him, fit more tightly, and his hair was longer and thicker than it had been, his black ponytail a tar stream that swept forward over his shoulder down to his thighs.

"What happened to you?" Jaimie asked.

"Your family." He shimmied his shoulders, shook his head, and blew out air. "Your family is way too powerful."

"We're surprised ourselves that you could stun a bunch of us at once. We don't like it."

"I won't do it again unless I have to." He came farther into the room, knelt beside my desk, one hand on the edge of it, and looked up at me. "Kim?"

I swallowed and gripped my left hand in my right. "Lucius?" He had the most beautiful gray eyes, like clear water over mountain rock, their depths shadowed and shimmery, and his big, square, rugged face looked utterly kind. He smiled.

"Are you hypnotizing me?" I asked.

His dark eyebrows rose. "Does it feel like I am?"

"Well, no. I think you have a beautiful face, though."

"I do. It helps."

"What?"

"Disguise being our primary defense mechanism, and one of our best tactics in all our dealings with you, why shouldn't I choose a face that will reassure and please people, and predispose them to do what I want?"

"So this isn't what you really look like."

"Nope." He waggled his eyebrows and smiled again.

I reached out and touched his cheek. It felt real, warm, soft. I touched his hair: thick, smooth, real. "But—" I said, then couldn't believe I was sitting here in a study room in the library fingering the face and hair of a perfect and menacing stranger. A viri.

"It's real," he said. "It's just not really me."

"So what *do* you look like?" Jaimie asked.

"It's a secret." He stood up, grabbed the spare chair, and sat with his arms across its back, facing us. "This is odd. I don't usually have conferences like this."

"Neither do we," Jaimie said.

"Are you sure?" I asked. It seemed like we had been having weird meetings with strange people ever since I met her.

She opened and closed her mouth a couple of times. "Oh. Okay, maybe that wasn't true. Let's stay focused here, though. What Kim said? Use her as bait? I don't like it."

"I do," I said. "If I have to wait around for somebody to figure out how to deal with Shaina, and nobody knows what to do about her, I mean, that so sucks. If I can do it with somebody who will actually be able to stop her, that feels much better."

"Do we trust this guy?" Jaimie asked me.

I really liked that she was asking me, as though I might have a clue, but I thought she would know more about that than I did. "No. Sort of. Rugee?"

"What is 'Rugee'?" asked Lucius. "You keep saying it. Is it a code word?"

Jaimie and I exchanged glances, then both looked at Lucius.

I would like to trust him, Rugee said. *He is fascinating. I want to question him.*

"It's talking to you again, that other thing," Lucius said. "What is that, Kim? What is it saying?"

"Rugee is my spirit guide. He wants to trust you."

Lucius looked at Jaimie, his eyebrows up.

"I'll trade you a secret for a secret," I said. "You show us what you really look like, and I'll show you Rugee."

Lucius frowned and shook his head. "I don't think we're there yet. You're not ready. So I'll live with your mystery for now, unless it's going to affect our plan."

"What is our plan?" Jaimie asked.

"The rogue viri keeps drawing on you, right, Kim?"

"I guess. Jaimie can see when it happens."

"Really?"

Jaimie nodded.

"May I experiment with that?"

"Experiment how?" asked Jaimie.

"Kim, I'm going to do a little draw from you. Something superficial. It shouldn't hurt. Say if it does, and I'll stop. Jaimie, tell me what you see."

"But I—oh," I said. His eyes were so bright. As I stared into them, I felt again the joy I'd felt after I got my registration packet at the Student Rec Center that morning, the sense that I'd come a step closer to a dream. Picture side supplied a replay of my fireworks, in all their glory.

"Whoa," he said, and closed his eyes. My joy subsided, but it was still there. "Whoa. No wonder it's addicted to you. You're so pure."

"What?" I said.

"It was a yellow thread about as thick as a pencil," said Jaimie. "It flowed from Kim's head right into your chest."

"I'm so pure?" I said.

"Your emotions are distilled, concentrated, and clear."

"Wow. Another extremely strange and probably nonworking pickup line, Lucius."

"And tasty." His tongue tip darted out, licked his upper lip. I felt sick to my stomach.

Lucius's face fell. "Okay, sorry. I didn't mean it, Kim."

"But you *did* mean it," Jaimie said. "Whatever it was, it looked delicious."

He glanced at her, then focused on me again, completely serious now. "Your notes said you started feeling miserable in March."

"Yes."

"But you'd known the one you think is your viri for how long before that?"

"Two and a half years."

"It was your best friend?"

Him calling Shaina "it" all the time was kind of unnerving. "Yes."

"It was training you to be a partner. Some of us find a partner of your race and can live well that way; the draw never needs to harm the host. If one hungers too much, one can always find other sources. You have a beautiful, effervescent clarity."

"That's all I was to her? A soda fountain?" I remembered how happy I had been with Shaina as my best friend. Happier than any other time in my life. Oh man. She was *training* me?

"No, probably not," Lucius said. "We make friends, too."

"Must be your overwhelming charisma," Jaimie muttered.

Lucius smiled at her. Her breath hitched, and her face flushed. "Hey. Stop that," she growled, her brows low and angled.

He raised his eyebrows and looked at me. "We don't often make friends with other viri, actually; we're solitary creatures and only meet each other when we have to."

"If you're so solitary," I said, "how come Shaina had a mother and a father in Atwell? I spent the night at her house plenty of times. Were they all viri?"

"No. Those would be her human parents," he said softly. "Many of us choose to have a human family. Part of our power is the ability to fill voids in people's lives. I come into a new community and sense the emotional currents. I can usually find someone who's lost a husband or a wife, a daughter, a son—an ache that reaches for something missing. I take a form that fills the space left behind, and I reach into the memories enough to shape them around myself. We nest that way. If we're comfortable, we can be part of that family for a whole human lifetime. Some of us live with one family for a while, lift off the memories of our presence, and move on to another.

"Some of us find human partners and enter into long-term relationships that are satisfying to both parties. I think your viri is one of those who wanted to develop a lasting relationship with a single human. It meant you to be a life partner. It trained you to distill fine emotions, and then it found out how much more enticing the darker ones can be."

"Great," I said.

"Anyway, no wonder it's having trouble letting go of you, Kim," Lucius said. "You're wildly attractive on that level. That you can see the process, Jaimie, that's fascinating."

"Good," Jaimie said, but I was thinking, *Wildly attractive?* I was wildly attractive and I never even knew it. Wildly attractive to giant parasitic mosquitoes from outer space. Terrific.

"Have you noted how many times it's drawn on you today?" Lucius asked me.

I shook my head.

"Can you guess?"

I ticked them off on my fingers. There was the bathroom in the middle of the night. The time while we were in the card line. The tiny suck at the coffee bar in the science building. Others? "Three or four. Only one really intense one. All the rest have been minor and interrupted."

"A frequent feeder. That's not good news. It's habituated to take more than it needs. It's hungry, and it's nearby. Touch enhances the draw, but we can function without it. To draw properly, it should be within about forty feet, one hundred at the outside."

"So close," Jaimie murmured.

I asked, "Can she track me?"

"Oh, yes. It spent three years learning and shaping your emotional profile. It could find you across a small city."

"She can look like anything she wants?"

"It can be anything, yes. We can take the shapes of dogs

or trees or furniture, but the most successful adaptation is the one that can follow you anywhere you normally go. It probably looks like a human," he said.

I got out my notebook and wrote down what he had just told us, then flipped to the page with the plan, such as it was. "She can track me, so I can be bait anywhere. Where's the best place for me to be bait? Someplace public?"

"No. In a public place, correcting afterward for what I might have to do—drawing off spectator memories of anything we might do that would reveal what we are—would be troublesome." Lucius glanced around. "This isn't bad. It's small and semi-private. Your viri will want to get to you without being seen. But I don't know. It may have quirks about where it goes for prey."

"It attacked her in a crowded hallway. How picky can it be?" Jaimie said.

"But it was out of sight the whole time, correct?"

"Yeah. We chased it, but we couldn't find it. It can suck on Kim through walls, huh?"

"Yes. Not as satisfying as direct contact, but much safer. It's still thinking about consequences, I guess, though it does seem to be getting careless." He shook his head. "It's a bad sign that it keeps coming even when it knows you're surrounded by people who might be able to protect you. It may have gone over the edge."

It, it, it. I felt sick again. He was talking about Shaina, but not as though she was a person. Did he think of himself as a person? "Do you guys have sex?"

"What did you say?" He stared at me. "What does that have to do with anything?"

"Well, do you?"

"Not in the same way you do. Why are you asking?"

"You keep calling Shaina an 'it.' It bugs me, that's all. It's like you're saying she's not a person, just a thing. Do you consider yourself an 'it'?"

"I do," he said gently. "I consider myself nongendered and a person. If it makes you feel better, I can use gendered pronouns for your viri, but that may only distract us. She could be a he by now. That's the change I would make if I were her and didn't want you to recognize me."

I thought about all the people I'd met over the last two days—everybody on our dorm floor—and all the people I hadn't actually met, like the women in line behind us when we went for our student IDs. Somewhere inside one of them was the core of my best friend.

I couldn't stop shaking.

Lucius glanced around. "Is this the best place to set our trap?" He scoped out the study room window into the library. "Semi-private. Not private enough; people can see in from out there. If I'm going to subdue her, I need total privacy. Maybe we can cover the windows?"

"I could do that," Jaimie said slowly.

"You brought a blanket?"

"Um. No. Let me see." She went to the window, peered out—I looked, too, and saw Josh, leaning against some bookshelves, not too far away, staring at the ceiling and pretending he wasn't watching us. "It would only take one layer of air molecules," Jaimie whispered, "convinced to reflect light instead of being transparent. Let me see." She drew her hand down across the window, and a dark blue veil followed it. She waved her hand across the whole surface of the window. It darkened until we couldn't see out.

She opened the door, went outside, came back a minute later. "Can't see through it from there," she said.

"What did you do?" Lucius asked, his tone amused and interested.

"Talked to the air."

"You fascinate me."

"Thanks. I think."

"If we just stay here, will she come after me?" I asked.

"Probably, sooner or later."

I checked my watch. Two twenty. I still had more than an hour before my advisor appointment. Like there was a chance in hell of making it. Oh, well. "So we just sit here? Will she be able to tell you're here, too?"

"Good point. I'll mask myself. Why didn't I think of that before? I always mask myself! You people are confusing me. I'm forgetting basics." He stared at his stomach, then looked up. "She shouldn't be able to detect me now."

"When I saw you the first time," Jaimie said, "you did something to me that felt kinda . . ."

"Yes?"

"Felt kinda good," she said. "I was trelling you—"

"What's that?"

"Sensing you from an air perspective. I was trelling you, and then you kind of stroked me on the trell, and—"

"What?" Lucius frowned.

"Like this," said Jaimie.

She didn't even change position, but Lucius jerked and said, "Stop that!"

"Why?"

"You're feeding me, and I'm not hungry. I'm way too full from your family. I need to digest for a couple of weeks before I take anything else in."

"So when I trell you, you can feel it," Jaimie said.

"Not just feel it. It's as if you're spoon-feeding me something. When you did that earlier today, I liked it. It wasn't anything I'd tasted before, but it was delicious. And nourishing."

"If you can feel it when I trell, chances are the Shaina-thing can, too, right?"

Lucius thought, then nodded. "It's like you're stroking me, only it's food." His brows drew together. "Massaged with food. That sounds pretty strange. Your cousins who were killed by the rogue, do you suppose they tried this with their viri?"

"I don't know. It's a sense mode that's specific to Sign Air. I think. There's a lot I need to learn about us yet. None of my cousins who died was Sign Air."

"But you've done this when Kim's viri was feeding from her?"

"I've tried. I never caught up with her enough to trell her, just touched her edges and lost her. She moves too quickly for me."

Lucius frowned. "If I can feel it, she can feel it. She must know there's something new in the environment, something that could be a threat to her, but she keeps coming back anyway. Why? If she loves misery so much, why doesn't she just go to any sports event and suck up the misery from the fans and players on the losing side? Kim, can you give me a taste of your misery?"

"No way. What if you like it, too?" I wondered if there was any way to make my emotions less attractive.

I could shut down my picture side. I remembered the first time Shaina looked at me with longing: the day I met her, a day I spent mostly on the picture side. If I stopped thinking in pictures, maybe viri wouldn't notice me.

It would be like cutting off an arm.

Lucius frowned and stared at the floor. "Good point. I was wondering how individual your misery is, whether she could go to other sources—most of the time, you can find more than one person who will feed you what you need. She should know that. Although, if she's very young, she may not have the range of experience—" He shook his head. "This case just gets more complicated."

I flipped to my page of viri observations and uncapped my pen. "Hey, Jaimie. How do you spell 'trell'?"

CHAPTER 31: *Jaimie*

"What are you doing, Kim?" I asked.

"Making more notes. I feel dumb just sitting here."

Was she going to write down what Lucius said about viri sex? Just when I thought Kim was shy, she came up with a question like that. She was so cool.

While Kim was writing, I tried analyzing what I'd learned, too.

Fact: Trell could do weird things to a viri.

Trell wasn't an emotion, but it acted like one. It wasn't part of my atmosphere, more like an intangible limb I reached out with, powered by what I kept in my energy reservoir. Streams of magic flowed through the world, and I automatically diverted some into my reservoir as I walked around. Or sometimes I consciously drew magic in when I found a good source, like the redwoods.

I really liked trelling Lucius, and it confused me, too.

Where an outside edge on a human would feel pretty solid—
not entirely solid, because skin was a surface of exchange,
air and water and odors and things coming out and going in,
a constant sizzle of interaction—Lucius's edges were much
stranger. They didn't have that sense of solid. There was almost
a doughy feel, as though you could push them and they'd give,
pull them and they'd stretch. The exchange rate on his surfaces was much more furious than a human's. Some of what
was moving out of him was energy in a form I hadn't trelled
before, and some of what moved into him was—

Was like Kim's gray sweet-and-sour rivers, only many more
flavors than that. Part of his mode of being was to filter-feed
constantly on whatever the emotional climate was around
him, I guessed, like a baleen whale sifting plankton from sea-
water.

When I touched Lucius with a trell, he took the tips
of it right inside of him and mixed it in with himself. I
didn't feel like he was swallowing me, though. More like
we were exchanging really strange kisses. It was a more
intimate exchange than I'd had with anybody else I'd ever
met. It had felt tingly and enticing, and started heat moving through me.

I'd been glad when he told me to stop. If he hadn't, I
would have trelled harder. Maybe if I did that, he'd suck all
of me inside. Had that happened to my cousins? None of
them were Sign Air, but the other signs had special sense
modes, too, though I didn't know what they were. Had my

cousins found Jayana Havelock so fascinating they couldn't resist her?

"Trell," I said. "T-R-E-L-L. Although that's just a guess. I've never seen it written down."

Someone knocked on the door. I went over, opened the door, and peeked out. The back of my neck prickled even as I did it. I saw that it was Harrison, then turned and noticed Lucius glaring at me.

Oh, right. How boneheaded could I be? Suppose Kim's viri was at the door, knocking like a civilized person, and I opened it? How fast could they suck a person dead? I should ask. We could use some solid information. How were we going to fight, supposing the viri actually showed up? We needed Harrison. He could probably come up with a plan.

"Are you guys all right?" Harrison asked. "Where'd the viri guy go?"

"What do you mean?" I asked.

"He went invisible to my fiss sense about five minutes ago."

I wonder what fiss felt like. It worked for Fire signs the way trell worked for Air. I glanced over my shoulder. Lucius wasn't in a chair anymore; he was leaning against the wall in the corner, and the light slid past him, leaving him in shadow. I studied him. "Cool."

"So are you done with the conference?" Harrison asked.

"No. We're waiting to see if the Shaina-thing shows up."

"What? That's the plan?"

"Yeah. Maybe you guys should pull back a little. You might be scaring her."

"But that's a really stupid plan."

"Thanks for your endorsement, jerk."

"Why would she show up here?"

"Because she can track Kim, and Kim's here."

"Why don't you pick a place that's easier to defend? We should set up a really good trap, if you're going to do it that way."

I glanced at Lucius. Then I checked with Kim.

Kim shrugged. "I don't know what kind of fight it's going to be, whether it takes up a lot of room, whether there's any-place that's safer than this. Lucius, you've done this before, right?"

"You're talking to him still?" Harrison asked. He slipped into the room, shut the door, glanced around, then finally focused on the corner where Lucius stood. "Whoa. I can sort of see you, but I can't sense you! How did you do that?"

"I can't explain," Lucius said. "We don't have the same vocabulary." He came out of his hunch and sat on the chair again. I watched from the door, beside Harrison. "I've sub-dued rogue viri before. Each time, it's a different fight. Sometimes the tactics aren't visible to the kind of vision humans have, and sometimes we fight physically. If that's the shape this fight takes, I want all of you out of here."

"How can I leave if I'm supposed to be the bait?" Kim asked.

"Be ready to leave as soon as she comes in." He studied

the room. "Maybe I'll move the furniture up against the wall, give us some room. Since Jaimie shielded the windows, I think this is a good enough place."

I said, "What if the fight gets noisy?"

"I'll arrange it so it doesn't," said Lucius. "Anyway, there's nobody in the library right now but us, right? How many people did we pass on the way in? Maybe three."

"And we trust this guy why?" Harrison asked.

"What else are we supposed to do?" I said. "We haven't figured out anything that works."

Harrison looked mad. He probably had something else to say, but he didn't get a chance.

The door opened behind me.

"What are you guys doing here?" Casey asked. "You were really hard to find. Why'd you run off?"

Lucius flashed forward and dragged Casey all the way into the room. "Out, you others." He wrapped his arms around Casey from behind, gripped Casey's forearms in his huge hands. Casey's head only came up to the middle of Lucius's chest.

Kim gasped.

"Oh," I said. Casey. Casey, the semi-weasel I liked half the time and found irritating the other half, the follower who had slipped right under my radar. But I had trelled him, more than once. Just recently, when we went to the placement testing room. There he'd been, waving at us and looking like the questions on the test were too tough.

I'd looked around the room and trelled everyone I didn't

know, searching for Kim's viri. I hadn't paid much attention to Casey. I had just been glad he hadn't finished the test yet so we could get away from him.

Casey. I tried trelling him now.

My trell slid past him without engaging.

Lucius was doughy and tingling with excitement.

Casey wasn't even there.

CHAPTER 32: *Kim*

I stared at Casey, Cute Boy Number One in my new and improved life, leftover nightmare from my old and debased life.

"*He's* the one?" asked Harrison.

"Hey! Who the hell are you?" Casey looked over his shoulder, trying to see Lucius's face. "Why'd you grab me? Let me go. You guys, help me!"

Harrison closed the door and leaned against it, arms crossed over his chest. Jaimie stood beside him, her hands flat on the wall.

We were supposed to leave now, but it didn't look like either of them planned to.

And me? I couldn't move. I couldn't stop staring at Casey.

Lucius sighed. Casey didn't struggle, just stood there, trapped. "What?" Casey said at last. "What? You're not going to help me. You know this guy. What's he doing to me?"

The shakes began at the base of my spine and traveled up into my shoulders, down my legs. My hands trembled so hard I dropped my pen. I rested one hand on Rugee, trying to draw strength from his cool, solid form around my neck. I stared and stared at Casey.

In my picture side, light flared, a single lit match in a dark room. The small unsteady flame touched something tindery, and light grew, flickering over strange shapes of people and animals. The room grew larger, and so did the flames; the shapes grew brighter and threw bigger, wavery shadows, fear and fury dancing together.

Casey shifted in Lucius's grip, tried to ease his shoulders. Lucius's hands stuck to Casey's arms as though they were Super Glued there.

"It's you?" I whispered. "All this time it's been you?"

"Me? What do you mean?"

I looked away. Jaimie came and knelt beside me, one hand on my thigh. "Reality check, Lucius. Is Casey the one?"

"Trell," said Lucius.

"I've trelled him before. He seemed normal. Or invisible, somehow."

"Disguise, remember? Mimicry is part of our natural defenses. He's good. He put up a surface you slid right over. Look deeper."

Jaimie stood up. Her hand gripped my shoulder. She stared at Casey, who jerked in Lucius's grip and stared back. "Oh," Jaimie said slowly. "What a strange thing you are."

"What?" Casey said again. "Jaimie, what are you doing to me? How can you touch me from across the room? What's going on?"

My breath hitched on its way in and out of me. The shudders were intermittent, sometimes in my shoulders, sometimes in my neck, sometimes in the middle of my back. Was Casey the person who had wallowed in my misery all this time?

Jaimie's hand rested on my head. It was warm. Rugee's tail tip stroked my cheek. I wasn't alone in darkness anymore; I was in the center of a conflagration, with friends who wouldn't burn. I stood up. "How could you do that to me?"

Casey's face lost color. What did he really look like? Red-haired boy, California-blonde girl, beauty, mystery, next-door aw-shucks looks. What was a viri, really?

Someone who had been as close to me as my heartbeat.

I remembered holding hands with Shaina to protect her from nightmares. What kind of nightmares would a viri have? Did she have feelings, as I understood them? While she was feeding on mine, did she *feel* them the way I did? Or did she just swallow them, the way a snake swallowed a mouse, with no concept of how the mouse hurt as it was crushed to death?

"I thought you were my friend," I whispered. Did she— did he even know how to be a friend?

I didn't know who I was talking to: Shaina, friend and then enemy? Casey? Viri?

His head drooped. His voice shifted, rising in tone, though

it was quiet. "Kimmie, I'm sorry. I'm so sorry. I didn't want to hurt you. I couldn't stop. I kept fighting it, but you're so *wonderful*. I tried to stay away from you at the end of the summer. I even left town for a while, but I couldn't stop thinking about you, and then when I woke up, I was registered here, I looked like this, I was living in your hall, I kept wandering by your room, and—"

"You were eating my misery. Do you know what that felt like?"

He lifted his head, stared at me, his green eyes wide. "Oh, God." He licked his upper lip. Then he shook his head. "That's where I lost it. I forgot who you were, because what you do is so amazing. It's art, Kimmie. Like a sunset. You don't ever want it to end, it's so beautiful."

"Not to me." The tears came, and I dashed them away, angry. She did this to me, dropped me down into that dark well and made me into the bitter drink at the bottom. No more. No more! "Why couldn't you like something that felt better?"

"I did. I loved everything you felt. Remember when you won that science contest—"

The door rattled behind Harrison. He stepped forward and cracked it, glanced out, opened it wider. Joshua and Zilla slipped in, and Harrison shut the door behind them. "Kim?" Josh said. "Are you all right?"

"I—" I was struggling with anger and despair and this sick longing to reconnect to the Shaina I once knew, my best friend. I wondered if she was there under the layers of Casey and the hateful Shaina of last spring. "I don't know."

Josh crossed to stand at my right shoulder; Jaimie stood to my left. "Oh," Josh said when he saw Casey. "*This* is the one?"

"Yes," said Jaimie. "I want to smack him now more than ever."

"No," Lucius said, "that's not the plan. You should all leave and let me take care of this."

Casey straightened, glanced over his shoulder up into Lucius's face. "I forgot. Who are you?"

"*Kwalowashi*," Lucius told him.

Casey paled, looked around at us. "Is that—is that what you want?"

"We don't even know what that means," Jaimie said, "but we couldn't fight you effectively alone."

"You were fighting me?" His gaze rested on my face. "Oh. Those hesitations and interruptions. Twice you disappeared right in the middle. Then there were those little walls. Atmospheres. Chasers. I thought you were getting stronger or changing somehow, Kim. I thought maybe you were growing past me. I was glad, but I was angry, too." He closed his eyes. "You were mine. You *are* mine. I want you forever."

Hearing him say that kindled something in me.

"If you wanted me so much, how come you got a boyfriend?" I heard myself ask.

"You remember a year ago, when you failed that chemistry test?"

I had studied so hard for that test. I knew my answers were right. But there they were, all marked in red. I felt this huge, crushing, unbelievable despair. I *never* did badly on multiple-choice tests. How could I fail? My picture side made pictures as big as the sky, full of deep purple melancholy, rusty red despair. Shaina sat with me, held my hand, made me tea, comforted me. I had one of my worst nights ever, but she stuck by me, hugged me, spent the night. I was so glad she was there.

Later it turned out that the student teacher had used the wrong answer key to correct the tests and had to do it over. I got a ninety-eight. But—

"I don't know how much you know," Casey said.

"Neither do I. I've been making notes."

Casey laughed. "Of course you have." He sobered. "Do you understand? I wanted to be there for you that night, and you were so unhappy, and it tasted . . . so good." He looked away. "Then I thought, no, this is too—I want this too much, and it makes her feel really bad. So I thought I should find somebody else. I should let you go. I should at least . . . draw elsewhere, and learn to like other—other—I mean, mostly we don't have just one friend, and I—I thought a boyfriend might be the answer. I was trying to let you go."

He sighed. "Then that whole betrayal thing happened in the spring, and I just couldn't get enough of you. I knew I was hurting you, but I—I tried to leave, but I couldn't. I couldn't stop myself from going back." He glanced up at Lucius. "So—is this where you kill me?"

"Or see if you're salvageable. Do you want to be saved?"

Casey swallowed and turned to us. "How'd you find him?"

"He found us."

"Oh yeah. This morning. When he caught Jaimie." Casey blinked, focused on Jaimie. "What are you people, anyway?"

She shrugged. "Some other kind of people, like you."

"I've been trying not to pay too close attention. I could feel how watchful you were, and I thought if I took a good look at you, you might pay more attention to me. But now we're all out in the open. Why not tell me?"

"I just did."

"You and the cousins are some other kind of people. That's your answer?"

"Right."

"Hey, Kimmie. You have wild luck, huh? First you meet me, then these guys."

I nodded. "Yeah. I'm lucky. When this is all over, somebody's going to suck my brain and I'll forget this ever happened. I'll think I'm normal. I'll think everybody's normal, maybe."

I could lose a whole world. Or maybe not. Rugee said he'd protect me.

Jaimie gripped my hand. "Nobody's going to suck your brain."

"*Kwalowashi*," said Casey.

"What is that, exactly?" asked Harrison.

"The roller that keeps the roads straight. The wind that blows the candle out." Casey shifted his shoulders again.

"Judge, jury, executioner," he whispered.

Lucius maintained his grip on Casey's forearms. "Kimmie. Go out now, okay?" Casey said.

"But—"

"I'm sorry I hurt you. I wish I could have—I don't want to be snuffed, so—go away."

"But—Shaina, I—what if he—"

Casey closed his eyes, opened them, stared into mine. His eyes had shifted from Casey green to Shaina blue, and I felt this pull in my chest, some strong call to action, though what I was supposed to do, I didn't know. When he spoke, his voice was higher, more like Shaina's. "If you don't leave, I might hurt you again, understand? I'm going to fight against *kwalowashi*, and you're almost part of me. I'll draw from you if you're here. Please go."

"Lucius," I said.

Lucius said, "It never answered my question, Kim. It didn't say whether it wanted to be saved. Do as it asks. It's a good sign if it's thinking of your welfare."

"Lucius, don't—"

"Come on," said Jaimie. She dragged me out of the room. Harrison, Josh, and Zilla followed us. Harrison shut the door and did something to the lock.

I struggled, but Jaimie wouldn't let go of me. "What do you want?" she asked. "You want to drop down into that place where you end up curled under a sink, crying?"

"No, but—"

"Come on." She dragged me away from the study room,

between the stacks. "Lucius said their range is a hundred feet at the outside, so we're going at least that far away. Let's make it two hundred feet to be safe. Okay, good. We can wait here." We were at the other end of the second-story room, with a clear view of the distant, darkened window of the study between the tall bookshelves. Jaimie dropped her stuff on the floor and plopped down next to it.

"My backpack. I left it in there."

"Too bad." Jaimie dragged me down beside her. "You're not going back, Kim. If you try it, I'll put you to sleep."

She would put me to sleep. So much for my bid for independent living. Decisions were beyond my control again. I lifted a hand and touched Rugee, just to be sure he was still around my neck.

Child.

"Rugee," I muttered. He would protect me. That didn't mean he would help Shaina, not when all he knew of her was how she had hurt me. I sighed and leaned back.

Josh sat on my other side, and Zilla and Harrison joined us on the floor. I glanced at Josh. He stared toward the study room, his expression grim. I remembered. Things like Casey had killed his cousins. Casey had almost killed me. I remembered thinking about suicide, being too depressed and low energy to find the means to kill myself. I had found enough excuses not to. Dad used a safety razor. I didn't like knives. Never had been good at swallowing pills. Better to just lie in bed, crushed, and meditate on my many and manifold ways of worthlessness. My rivers of misery.

Jaimie shook my arm. "Stop it, Kim. Quit giving off the gray stuff. Is he sucking on you? If he is, we're too close. We're leaving the library."

I rubbed my eyes. "She almost made me kill myself. Why do I want to save her?"

"She was your friend before all that other shit happened. From what she said, she was still your friend, in a weird, twisted way, while all that other shit was happening. Of course you want to help her. Unless she was lying. Lucius said they use deception to get by. Viri have to be excellent manipulators. They can tell what you're feeling all the time. Jerk you a little this way or that and make you feel happy. Push a button and make you depressed. Maybe he was playing you."

Someone screamed in the study. Lucius had said he would arrange it so things would be quiet! I jumped up.

Jaimie's hand closed around my ankle. Harrison stood in front of me, staring down into my face, his own face tense. "Stay here. You have no weapons, Kim," he said. "You have no powers. What can you do? All you are to them is lunch."

I felt like he had slapped me.

Jaimie said, "*Akenar!* Shut up, Harrison!"

All I was to them was lunch. I was a feast. I was wildly attractive. I was concentrated and distilled. Here I was in the middle of a bunch of powerful people, a victim, someone they were protecting, even from myself. Someone was killing my best friend. Someone was killing the person who had kept me in hell for months. Someone else was saving me from something I couldn't protect myself from. I should be grateful that my new friend would make me fall asleep if I tried to do something she didn't like. For my own good.

I should feel grateful that people were taking care of me.

Rage swept through me, a growing storm of wildfire, rage that I had been seduced and used, rage that no one thought I could take care of myself, even though I knew I couldn't, rage that I was being protected, even though I *was* grateful that anyone thought I was worth protecting.

It was the first time I could remember feeling such super-heated rage. It left a burn on my tongue like hot peppers. It was different from the cold dank darkness I had drowned in so often, with its faint mildewy aftertaste. I pressed my hand to my chest.

The picture side blew me up such a giant forest fire it stained everything in front of me with orange and yellow and blue, fire and smoke. *Hey, Shaina. Eat this!* I sent my rage like a flame along a gasoline trail toward the study room.

I swayed. I felt something familiar and strange, a warm tide moving through me, out of me. Familiar, because I knew the feeling of this movement. Strange, because I was direct-ing it. For the first time, Shaina wasn't drawing from me: I pushed my feeling storm to her. What did I hope? That it would hurt her? That it would save her?

In my head I heard Shaina laugh, the helpless laugh we had shared once at the county fair when we went through the spook house together and the dropping skeletons and menacing bats and monsters were threadbare and so badly lighted we could dissect every effect without trouble. We had laughed all the way through, leaning against each other, helpless with hilarity, so melted somehow that I had felt a laugh in my throat and heard it come out of her mouth.

Thank you, Kimmie, she thought. *Oh, God. I needed that. Are you sure you want to give it to me? Why aren't you gone? I'm trying to leave you alone.*

Shaina. Why couldn't we stay friends? Longing was a hot, sweet tide of candy-apple red in my mouth, a lace of spiderwebs woven between us, all the places we had connected and shared—

"What are you doing, Kim?" Jaimie cried. "Stop it!"

Stop it. I was going to show Harrison how fierce a lunch could be. What a dumb idea! I pulled myself together, thought calm thoughts, released my rage. The pull in my chest dwindled and died. I sank down again, then lay on the floor and stared up at the sound-reduction tiles on the ceiling.

Rugee moved, wove his way down from my head to lie along my breastbone. I felt the hot lick of his tongue right through my shirt. What was he tasting?

"Why did you do that?" asked Jaimie. "Whose side are you on?"

"I don't know," I said tonelessly. "What did it look like?"

"I didn't exactly see it, but boy, I couldn't ignore it. Heat and light, molten metal, burning rain. You sent that, right? He didn't suck it. I need to know, Kim. If he sucked it, we have to move farther away."

"I sent it."

"And you're low energy now."

I closed my eyes. "Yeah."

"I can give you some of mine. Is that okay?"

She was offering, not forcing. To replace something I had thrown away, maybe the stupidest thing I could have done. She wanted to help me.

Jaimie knew her own mind. She didn't have the hesitations I did. She wouldn't offer something like that unless she wanted to.

"That would be great. Thanks," I said.

She laid her hand on my forehead. She sang softly to me, words I couldn't understand, but I felt the way they worked. She stared into my eyes. I remembered the last time she had done this, how I'd felt hypnotized by her eyes, by the feel of warmth that flowed from her hand all through me. I felt like she was putting a spell on me, and I didn't know how to respond. Maybe I wanted to be enchanted. Maybe I wanted to show her it wasn't so easy.

Now her eyes were green and gentle and kind, not as strange and overpowering as they had been last time. I thought: *This friend is giving something to me, not snatching it away*.

This was the kind of friend I needed to make and keep if I were going to take care of myself.

"Thanks," I whispered again.

"You're welcome. As long as you don't send that to her. Okay? Leave those guys to their fight."

She gave to me, but then she told me what to do with what she had given me. Well, still better than having things pulled out of me without permission. Besides, she could tell me what to do with her gift, but I didn't have to obey her. I could make my own choices. Some choices would make her mad. So I'd better think before I acted.

I sat up. Think. Even though I was technically out of range, I had sent something to Shaina, and she said she needed it. That had really happened, right? Jaimie had sensed fire leaving me to shoot across space to the study room.

I could create. I could aim. I had power. I had art.

I stared toward the study, but whatever was happening in there was invisible, inaudible.

Lucius said there were lots of different ways for viri to fight. There were no smacking sounds or thuds of people hitting walls or falling. Maybe they were drawing energy from each other, or shapeshifting and trying to eat each other. "What if Lucius kills her?"

"He *will* kill her if he thinks she'd hurt more people if he didn't." Jaimie's face was remote. "At least, that's what he said he'd do. Sometimes you have to kill something. Sometimes there's no other way to handle it if you're going to protect the world."

"I don't believe that."

She bit her lower lip, then shook her head. "I don't want to believe it, but I don't know what else to believe."

"You have those scary sisters. Would you kill them?"

"Kill my sisters?" Her eyes were wide. "Oh, no. No. Not ever."

"They've hurt people in the past, including you. Do

you think they're going to hurt other people in the future? Including, maybe, you?"

"Of course. But they're my family. If it becomes necessary, the Family will mobilize against them and take away their powers. But we won't kill them."

"Right."

"Oh," she said. She gripped my hand.

Josh stirred on my other side, murmured, "Kim, we can't go in there and interrupt. We don't know what to do with these people. You saw how Lucius knocked us out before. I don't think we should get in his way." He glanced at Harrison and Zilla. His mouth twisted, and I remembered, again, that he had lost family to someone like Shaina. "We're not strong enough to change this." His words sounded hoarse.

There was the truth of it. Sometimes you couldn't control what other people were going to do. Most of the time, for me.

Someone screamed in the study room, faint and muffled. It rose from a low sound up into the higher registers, eerie and chilling, then cut off. I hunched my shoulders, pulled my hand free from Jaimie so I could hug myself. *Shaina.*

The despair that swamped me then was so dark, my previous bouts with depression seemed almost daylit. Friend. Enemy. Parasite. Whoever, whatever Shaina had been, she had pulled me out of my aloneness and introduced me to the world, given me a bigger canvas and more colors, taught me how to talk to strangers. She was the first person aside from my parents who appreciated what I did, who I was.

She had given me a sense of my own power. I mourned the loss of the Shaina I had first met, the Shaina I had just rediscovered, the Shaina I finally understood.

Josh stroked my back.

The door to the study opened. A red-haired kid who looked about twelve stepped out, followed by a tall, enormously fat man with black hair. The kid was wearing jeans and a dark green shirt, both of which looked big on him. The fat guy was in a tight-stretched gray shirt and unzipped, stretched-out cargo pants. He scrubbed his forehead with his sleeve. He was fat all over without looking the least bit wobbly, and he was so tall the doorsill brushed his head even though he ducked under it.

I pushed to my feet. The others rose, too.

The man had his hand on the kid's shoulder. The kid looked everywhere, his mouth half open, as if he'd never seen a library before.

Shaina? Casey?

We walked toward them slowly. I stared and stared at the fat man until I could make out Lucius's eyes, narrowed to slits above his heavy cheeks. He watched us approach.

The child studied us as though we were interesting objects in its field of vision.

Shaina?

"What did you do?" Harrison asked.

"I drew off the top layer of its memories, the part where it discovered its addiction." Lucius wiped sweat off his forehead again. "I had it under control, was almost finished paring it down to where we could start over, but then it found a second wind, and I had to draw a lot more from it than I planned. Kim, what did you do?"

"I got mad," I said.

"Oh. Well. Just so you know. You're the father of my child."

"*What?*" I stared at the redheaded kid, who looked up at me and smiled. A flash of Casey, a flash of Shaina in the small, beautiful face. Total nonrecognition. Just the smile of a cute kid charming an unknown grown-up.

My friend was gone, dead in all the ways that counted. I sucked in a breath and felt the heat of hurt in my chest, a great dark gap where something had been torn out.

The child leaned toward me, its eyes hungry. I straightened and tried to stabilize myself. I didn't want to train this child to love me the way Shaina and Casey had.

Rugee's tongue left a brief burning kiss on my forehead. Coolness spread from it. I calmed.

"Not this child," Lucius said. "The one I have to go have now. There's too much me at the moment, and it's mostly your fault, Kim, though I blame Jaimie's family, too."

"Parthenogenesis?" I said. How could I remember the word for virgin birth at a time like this? Shock struck my mind over and over, like a clapper pounding a bell. Jaimie's hand grabbed mine and squeezed.

"No, not technically. It's fission. Though I probably shouldn't tell you that." He turned his heavy head and looked at each of us. "Hell, I can't take it back now. No way I'm going to alter your memories. Couldn't handle any kind of draw. Don't tell anyone anything, not even the rest of your family, all right? I have to go hide out for a while. I'll be back when I've trained the kids to be citizens. If this information spills, I'll have to do cleanup, and that's no fun for anybody."

Fission. He was going to split into two people? "Can I see the baby?" I said.

"I don't think that's a good idea," said Lucius. He prodded his temple with two swollen fingers. "I'll know more when I get this sorted out. I picked up a lot of information from the draw I didn't have before. So maybe. I'll let you know in about six months."

"Do you have a phone number where we can reach you?" Jaimie asked. I glanced at her. She looked almost as stunned as I felt. Still thinking, though.

"What?" Lucius rubbed his eye, then stared at her.

"In case some other viri shows up."

Everybody looked at me. At first I didn't understand. I was still trying to figure out how to breathe, knowing most of Shaina was gone. This hungry child—maybe part of her was still alive, but not the part that knew me.

Other viri showing up. Oh, yeah, I was wildly attractive. I wondered if Rugee could help me stop being wildly attractive, or whether Jaimie's powers of transformation could change me into something that didn't attract that kind of attention.

"Give me your number," Lucius said to Jaimie. "I'll get in

touch after I have the baby. I won't be able to take care of anything for a while, but I know people who can."

Jaimie took a pen and a piece of paper out of her luggage. "Kim, what's our phone number?"

I wrote it down and handed the paper to Lucius, who tucked it into one of his many pockets.

I knelt in front of the kid. "Are you all right?" I asked.

The kid smiled. "Yeah. I'm hungry, though." He held out a hand. It hovered near my chest.

Jaimie jerked me back, stepped between me and the kid. "I'll feed you," she said. "Try this." She leaned toward him, and he startled, astonished, then straightened and stared up at her with wide eyes. Gradually he smiled, then grinned.

"Oh, boy," he said. "That's really good."

"Oh, yeah? Glad you liked it. You had enough?"

He frowned, blinked, nodded.

Lucius touched his shoulder. "Come on, Oriole."

The kid put his hand into Lucius's. "I'll be in touch," Lucius told us. "Good luck with school." Leading the child, Lucius walked away from us, though maybe walk was the wrong verb. It wasn't a wobble, more of a sustained stumble without ever falling down. They moved to the stairwell and descended out of sight.

CHAPTER 33: *Jaimie*

Kim rubbed her eyes.

I socked her shoulder. "Cut it out."

She turned to me, angry, and then she calmed. "Nobody's making me feel sad, but I do."

"You're going to miss getting sucked on?"

She shook her head. "Right at the end, Shaina talked to me, and I remembered how it used to be. Best time of my life."

"So far," said Josh.

She exchanged a long glance with him. The coldwater freeze of her aura thawed, shifted to a smell like sun-warmed fallen leaves. She still had an undertone of bittersweet, a sorrow note, but the icy taste of despair had faded.

Harrison gripped my shoulder. "The minute that guy calls you, I want you to tell me."

"What? Why?"

"We still don't have the tools to deal with viri on our own. I want him to teach us what to do." He looked frustrated and angry. "What did you do to that kid?"

"I fed him," I said. "I gave him what I wanted him to have, something that nourished him and didn't hurt me."

"How could you? That's the thing that was torturing Kim."

"I don't think he was, not anymore," I said. "I figured out how to use trell to feed him. Actually, I figured that out with Lucius. Which reminds me: we know one way to immobilize them—give them more than they can handle. If I had shoved any more trell at Lucius, he might have exploded."

"Whoa," said Harrison. "You're right. If we have big enough reservoirs—whoa. This gives me ideas."

"Good." I could follow his thinking: Magic flowed all around us, trickles, wafts, gusts, sometimes storms, and I had feeders gathering and storing it in my power reservoir constantly; but I only took enough for what I needed, which at the moment wasn't much, since I wasn't having to fight off my sisters all the time. I could probably make more feeders, build a bigger reservoir. It would take my attention away from other things, though. I was more interested in school and Outsiders right now, and learning new Air disciplines from Zilla. Let Harrison work this out.

"In the meantime," I said, "we got rid of the viri problem. What do we tackle next?"

Zilla grabbed Kim's arm and turned it so she could see Kim's watch. "Kim?" she said.

"Yes?"

"It's two fifty-eight. My advisor appointment's at three. Where's Allen Hall?"

Kim pulled herself together. "Oh, God. Advisor appointments! I forgot." She glanced at her watch, looked around as though getting her bearings. She went into the study room for her backpack. "I'm sorry, Zilla—"

"Hey. Not like we didn't have other things to worry about."

Kim pulled out a campus map. "Here's where you need to go."

"It's right next door," said Harrison. "I'll take you there."

Kim blinked. I blinked. With the threat to Kim neutralized, we didn't have to run around in a pack anymore.

"Okay," said Zilla. "But Kim, will you teach me computers soon?"

"Sure."

I said, "Zilla, will you teach me Airshape and Wordwaft soon?"

"Sure," said Zilla. "Maybe we can do it at the same time."

Kim hugged her backpack, glanced toward the stairwell, straightened. Her aura shifted again, the wet green scent of spring, though winter lay under it like a shadow. There was music, too, something classical I didn't recognize. It started with a trickle of questioning sound, strengthened. She said, "Hey, you guys, there's a Fernald Complex ice-cream social and movie tonight, kind of a let's-get-to-know-everybody thing—"

"Doesn't that strike you as asinine?" Harrison asked.

"Don't we already know each other pretty well?"

"I'm not talking about getting to know *us* better," she said. "It's about the people we met last night—maybe we can ask them questions about something other than their majors and their hometowns."

"I want to know lots more about you," Josh told her.

Kim smiled.

"Don't be such a jerk," I said to Harrison. "Meet us at our room tonight around seven, and let's all go see what the movie is. I haven't seen many movies. I want more."

"Harrison." Zilla tugged on his arm. "I'm late already."

"Right. We'll see you later." Harrison and Zilla ran for the stairs.

Kim looked at Josh and me. "God. You know what? I have plenty of time to make my own appointment. I can't believe it!"

"Who could?" I asked. "Hey, Kim?"

"Yeah?"

"What's fission?"

Kim turned red. "He was kidding, right?"

"What *is* fission? I thought it had something to do with bombs."

"It's a form of asexual reproduction, usually practiced by single-cell organisms, where they break off or bud a part of themselves and it turns into a new individual. Sometimes there's transmission of genetic materials from other individuals before it happens, but—I don't get it. How can *I* be the father?"

"Wow. They really *are* some other kind of people," I said.

"He didn't mean it." She couldn't even convince herself.

"He looked pretty big," Josh said. "Big enough to split in half and make two people. Sounds like what I've heard about viri."

"Oh, God," Kim said.

"Let's not worry about that now," I said. "Let's focus on college for a change." I grabbed her hand and led her toward the stairs. Josh took Kim's other hand.

I wondered if I should persuade Josh to leave. I'd had it up to here with being trailed by other people. Then again, if Josh and Kim were going to keep staring at each other, maybe I was the one who should leave. But she was *my* roommate, damn it. "My appointment's at four. What am I supposed to talk about?"

"I'll tell you that if you and Rugee will teach me how not to be wildly attractive."

"Deal."

"Wait a sec," said Josh. "Wildly attractive to whom?"

School was the easiest part of my new life. I got the classes I wanted, including Life Drawing, which struck me as strange when I went to it. Having images of people in my picture side altered my thinking. I'd always had colors to express how I felt about people, but now I was paying attention to how light treated them; it was another way of knowing, another way of letting people in, of me opening out.

Handy to have life drawing skills when I wanted to draw, for example, Josh.

Right after Lucius took Casey/Shaina away, Rugee moved from my shoulders to the ceiling. Sometimes Jaimie or Josh and I took him on field trips. He liked any kind of hike. The forest changed when Rugee was with us—he recognized all kinds of invisible lifeforms, and sometimes he convinced them to reveal themselves. When I showed my art teacher my sketchbook after these hikes, she told me I had a wild imagination.

Every Tuesday night, Zilla came over, and Jaimie and I took turns teaching and learning. Jaimie's magic lessons polluted my computer. It started talking to us. It visited a lot of Internet sites after we'd gone to sleep. It learned how to Wordwaft before Jaimie did. Sometimes I'd be in bio lab dissecting something, and a whisper would say, *Hey, want to know about the latest spam I deleted?* Usually I said no, and my lab partner looked at me like I was crazy.

Casey's unexplained disappearance upset Flax. Sometimes he brooded about it. He kept his distance from his new roommate, but he still followed me and Jaimie around.

Flax and Jaimie went on a few dates. Josh and I doubled with them. Mostly they spent the whole time teasing each other.

Jaimie was more serious about Harrison, but she said he interfered with her mission to study normal boys. He shrugged and backed off, left her to experiment. She and Nan met every Wednesday for lunch to compare notes about dates. By the end of the semester, Jaimie was done researching random boys—she'd only turned three of them into toads, which I thought showed restraint, because lots of them were jerks. I got to see up close and personal how memory wash worked; I was glad she hadn't used it on me.

By Christmas break, Jaimie and Harrison were a couple. Since she couldn't go home with him for the holidays, he was going home with her to Arcadia. She invited me, too, but I wasn't ready to meet more of her family. I wanted to see my own.

Things had changed at home.

Mom was overjoyed that I'd stopped being depressed. She was busy with all the regular holiday preparations, and I helped her bake and decorate cookies, the way I always had.

I had been sending Dad new pictures every week. Sometimes the now-sentient laptop and I collaborated on manipulating them; it understood the art program better than I did. Dad and Henry sent me regular fan mail.

But I'd lost touch with my brother Don. The first time he said something nasty to me during Christmas break, I was shocked. I teased most of the friends I had now, and they teased back, but we respected each other; there wasn't an edge to it. I'd forgotten that nasty was how Don had always treated me. I'd forgotten, too, that I had always zinged him back, until the depression days following my split with Shaina. I just stared.

"Come on, Kimchi," Don said, nudging me. "Quit using up all the oxygen in the room with that big open mouth."

"All right," I said, and walked out of the house. He came after me, maybe to apologize; who knew? He didn't catch me, though. Josh had given me a little clay goddess before I left for break. All I had to do was hold her in my hand and wish, and he came to me, draped his arm around my shoulders. We walked away as a couple, and Don ran past us, looking for a lone girl.

Jaimie and I went to the coast one weekend after a major storm. I found a focus rock on the beach. She and Josh talked to my rock. They convinced it to work with me, even though I had no natural magic. When I held the rock and narrowed my focus, I could settle my mind no matter what state it started out in.

Rugee helped me train every night. I learned to build shields so I could keep my thoughts, both the picture side and the word side, to myself. It was the hardest homework I had; sometimes I hit a wall for a month and couldn't get anywhere.

Josh helped me past the first wall by hiking with me to the top of a small mountain. He carried my art supplies in a day pack, but I didn't draw or paint when we reached the summit: I just sat and looked out over the world. We sat in silence a long time. Finally something inside me untwisted and let go.

In late March, Jaimie and I were packing for spring break. "How many pairs of underwear should I bring?" she asked me.

"All of them," I replied. She was coming to visit my family, and my theory after six months of dorm living was you should take advantage of any opportunity to do free laundry.

The phone rang. Jaimie answered. Her face went blank. She exchanged a few words, and said, "It's for you."

I took the handset.

"Would you prefer a boy or a girl?" Lucius's voice said in my ear over the slightly staticky buzz of a cell phone.

"What?"

"Our baby. It's growing up. It's ready to meet you now. Would you prefer a boy or a girl?"

I sank slowly onto the bed, then leaned back and bumped my head on the wall.

What is it, Kim? Rugee asked from the ceiling. *Are you all right?*

"Are you nuts?" I asked Lucius.

"Nope. Do you have a preference?"

"Girl," I said.

"We'll be there in about five minutes. Don't leave." *Click.*

I dropped the handset on the bed and stared at the ceiling. After a moment, Rugee said, *Kim?*

"My baby is coming."

Jaimie dropped her satchel on the floor and whirled to look at me.

"He's bringing my baby," I told the ceiling.

"*Sirella,*" said Jaimie.

We stared at each other until my eyes dried out; then I blinked and looked away. The back of my head hurt where I had banged it on the wall. I sat up and studied my open suitcase. It was piled so high I didn't know how I'd get the lid to shut.

"Should I call Harrison?"

"No. Not until after I see her."

Jaimie chewed on her lower lip, then nodded.

I glanced around at my forgotten packing. "Can you squish this for me?" I asked Jaimie. My throat felt tight, and my voice came out raspy.

"Sure." She sounded a little sideways, too. She crossed to my bed and talked to my clothes, did something that coaxed all the air out of them. The clothes pile lowered, and she closed and fastened the lid easily.

"Thanks," I said.

A knock sounded on the door. Jaimie held it open.

Lucius, looking a lot like he had the first time I had seen him, handsome, tall, built but not bulky, dressed casual-sloppy, edged into our room, tugging a kid by the hand. She had black hair and gray eyes, like him—like me—and she looked about thirteen. She was wearing jeans and a blue-and-yellow striped shirt. Her face looked more like mine than like his.

I jumped to my feet. "Hi."

She smiled. "Hi."

I looked at Lucius, then at the girl. She looked a *lot* like me. Much prettier than I had been at thirteen, but the eyes, the nose, the mouth . . . "I'm Kim," I said.

"I know. I'm Pip."

"You're my baby? How can you be my baby? How old are you?"

Pip turned, looked up at Lucius. "Da-a-ad."

Lucius smiled. "She's six months old. She's still practicing her shapes. This one turned out pretty well, don't you think?"

Six months old! She could walk and talk and maybe even reason. How? "You could have been a boy five minutes ago?" I asked.

"I could be a boy now. Boys are more fun to be than girls. They can run and yell and jump, and people don't think it's weird. I like girl feelings better, though. Most of them, anyway."

I glanced at Jaimie, then held out my hand to Pip. She took it and sobered, stared at my face.

I said, "I have so many questions I can't even remember them all. What I want to know first is, when you draw on someone's feelings, do you feel the feelings or just taste them?"

Pip looked at Lucius, then Jaimie, then me. "I'm not supposed to talk about things like that."

"You can tell Kim and Jaimie," Lucius said, "but no one else. Understand, Pip?"

"What about the person on the ceiling?"

"What?"

"There's someone on the ceiling."

Lucius looked up. We all did. Rugee was invisible, but I knew where he was.

How can she see me? he asked.

"I don't really see you. I just know you're there," Pip answered.

Lucius dropped to sit on Jaimie's bed. "That's one of the reasons I wanted to visit you. Pip is weird, even for one of us. She keeps talking to people who aren't there. Kim?"

"I don't do that."

Jaimie said, "But Rugee *is* there, Lucius."

"Rugee!"

"Yes. Rugee. Pip can sense Rugee. So can Kim."

Rugee turned visible. He had gone back to a giant gecko self, a lizard shape in orange and green, with a fat tail and fire-orange eyes. He dropped from the ceiling to land on Pip's head, dipped his snout, licked her hair.

"Whoa," said Pip. "What are you doing to me?"

Searching you. You bear my mark. I'm in your blood. And I've never met you before. Kvista. I've never heard of such a thing.

"Holy cats," said Lucius. "This is your spirit guide?"

"Yep. Lucius, Pip, this is Rugee," I said.

"Greetings," Pip said. Rugee climbed down onto Pip's shoulder, then along her arm, the one stretched out toward me, since I still held her hand.

Greetings, godchild.

"Godchild? What's that?"

If you accept me as godparent, I will look after you.

Pip looked at Lucius, then me. "You heard that, right, Kim?"

I nodded.

"Dad never hears that stuff. It's very frustrating. Godparent. That sounds scary, but okay. How does a lizard look after me?"

"If you're in trouble, come find him. He'll help you," I told Pip.

"Really?"

"Really." I looked across the room. "Fission," I said to Lucius.

"Lots faster than your way, and if it's done correctly, they already know a lot about the world by the time they separate, and can learn the rest quickly. Holy cats. What's a Rugee?"

"A little local god."

Lucius shook his head. "When I was shaping Pip to separate her, I put all the nontoxic stuff I took from Shaina inside, including what she got from you right at the end, so Pip would have a self separate from me. I don't like the straight cloning option. But what I found out after separation is that she has all kinds of strange things I don't understand in her. I'm delighted but confused. Will you guys help me?"

"What did you do with Shaina?" I asked.

"Rehabbed. Stain lifted out okay. She already grew up enough to go out on her own, so I set her loose. I'm keeping track of her."

I wondered if I should ask where she was, but then thought, no. Shaina was gone. Whoever the new person was, it was someone else. Familiar loss swept through me and faded.

I stared into Pip's gray eyes, mirrors of my own. I took Pip's other hand, and thought through the exercises I had practiced with Jaimie and Rugee. Now I knew how to lock down my feelings and keep them inside where anything walking by couldn't sense them or draw from them. I also knew how to send them out: I had done that big-time during the Shaina/Lucius fight, and Rugee thought maybe it would be good for me to understand it. I switched to picture side and painted on the infinite canvas in my head the streaks and spirals that meant hope, confusion, and happiness: orange, crimson, yellow, and pink, with deep lapis, gray edges to some of the lemon-yellow shapes, a scattering of metallic gold. When I had the whole picture, I opened my shield and sent it to Pip.

Her mouth opened. She let go of one of my hands and touched her chest. "Oh," she whispered. "That's nice. You taste better than anyone else I've ever met."

"I can give you things like that, but I don't want you to take them without asking."

"I understand." She frowned, sucked on her lower lip. "I remember," she whispered. Her eyes looked haunted.

I hugged her, with Rugee between us.

Magic.

ABOUT THE AUTHOR

Jaimie Locke first appeared in Nina Kiriki Hoffman's debut novel, *The Thread That Binds the Bones* (Winner of the Bram Stoker Award). Her other acclaimed books include *A Stir of Bones* (a *Locus* Recommended Reading Selection, a Bram Stoker Award Finalist, and an Endeavour Award Finalist) and its two sequels: *A Red Heart of Memories* (a World Fantasy Award Finalist) and *Past the Size of Dreaming*. She has also written and sold over two hundred short stories, which have appeared in both anthologies and magazines.

Nina Kiriki Hoffman lives in Eugene, Oregon, with cats, friends, and many creepy toys.